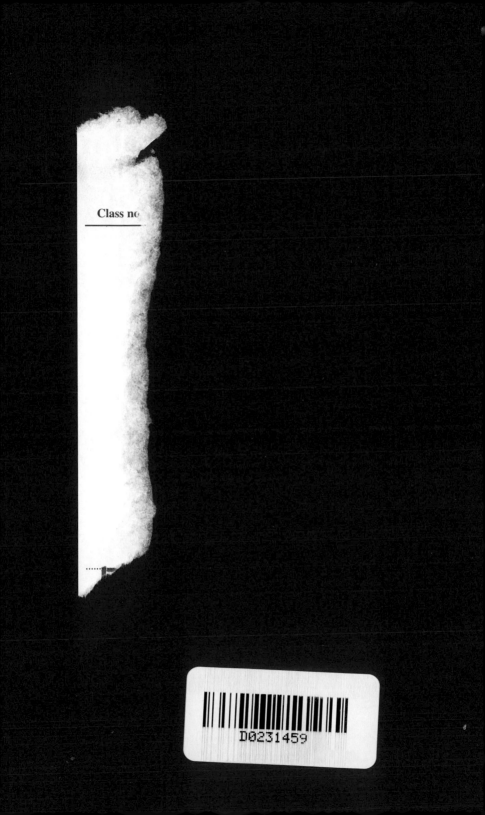

MOBIUS DICK

MOBIUS DICK

ANDREW CRUMEY

PICADOR

First published 2004 by Picador
an imprint of Pan Macmillan Ltd
Pan Macmillan, 20 New Wharf Road, London N1 9RR
Basingstoke and Oxford
Associated companies throughout the world
www.panmacmillan.com

ISBN 0 330 41991 9

1 3 5 7 9 8 6 4 2

A CIP catalogue record for this book is available from
the British Library.

Typeset by Intypelibra, London
Printed and bound in Great Britain
by Mackays of Chatham plc, Chatham, Kent

For my beloved Mary, Peter and Katia

This novel was completed with the assistance of an Arts Council Writer's Award.

CALL ME

CALL ME: H.

The text arrived on John Ringer's phone as he worked at his desk in the university. He heard a beep, brought his Q-phone from his pocket and read the cryptic message. *Call me: H.* Nothing more. No indication of who H was, or how he was supposed to get in touch. Only a 'user not found' when he hit 'reply'. Immediately he thought of Helen.

He recalled having read something in the manual about a 'call trace' feature, but since even changing the ring-tone on this next-generation device was beyond his abilities, there was little chance of his implementing it. Clutching the slim phone in his hand, stabbing awkwardly at tiny keys designed for teenage fingers, he went through several menus – in the random, empirical fashion modern technology dictates – and by way of a few adverts and a shopping channel found himself looking at the campus events listings. *Lunchtime lecture (Modern Literature): Vicious Cycloids.*

He wanted to know about H, not the entertainment programme of the arts faculty. He tried backtracking through the menus, regretting that he, a theoretical physics professor in his forties, did not himself belong to the 'next generation' who could not only navigate these contraptions with ease, but could do so while simultaneously chewing gum and talking in tutorials. The caller, he reasoned, could not be Helen. He had not seen or heard from his former lover for many years. But perhaps what the message meant was: 'Call me regarding H'. Some important news. Even a chance to meet again.

Or more probably a stray text, a wrong number. A tiny, trivial piece of another person's existence that had inadvertently dropped itself into his, forcing him to make sense of it. We are a species of pattern finders. Evolution made us so.

It was like the lecture title he'd stumbled on: *Vicious Cycloids*. Ringer found it again on his phone, and this too seemed addressed to him. The cycloid is a geometrical curve; not what you'd expect in a talk on literature. Perhaps Ringer's Q-phone (like his brain) had a way of filtering relevant information; it knew the cycloid to be a classic example of mathematical beauty: the place where art and science meet. He might even once have told Helen about it.

He decided to go to the lecture. As one o'clock approached, armed with his lunchbox, Ringer ventured out of the physics department to a region of the university he had never previously explored; one whose walls lacked the Hubble photographs and conference posters so familiar in his usual scientific domain, yet which nevertheless exuded its own kind of intellectual intimidation, its narrow corridors suggesting the ill-planned labyrinth of a doctor's surgery. Eventually finding himself at the appointed seminar room, he took a seat – surrounded by humanities postgrads and staff who presumably, like him, had no better way to pass their lunch hour – and waited with high expectations for the show to start.

The speaker – a well-bosomed but disappointingly plain woman, lecturer at some university or other – immediately launched into a discussion of *Moby-Dick*, whose ninety-sixth chapter is about 'try-pots': large cauldrons for rendering whale carcasses. The hero, Ishmael, finds himself inside one, cleaning its shiny metal surface, and its specially curved shape prompts a remarkable discovery. 'In geometry,' says Ishmael, 'all bodies gliding along the cycloid, my soapstone for example, will descend from any point in precisely the same time.'

Herman Melville evidently knew that a pendulum, if it sweeps a cycloid, will keep perfect time. Unfortunately the lecturer hadn't done quite so much background research. The real significance of the passage, she announced, is that 'cycloid' is an old-fashioned word for the personality-type later called manic-depressive or bipolar. So chapter ninety-six of *Moby-Dick* is not about geometry; it's about mental health.

At this point Ringer's attention lapsed. He suddenly understood the difference between the speaker's discipline and his own. She had latched onto a verbal coincidence and was treating it as a profound insight. Ringer was only here because of a glitch in his mobile phone.

The same random leaps were the basis of this woman's mind and career.

His affair with Helen was a matter of chance, too. They met over lunch; not sandwiches in a seminar room, but a crowded university canteen where they found themselves sharing a table. They each placed a book beside their food as they sat down opposite one another, preparing to dine in polite, mutually oblivious silence. Hers was *Doktor Faustus*. His was *Quantum Fields in Curved Space*.

Perhaps, when she finally spoke, it was simply because she'd grown tired of her quiche. 'I wish I could understand that,' she said suddenly, her mouth not entirely free of food, nodding in the direction of Ringer's book. 'But I was always terrible at maths.'

'And I've never been good with novels,' he replied.

She looked puzzled; her smooth brow became knotted with a bemused wrinkle. 'What's so difficult about reading a novel?' she asked, following the remark with a mouthful of salad while he paused over his fish and chips.

'They bore me,' Ringer said. 'All those made-up stories about people who never existed. Where are the facts? Where are the ideas? I want a book to give me a window on a new way of thinking; not mirror things I already know.'

'Then perhaps you should try this novelist,' she said, tapping the book beside her with the base of her fork. 'Thomas Mann. Plenty of ideas there, believe me.'

Mann, she explained, was fond of bringing a great deal of background information into his stories. 'For example,' she said, 'take this part here.' She put down her knife and fork, lifted the German novel and leafed through it. Ringer noticed how pretty she looked, her dark hair tumbling across her forehead, making her resemble a serious schoolgirl before an audience of parents as she carefully located one of several parts labelled with protruding bookmarks of yellow paper. She then began to translate for him a passage that slowly assembled itself into what he recognized to be a reference to cosmological expansion, buried in a novel about a composer who invents a new kind of art and pays for it with his sanity.

'Perhaps I ought to read *Doktor Faustus*,' he said. 'It sounds better than most novels.'

'First try *The Magic Mountain*,' she told him. 'That's about a man who goes to a tuberculosis clinic in the Swiss Alps. It came out in the nineteen twenties, and Mann got the Nobel Prize not long after.'

'That's a striking coincidence.'

'What is?'

'The fact that we should both be sitting here, you with your Thomas Mann and me with my physics. Because the main subject of my book is something called the Schrödinger equation. It's the fundamental rule of quantum mechanics. And do you know how Schrödinger found it? One Christmas in the nineteen twenties he went to a tuberculosis clinic in the Swiss Alps.'

Coincidences mean only whatever we want them to. Thomas Mann wrote a novel about a sanatorium, then a year after it was published, Erwin Schrödinger went to a similar establishment and made his famous discovery. Both got the Nobel Prize for their efforts and became celebrated as philosophers of their age. Is there any connection? Absolutely none.

That's not how Ms Vicious Cycloids would see it, though. When Ringer tuned in to her lecture again, they'd left Melville altogether. Now the subject was the composer Robert Schumann; a manic depressive whose 'cycloidal' personality manifested itself in cyclical works like the piano suite *Kreisleriana*, whose name comes from the German for 'circle maker'. Or should that be – as the lecturer now asked with a piquant, rhetorical smirk – 'cycloid maker'? This, Ringer understood, was what counted for logical argument in her line of work: random hyperlinks as arbitrary as skipping from one menu to another on a Q-phone; as fortuitous as sitting down for lunch opposite the person who will become your lover.

With Helen, finding such links was no more than an erudite form of flirting. *Vicious Cycloids* was a similarly rhetorical exercise in social manoeuvring. The speaker did, to be fair, mention pendulums – but only as a way of then hauling in the name Foucault, and hence another avenue of pointless associations. For her, Ringer realized, there was no truth or falsehood, only 'texts' to be 'deconstructed'. Too bad if any of those texts should happen to be a wrong number, and all interpretation consequently wrong.

He brought out his Q-phone and tried to pull the mysterious message back onto the screen, his menu-hopping instead sending him to the leisure section where a sudden loud and fully orchestrated burst of *Rhapsody in Blue* caused heads to turn in anger. He sheepishly switched off the phone and put it back inside his pocket. *Call me: H.* What did it mean? Almost certainly nothing. And yet there was a chance – only a chance – that it really was connected with Helen.

'It's an interesting parallel,' she'd said to him, pushing a lettuce leaf with her fork. 'Mann and Schrödinger. I might even be able to work it into my thesis.' She was studying German literature in relation to philosophy. 'But how do physicists get their inspiration? I'd be fascinated to know.' Helen looked at him across the table with eyes that suddenly promised more than conversation.

Sex was Schrödinger's inspiration. Holidaying at the sanatorium where he had formerly been treated, he arranged for a lover to join him. And somehow this obscure physicist, who had hitherto done nothing of outstanding value, discovered the equation for quantum waves.

Maybe it was a fluke. Who knows, perhaps the great message was really meant for someone else. God misdialled, and it was Schrödinger, not the intended recipient, who came down from the mountain with $H\psi=E\psi$ in his pocket. His ticket to world fame, a place in history. Like Mann – like everyone – he never entertained the possibility that his success might be due to luck. When events work to our advantage, we prefer to call it destiny or talent.

'Perhaps there's something magical about mountains,' Ringer suggested.

'It's like Nietzsche,' Helen said. 'He was hiking in Switzerland when he had his vision of Zarathustra.'

'And he went totally mad,' Ringer recalled.

'Nietzsche lies behind *Doktor Faustus*,' she told him gravely, and while her face was lowered he divined, like a faint galaxy, the protrusion of a nipple beneath her red pullover. 'Nietzsche saw music as expressing the essence of existence. This was Schopenhauer's notion: it became Wagner's creed. But Mann realized that with its mysticism, its irrationality, this philosophy of idealism could only lead in the end to the collective madness of fascism.'

Like the cycloid story Ringer found himself listening to years later, this was a neat and entirely untestable theory (unless one could rerun history without Nietzsche and see if Hitler still rose to power). But with Helen he had been more patient, because none of it was about fact or reason. It was about the promise of her naked body; the promise – soon to be fulfilled – of chance and beauty, and the momentary sensation of being truly alive. We are irrational animals: nature made us so. Thus each of his and Helen's words, no matter how coolly abstract, was only a coded form of a more important communication that read: 'There is a point in spacetime where you are commanded to make love, and you must find it.'

Or else it said *Call me: H.* Years after last seeing her, Ringer's Q-phone had picked up a signal that had traversed the cosmos, and now here he was, listening to a lecture that reminded him of Helen. It was a meaningless coincidence; and the same fictitious force was what kept *Vicious Cycloids* trundling along.

The lecturer was describing how Ishmael, crouched in the metal try-pot, would have seen his own distorted reflection beneath him; so for a moment he would have acquired a cycloidal doppelgänger and gone slightly mad – just like Schumann, who based *Kreisleriana* on an E. T. A. Hoffmann novel about a crazed musician scared at one point by his reflection in a curved mirror. This took them to Lacan's 'psychoanalytic topology' – in which the male erectile organ is equated with the square root of minus one – and then on to another chain of absurd connections.

Ringer had heard of E. T. A. Hoffmann, though, thanks to Helen. So anyone might guess it was all terribly significant, this lecture he'd blundered into, with its multiple cross-references. No doubt some imaginative novelist could conceive a logical scheme linking everything: Hoffmann, Schumann, Schrödinger, Mann. Some grand unified theory in which Helen and Ringer would be quantum resonances; their lovemaking (that first time, on the rug before the sputtering gas fire in his flat) a narrative inevitability.

But life is not a novel, except for those vain enough to consider themselves creatures of art. Ringer knew otherwise. The experiencing of his life came to him by means of a mental search engine that sifted and filtered according to subjective relevance. Finding patterns in the output was as easy as seeing faces in clouds.

This was why he had so often seen Helen: strangers who looked like her from behind, or were glimpsed by him through the reflections of a bus window as it set off and sped from view. Women who, if he could look at them properly, would be totally unlike the one he first met in the university canteen, pushing her uneaten salad to one side as their encounter reached its critical moment, then resting her chin on steepled hands and saying simply, 'So?' as her eyes flashed their celestial promise once again.

Call me: H. It could not be Helen, because after the end of their affair she abandoned her studies, went abroad, and eluded his every effort to contact her. It was as if she had disappeared from the earth; her name, in the following years whenever he had searched for it, was absent from every phone directory, even the Internet. She might have died, or changed her identity. More likely, she had simply slipped over the horizon of his existence, in the same way that most acquaintances pass unnoticed.

What if he were ever to see her again? She would probably be married with children, like Ringer. Their shared past would be laughably irrelevant; they could instead become passionless friends. Probably best, then, if he never saw her.

The lecture was still rolling on as he rejoined it. In *Moby-Dick*, Ishmael watches the try-pot, filled with greasy whaleflesh, burn and bubble through the night, prompting morbid thoughts of death and insanity. In the end Ishmael's not even sure if he's awake or asleep – the world has become 'in some enchanted way, inverted'. And that, the speaker explained, is why Melville, in his densely meaningful little episode, made the gleaming try-pots cycloidal. They are a symbol of time and madness, of multiplicity and reversal: themes pursued elsewhere by Hoffmann and Schumann. Three years after *Moby-Dick* was published to murderously hostile reviews, Schumann starved himself to death in an asylum. He was posthumously diagnosed as suffering from dementia praecox – schizophrenia – by the psychiatrist Paul Möbius.

And this, it turned out, was the punchline they'd been heading for all along; for now they came – as the speaker triumphantly declared – 'full-cycloid'; but with a twist, as in a Möbius strip. Melville based his story on a legendary whale called Mocha Dick. Surely, when altering the name for his book, he made the wrong choice. A novel that has a mirrored double-personality at its heart should rather be called *Mobius Dick*.

And there the lecture ended. Some audience members were able to summon up a question, but the only one in Ringer's mind was: 'What the hell was all that about?' He picked up his empty sandwich box and headed back to the theoretical physics department, fully convinced he had chosen the right degree subject thirty years previously.

Forget the text, he decided. *Call me: H* meant nothing. Life is not a narrative. To think otherwise is a game novelists play in order to delight and entertain; some professors play it too, but only so as to confuse. Ringer sat down at his desk, and when he brought his Q-phone from his pocket not long afterwards, he saw to his surprise that the text, immune to all his fumblings, had decided to display itself again. Had it resurfaced like a restless ghost? Or had the unknown caller sent it again?

FROM *THE ANGEL RETURNS*
by Heinrich Behring*

Not an easy journey for a woman of my age, but I made it twice. The first time, in May of 1855, I found Schumann unwell, though not beyond hope. A year later, all hope was gone. Dr Richarz had clearly done a fine job on his most illustrious patient, having made him every bit as sick as the good doctor always guessed him to be.

Richarz is supposed to be one of the more enlightened physicians, but Endenich is a dismal place. A dreary courtyard leading to a dreary house, where a dozen or so patients have their days of madness measured out in grains of sedative. Schumann's suite was upstairs, offering a view of nearby Bonn he sickened of, and a piano he played seldom, and badly. On my first visit he longed only for escape. On my second, it was clear that one exit alone was left to him.

Richarz is amiable, incompetent and somewhat deaf. Overwhelmed by the success of his unique private

* English translation by Celia Carter. Cromwell Press, British Democratic Republic, 1949

hospital, he has had to delegate much of the work to subordinates trained at public asylums; warders who think it therapy to sit silently with their mournful charges in local taverns. At least Schumann was spared this. Instead, while still able, he was taken for long, pointless walks: visiting Beethoven's birthplace, or picking violets at the roadside.

'There was really no need to come again, Frau von Arnim,' Dr Richarz said, mildly flustered, as he received me in his office. 'Your journey is entirely unnecessary.' Medical notes burdened his desk in disarray. He sat down and tried putting them in order, peering at me over his spectacles as he rustled the stiff, useless documents.

'So much paperwork, Herr Doktor,' I observed.

'Indeed,' he said, squaring and at last mastering the heap before disposing of it in a drawer he slammed shut. 'The essence of science is exactitude. Precision of habit,' he elaborated, now contemplating the open lid of his silver inkwell, becoming quickly distracted by it, 'engenders . . . precision . . . of . . .' He closed the lid, fell silent.

'Thought?' I suggested.

'Exactly, madam,' he declared, recapturing his thread. 'Precision of thought. The kernel of science. The artist's mind, on the other hand, is characterized, so to speak, more by . . . by . . .' The position of the inkwell on his desk appeared to be causing him some disquiet; he slid the object from left to right, as if unsure which hand was meant to dip a pen in it.

'Vagueness?' I offered.

'What's that you say?' Richarz squinted at me. 'Madam, I'm afraid you'll have to speak up a little.'

I therefore suggested to him, mezzo forte and with clarity: 'The artist's mind is characterized by imprecision.'

'Really, what nonsense!' Richarz chuckled heartily to himself, almost breaking into a chesty cough. 'Madam, though you have known the affections of the greatest artists of our age, it seems your feminine charms have served only to make those artists hide from you the very root of their genius. No, my dear Frau von Arnim, the artistic mind has, at its foundation, something very precise indeed. I mean the condition of melancholy.'

Then he sat back, creaking heavily in his chair, and from his waistcoat drew a snuff box with which he began to fiddle. In this way he could at least forget about the matching silver inkwell, which had by now come to rest in the middle of his desk, directly before his myopic gaze.

'Yes, madam, melancholy,' he said grandly. 'Of course, I readily grant that a thousand men might have all the sorrows of Werther, and none of the talent. Melancholy is, as we scientists say, a necessary but insufficient condition of genius. Moreover there appear to have been one or two artists throughout history in whom the melancholic disposition has been suppressed to such an extent, and with such uncanny skill, that to their earthly companions these inspired men seemed almost happy. Oh, yes, I could describe a dozen case histories – poets, composers, painters – all of whom were men of public laughter and good cheer. But look into the dark privacy of their souls, madam, and you will always find a streak of despair where none suspected it; and this hard, thin sliver bears the very sap of genius.'

'Which brings us, does it not,' I reminded Dr Richarz, 'to our friend Robert Schumann?'

The doctor, having spilled more snuff than he had rubbed, now poked some into his nose. 'His is a very typical case,' Richarz told me, his eyes watering, though not with emotion. 'His sap, so to speak, has run dry. It is the inevitable concluding state of his condition.' He spoke with the satisfaction of one who has completed a difficult calculation, arriving at exactly the required total.

'If he has reached the final stage,' I said, 'does this mean his wife Clara can expect to see him discharged soon?'

Richarz was suddenly deaf again, and ignored my question. Wiping a moist eye, he told me, 'For some time now we have been offering only basic supportive care. He refuses to eat, and has almost completely lost the power of speech, or of comprehension. Such vegetative degeneration is wholly to be expected, given the causative factors and overall pathology. He'll be dead in a month or two.' Richarz turned his head and gazed complacently towards the window's sickly light. 'It's all very sad, of course,' he said. 'But Schumann's end, one might say, is something of an occupational hazard, as much as the hardening of a miner's lung. Genius and melancholy, inseparably bound, are like . . . how should I put it . . . ?'

'Two sides of the same coin?' I suggested.

'What's that? A coin? Yes, Frau von Arnim, you circumscribe it very amply indeed.'

The asylum of Dr Richarz had been earning a great many coins from Schumann's illness, most of them donated by sympathetic friends and fellow musicians, since Clara's earnings as a pianist could not cover the heavy costs in addition to feeding seven children. The last of them, Felix, was born three months after Schumann came to Endenich. Now Robert had been here for more than two years, and in all that time, Richarz had never allowed Clara to see him. It was a drive of several hours: too far to undertake, Richarz insisted, unless strictly necessary. At first he told Clara that emotional stimulation would only further damage the composer's fragile organism. More recently, Richarz had advised all visitors to stay away, so that they need not witness his patient's irreparably pitiable condition.

'A coin, yes,' Richarz murmured. 'You speak with the voice of a poet, Frau von Arnim. You, who have known Goethe.'

During my previous visit, Richarz quizzed me endlessly about my most famous friend. Was Goethe's melancholy manifest, the doctor wanted to know, or else suppressed? Tell me, Richarz had asked, pen in hand; was Goethe's love, in your opinion, a form of self-punishment?

Then there was Beethoven, of course. Richarz had diagnosed his period of 'organic instability' quite precisely. It occurred, he informed me, only a few years after I brought Beethoven and Goethe together for their historic meeting. And do tell me about Liszt, Richarz had added, showing me the piano Franz once played, which Schumann now ignored. For Richarz, these names – men whose company and even love I shared – were merely illustrious specimens, in need of proper cataloguing.

During that first visit, I made it clear to Richarz I was only interested in discussing Schumann. But Richarz was after bigger game, and now once more he raised the hallowed icon of my greatest love.

'We should not speak of Goethe,' I told him. 'It would be indelicate of me; like the gossiping of a physician about a patient.'

Richarz was not too deaf to raise an eyebrow; he knew my meaning. His wagging tongue had made it common knowledge round here: Schumann's wife had taken as lover the promising and beautiful young Brahms, whom Schumann himself unnaturally doted on. Family problems, Richarz reckoned, were what had made Schumann throw himself into the Rhine only months after Brahms showed up on their doorstep in Düsseldorf and made himself at home. A domineering wife whose performing success eclipsed Schumann's own failed career as conductor; and now she was unfaithful too. My friend Joseph Joachim tried to save him, but it was too late. Joachim and Brahms were allowed to visit Endenich, but not Clara.

'Gossip is a vice that does not tempt me,' Richarz said smugly. 'I leave that to the fairer sex. But regarding Goethe, whom you knew so intimately, I was thinking only that the two-sided coin with which artists pay for their immortality is a pact the author of *Faust* must clearly have understood. He, more than anyone, must have known the deep, dark chasm of despondency from which all art springs.'

I left Richarz to pursue this reverie in the seclusion of his own meandering thoughts, but soon found the doctor quoting the poet's words: '*Brief joy must be our lot, that woes overwhelm.* A flicker of happiness is all we can hope for, Frau von Arnim, followed inevitably by darkness. Such is Faust's realization. Granted his every wish, he has Helen woken from the Trojan dead: the most beautiful and desirable woman in all history. Yet what can he enjoy with her, except a moment of dream-like pleasure? And after that, oblivion.'

Richarz looked at me with the hollow wisdom of a man who takes as truth exactly whatever he has found written in some other man's book.

'I wonder who Goethe's Helen really was,' Richarz then asked teasingly. 'Who was the lost love he raised from the past in his great poetic drama? Or does Goethe perhaps mean Eternal Woman: the spirit that drives men to art, and to despair?' Richarz waited for me to answer; I gave him none. So he continued, 'Goethe's early love for your mother is a story as famous and touching as the one you yourself have told of his later affection for you.' Still I remained silent. 'And Beethoven, of course, had his own Immortal Beloved, did he not? Some allege the unknown woman who inspired him was you, madam. My, what a veritable stable of earthly muses!'

Again Richarz chuckled, and again I ignored him. Yes, I – Bettina von Arnim – was Goethe's lover: my late husband Achim and the whole world knew it. Nature never meant me to be a wife, or a widow; and if now, an old woman past my seventieth year, I should still find myself charmed by a fine young man such as Joseph Joachim, what of it? Richarz would no doubt have been shocked beyond words had I admitted to him my love for the musician who was himself spurned by my own daughter. But I have lived long enough to know that in this world anything is possible, and that everything, if only it can be understood, can be forgiven. Goethe loved my mother before he ever fell for me; and I do not dismiss the idea that love can leap generations in the other direction too, so that after a daughter, a mother is loved, even if she is old.

Very well then, I have adopted young Joachim, just as the Schumanns adopted Brahms. And yes, it was only out of consideration for Joseph that, like him, I visited Endenich; just as Brahms did only in order to please Clara. But should we then conclude, as Richarz apparently did, that the melancholy of geniuses is precipitated always by the fickleness of women?

'Why do you resist visitors such as myself and Clara,' I asked him, 'but not Brahms or Joachim?'

Richarz rocked uneasily in his chair. 'I would prefer those gentlemen not to waste their time coming here, however I am in no position to resist. They have a legal right of access.'

'And Schumann's own wife does not?'

'Madam,' Richarz said, 'please do not put me in the position of having to speak of matters which might embarrass you.'

I was having none of this. 'Dr Richarz,' I told him, 'I am seventy-one years old, a widow, an author of considerable renown, and a woman who has seen all that the world has to offer. If there's anything you could possibly say that would embarrass me, I think I'd be quite interested to hear it!'

Richarz, his mouth hanging open with surprise, was saved by a knock at the door.

'Ah, this must be Dr Peters,' Richarz exclaimed with some relief. 'Come in!'

The fellow who entered was tall, thin, grey faced, and wore the sorrowfully expectant look of an undertaker. He greeted me civilly, then seated himself near the window.

'Dr Peters is in charge of Schumann's day-to-day treatment,' Richarz explained to me. 'He can tell you far more than I about the patient's demeanour.'

I looked from one man to the other, not knowing which of them I trusted less. Peters was waiting for someone to prompt him.

'How is he today?' I finally asked.

Peters was unsure how to answer. 'As before,' he eventually told me.

'We shall wait until Schumann is soundly asleep,' Richarz explained to me, 'before going up to see him.'

I was puzzled by this. 'Would it not be better for me to see him awake?'

Richarz and Peters looked at one another, then again at me.

'No,' said Richarz. 'It would not.' Then he turned to Peters again. 'Have there been further hallucinations?'

'Yes, sir.'

'And is their content unchanged?'

'It is, sir.'

I began to understand that Richarz's dialogue with his subordinate was a way for him to ease his own embarrassment in clarifying for me the nature of Schumann's latest illness.

'Tell me, Dr Peters,' Richarz continued, 'would it be accurate to say that the patient's hallucinations principally concern an individual, or individuals, of the female sex?'

'It would, sir.'

'And would it therefore possibly be inadvisable for any living individual of that sex to be present while such hallucinations were in progress?'

'Indubitably, sir.'

Richarz clearly felt he had said enough. He straightened his waistcoat with a victorious air, then slid his inkwell definitively to the edge of his desk.

I turned and said to the cadaverous Dr Peters, 'Does Robert imagine he is with his wife?'

Peters was uneasy, and spoke quietly. 'It's hard to say, madam.' He looked to Richarz for encouragement, received none, and hence was forced to continue. 'The patient came to the conclusion some time ago that his wife – as she has never written or visited – must be dead. Since then, he hasn't been eating. We have to use a tube.'

'A tube?' I exclaimed, loudly enough for Richarz to hear.

'That's enough, Dr Peters,' he instructed. 'We should not expose our distinguished guest to the distasteful physical details of our patient's medical treatment.'

I interrupted angrily. 'Are you telling me that Schumann is being force-fed?' Searching the faces of the two men, I saw nothing but indifference. 'Has isolation from his family made him lose the will to live? What kind of doctors are you? This is not care, it's mediaeval torture!'

'Enough!' Richarz silenced me, then continued more calmly though with evident irritation. 'This is no place for hysterical outbursts. We have ways of alleviating such conditions. I assure you, madam, that if you were as fully qualified and informed about the matter as we are, then you would not use such slanderous language.' He stood up; Dr Peters did likewise. 'I shall leave you for a moment, Frau von Arnim, while I and my assistant go upstairs to assess the patient. I hope that when we return you will have reconsidered your opinions about our establishment. Otherwise I shall have no alternative but to terminate your visit.'

Then he came out from behind his desk and marched stiffly to the door, followed by Peters who closed it behind them, leaving me to try and guess what state poor Schumann must be in.

Twelve months earlier, when I had last visited, I had found very little wrong with him apart from an excess of nervous energy that the boredom of his confinement had greatly aggravated. On that occasion too, Richarz would not allow me to see him until I had first endured a long delay whose only purpose, it seemed, was to make sure I knew whose will it was that shaped things here.

Then, as now, Richarz had begun with a lecture. 'The human mind,' he informed me, 'is somewhat like . . . ' And he lapsed into his habitual academic silence, leaving me to try and supply the necessary metaphor.

'A book, Herr Doktor?' I suggested.

'What's that? No, no,' he said. 'A book is written in advance and demands only to be read.'

'Then is the human mind like the author of the book?'

Dr Richarz laughed. 'Since you are an author your-self, Frau von Arnim, I can see that the analogy must be appealing. But no; we are not the conscious authors of our thoughts. Why, even from his earliest years, Schumann claimed to possess two separate personalities with separate wills of their own. And he heard the voices of angels, dictating music to him.'

'Does he hear them still?' I asked.

Richarz frowned then. Now, waiting for my second encounter with his patient, I recalled that frown and wondered what it meant. Were those angels the stuff of his latest visions?

Joseph Joachim has the face of an angel. So does Brahms, of course. They will be the great men that some old lady like myself one day remembers; and in Brahms's case, that greatness was bestowed by Schumann himself, in print. *New Paths*, Schumann called the article where he announced the arrival of a Messiah to counter the Wagnerites. '*He is come, a young blood by whose cradle graces and heroes kept watch. He is called Johannes Brahms.*' Not bad, as first reviews go. And that's all it takes to launch a career. Oh, people like Richarz can ponder their lofty nonsense about genius and melancholy, but I've seen enough of the world to know how it is that people make it onto the pedestal in the first place. Opinions are formed by intelligent people such as Schumann, or myself. Then they are repeated by common fools like Richarz who turn them into great truths. If Brahms were not so handsome, would Schumann have been quite so indiscreet in his admiration? If Brahms had not knocked unannounced on Schumann's door one day and made himself a house guest, would anyone ever have heard of this girlish twenty-year-old; this blond blue-eyed lad who they say perfected his piano technique in a Hamburg brothel?

It doesn't take much to put an angel among the stars. In Brahms's case, as in so many others, it was merely a matter of the right word from the right authority. Schumann's prophecy is sure to fulfil itself, and one day busts of Brahms, grown old and famous, will adorn respectable parlour pianos everywhere. Of course I'd heard the rumours: that for Brahms and Clara, Schumann's imprisonment here was quite convenient. Or even that the seventh child whom Robert never saw is not his own. I leave such matters to the likes of Richarz: the quacks and scholars who need great men as fleas need dogs.

Still no sign of him and Peters. They were making me wait, just like before. Such games must afford them welcome entertainment in a place where mental stimulation of any kind is strictly banned. Even Richarz's office, where I sat, was largely bare. Uncluttered surroundings, Richarz told me, make for an uncluttered mind. What he really meant, I think, was empty.

Schumann began writing his article about Brahms almost as soon as the young Apollo walked into his life. And a few weeks after that, Schumann conducted his last concert. Joachim told me what a disaster it was. In the rehearsals, Schumann kept dropping the baton, eventually having to tie it to his wrist with string. The Düsseldorf orchestra had seen Schumann grow increasingly erratic in recent months, but now he reached the limit. He was spilling sheets of music from the lectern; he didn't know where he was. An important horn solo never happened, since Schumann had lost count of the bars and failed to cue the player. Could love alone so turn a head? Was the angelic Brahms, lounging on Schumann's hearth rug, the cause of such distraction?

The musicians begged Joachim to conduct the evening's performance, but he refused: he could never do

such a thing to a friend. Schumann raised the baton that
night, and it was a shambles. Afterwards he was effectively dismissed from his post.

So when Schumann published his article on Brahms,
he was not only heralding the arrival of a new genius but
also announcing the end of his own career. He was passing the crown to his heir; passing his wife too, perhaps.
Four months later he leapt into the Rhine, was dragged
out by fishermen, and his incarceration at Endenich
began.

Richarz kept me waiting the first time, just like he did
again now, possibly hoping I would give up and leave.
'Frau von Arnim,' he said to me on that previous visit,
'how exactly can I explain to you, in terms you might
understand, just what it is that the human mind most
closely resembles?'

We'd already dismissed books and authors. 'A cabinet
of precious jewels?' I wondered.

He thought about it for a moment. 'Not really.'

'A flower?'

'Heavens no.'

'A city?'

Dr Richarz appeared to like this; he rubbed his chin,
but then said, 'No, I don't think that will do.'

'Is the mind perhaps like melting snow; or the wheels
of a carriage?'

I don't know how many metaphors I offered him; I
could feel my own poetic stock run almost to exhaustion
when at last the doctor's face became illuminated by a
happy thought.

'I have it!' he declared. 'The human mind is like . . . is like the universe itself!'

Well, this was good to know.

'You do recall, after all,' he said, 'that our great poet once set himself the task of writing a novel about that very subject.'

Yes, of course I knew of Goethe's failed ambition, but I was not to be drawn back to Goethe again. 'If the mind is like the whole world,' I said to Richarz, 'then I can see why your task as healer of minds is as futile as the poet's lofty goal.' Of his novel about the universe, Goethe managed little beyond an essay on granite.

'The world; the spirit,' Dr Richarz enthused, 'our philosophers have shown beyond doubt that they are identical and commensurate; that they are inherent within one another and stand in a necessary relation of indiscernible identity . . .'

'Yes, Herr Doktor,' I said patiently. 'I am quite familiar with Hegel and Fichte and Schopenhauer. But I do sometimes wonder if there really is any more wisdom in them than in the tales of elves and fairies my grandmother used to tell me on her knee.'

Dr Richarz laughed loudly. 'My dear Frau von Arnim,' he chuckled, 'you are one of the most esteemed literary figures of our times; and your late husband, if I may be so bold as to say, must have been one of the luckiest men alive. But really, madam, though you have commerced with geniuses like a shooting star amidst the heavenly constellations, you speak, after all your years of rich experience, with the simple, delightful voice of a schoolgirl.'

That was when he got up and left me; cordially, on that occasion, but with just as much determination to make me wait. That's what we do at my age: wait. We count the days and think how many have been counted for us already.

Schumann had been at Endenich for a year when I made my first visit. In that time he had made what Richarz considered modest progress, thanks to warm baths, enemas and walks in the woods. Joachim, on the other hand, told me Schumann was so starved of company he had nearly forgotten how to speak. A whole hour passed until at last I saw him then, poor Robert, coming into the room, his face instantly transformed when he recognized me, rushing to embrace me and at first barely able to form a sentence. Once he mastered his tongue, he was like a musician long separated from his instrument, the words beginning to pour from him. Soon he was talking almost too quickly for me to grasp what he was saying, about places he had visited in the past, about his family, and above all about the wonderful music of Brahms.

After that first visit, I wrote to Clara straight away, told her my concerns about Richarz and his establishment. Clara came to Endenich, spoke with Richarz, then went home again without even seeing her husband. In the interests of what she considers right, she can show the cold determination of a well-sharpened blade.

Joachim saw how Clara teaches her pupils. A young

girl was there at the Schumanns' house one day for a piano lesson; a girl with some mechanical talent but not the slightest shred of musicality. The kind, in other words, whose parents provide real musicians with a living.

This pupil was sitting bolt upright as required. All unnecessary movement of her limbs had been solved long ago by making her balance coins on the backs of her hands while playing the preludes of Bach. Now, whether it was a Beethoven sonata or a Schubert waltz beneath her fingers, this girl performed with an aloofness born of terror. Should she ever dare love what she played, the imaginary coin might slip from her hand, and she would feel the sharp lash of Clara's displeasure.

On this occasion they were studying Robert's music, Joachim told me. The pupil had mastered *Kinderszenen* before she was twelve or thirteen; Joachim listened as she played 'Chiarina' and 'Estrella' from *Carnaval*, then was coached in the suite *Kreisleriana*, which, like the *Nachtstücke* and *Fantasiestücke*, takes its title from the composer's beloved E. T. A. Hoffmann.

Joachim sat listening while the girl began the final movement, so humorous and macabre: a ghost story in music. It depicts Hoffmann's fictional hero Johannes Kreisler creeping softly through the night. Joachim says that when he once heard Robert play it, it made the hairs on his neck stand up. Clara's pupil, unfortunately, could not produce the same effect.

Schumann instructs in the score that the left hand be 'light and free'. According to Joachim, Clara's pupil was taking the instruction quite literally; she was playing with the intended rubato, making the left and right hands almost disconnect. Joachim thinks this spectral finale shows Kreisler haunted by his double; or perhaps the lower stave is Kreisler while the upper is his cat Murr, the comical feline philosopher, tripping over moonlit rooftops. Either way, Joachim says, the player's hands must be allowed a degree of independence, as if telling two different stories at once. But Clara was having none of it.

'The left,' she bluntly announced, interrupting her pupil. 'Observe all note values carefully.'

The flustered pupil was allowed to continue. It sounded even worse than before.

'Halt!' Clara cried, so suddenly that the pupil gave a start, tearing her hands from the keyboard as if it were a hot stove. Such was Clara's own distress at the incompetence she had to deal with that for a moment she could not find her words. 'I was not hitherto aware,' she finally said, grandly, 'that my pupil is come of the people of Nineveh.'

The girl looked down at her lap, where her useless hands were folded, with an air of resignation.

'Do you not know your left from your right?' Clara said witheringly. 'Do you not know how to count? Do you not understand that when I ask you to observe the note values in the left hand, it is not my wish that you should instead shorten yet further the already unpleasant staccato it pleases you to peck out with your right?'

Joachim told me the girl was almost crying by now. He wasn't surprised.

'Young lady,' Clara said to her, more softly but with undiminished firmness. 'We are here not to make merry, but to serve a higher purpose in which our own insignificant feelings and sentiments can have no place.' Then Clara sat down at the other piano. 'Let me show you how it must be.'

She began to play the same passage, her hands gliding with absolute confidence and control across the keyboard, and Joachim said it was like the sudden opening of a window, such was the purity and exactness of Clara's touch. It was the sound of a truly great musician; yet it was a voice that was hers alone. Clara's way of teaching is to try and make all her pupils sound just like her. In other words, to drain from them every last drop of individuality, turning them into brilliantly polished imitators.

Joachim, dispirited, stood up and excused himself from the lesson. He had heard enough, he said to Clara; a remark that apparently left her pupil weeping inconsolably once he had vacated the room, since she had hoped to receive the famous young violinist's blessings on her own musical career. What he had heard, he told me, reminded him more of the chess-playing automaton that once amused Voltaire.

Clara won't allow her pupils to make their own mistakes; instead she makes them faithfully reproduce her own. But there can be no art without love, Joachim told me, even if it is a love that is flawed; and I knew from his eyes that he was thinking of Gisela, my daughter who refused his offer of marriage, though I advised her to accept. There must be love and despair, he said, humour and anger, reason and madness, jealousy and pride. *Kreisleriana* has all of these.

When Schumann wrote it more than twenty years ago, he dedicated it to Chopin, whom he had praised in print just as he would later hail Brahms. Chopin, I'm told, took one look at the score and said the cover was very pretty. That is the scorn of a true artist: like the way Goethe shrugged off Beethoven after I brought them together.

Perhaps when Brahms arrived on Schumann's doorstep, a genuine artist would have had the upstart kicked back onto the street. But Schumann let him in, this beautiful young brothel pianist who signed his musical works 'Kreisler' after his favourite fictional character. Yes, Brahms too is besotted with Hoffmann's supernatural tales: he arrived at the Schumanns' house like a creature of Robert's imagination made magically flesh. Some say Brahms was moved to visit after coming across the score of *Kreisleriana*, which he read as if it were about himself. So perhaps the ghostly figure in the last movement is Brahms, light and free, preparing to creep up on Schumann years later. Preparing to enter the house, steal the wife, sink his teeth into Schumann's neck and drink the master's blood. This was the ghastly vision Clara wrested from her pupil, then played so smoothly.

But what had happened to Richarz and Peters? What could be taking them so long, upstairs with their patient while I sat waiting like a servant? Twelve months previously, Schumann had been allowed down to see me. Now he was permanently confined to bed, slowly starving himself to death.

The door opened and I saw Richarz. 'Frau von Arnim,' he said. 'Are you prepared to see the patient?'

I gave a silent nod.

'And do you undertake to restrain yourself in the patient's presence from any form of behaviour which might exacerbate his condition?'

Again I nodded.

'Then you may come with us,' he told me, and I rose to follow the doctor upstairs.

'Does he ever compose now?' I asked Richarz as I clasped the banister and slowly mounted the steps, feeling every year of my long life in the stiffness of my joints.

'He has jotted a few scraps,' Richarz told me, turning to watch my ascent behind him, though not offering any help. 'Herr Brahms collects everything, yet none is worthy of inclusion in the composer's collected works. Herr Brahms considers it better to destroy these last sad outpourings.'

We reached the top of the stairs where I regained my breath. So Brahms was already editing the complete edition. All that was left was for Schumann to die and then the final inconvenient detail would be resolved. The composer's life had effectively ended only a few months after his last concert, when he threw himself into the Rhine. That was when his life as an artist – the only one anybody cares about – was extinguished.

We reached Schumann's door, where Peters stood waiting. There was a metal panel fixed upon it, which Peters slowly drew aside, making a sound like the grinding of a knife. A peephole was revealed through which the captive could be observed.

'Look for yourself, Frau von Arnim,' Richarz told me.

Peering into the room, I saw a figure lying unconscious on the bed. His face was not visible to me; all I could see was a thin hand projecting from the bedcovers, which I would not have recognized as Schumann's had I not known whose it was.

'I wish to be allowed inside,' I told Richarz.

'I would prefer the patient to be left undisturbed,' the doctor told me; but I had no more time for his prevarication.

'Unlock this door for me,' I said to him. 'Until you do, I promise you I shall not move from this spot.'

Richarz was annoyed, but another glance at Schumann convinced him the patient was safely sedated, and so he instructed Peters to let me in. With a jangling of keys, Peters opened the heavy door and the three of us went inside and approached the bed. I stood flanked by the doctors as we gazed silently upon the pitiful sight.

Schumann's face was changed. It was the emaciated mask of an unburied corpse. I gave an involuntary gasp of horror.

'You can see why it would have been better for you not to come,' Richarz whispered. 'And why his family must be spared such a spectacle.'

Then, as I watched, I realized that Schumann's lips were trembling, almost imperceptibly. He was trying to speak. I bent to listen.

Richarz hissed at me, 'Madam, please!' But it was too late. Before he could restrain me, I had brought myself close to the bedside, stooping to feel the composer's faint breath on my cheek as I listened for his words.

'Robert,' I said, 'it's me, Bettina.'

'This is most unwise!' Richarz anxiously whispered, trying to draw me back.

'Robert, your family and all your many friends send their warmest greetings.'

Richarz and Peters were tutting behind me like a pair of old fishwives. I silenced them. Robert was saying something. At first I thought he was complaining about a lack of air; I tried to loosen the top button of his night-shirt. Then I heard more clearly what he was saying. *Angel.*

'I'm not an angel, Robert. I'm your friend Bettina.'

His words became clearer; perhaps only because I was growing accustomed to the weakness of his voice. 'Where?' he said. 'Where angel?'

He must be looking for Brahms, I supposed; his eyes were partly open now. Pale and watery, they directed themselves towards a table behind me, and when I turned I saw on it some pages of music that Brahms must have assembled there for destruction. Did Schumann perhaps want me to save them?

'Angel,' he said again. 'Came before.'

36

'Madam,' Richarz interrupted, 'please do not encourage the patient's fantasies.'

Yet Robert's voice grew more urgent and insistent. 'The angel will come again,' he said. 'She promised me.'

He wasn't speaking of Brahms after all. 'Clara is well,' I said, hearing a groan from Dr Richarz. But she, too, was not the angel Robert spoke of. Instead he became still more excited.

'*Is it as wife she comes?*' he said. '*Comes she as queen?*' It was a line remembered from long ago.

'You see the extent of his delusion,' Richarz said gloomily, and as Robert had now fallen silent and closed his eyes, I raised and straightened myself to hear the doctor's explanation.

'You might recall,' Richarz told me, 'that Schumann laboured for many years over a musical setting of Goethe's *Faust*. He completed and published some scenes before he became ill. The project has not died in his imagination.'

I was amazed. 'Is he still composing further sections? And is this the music Brahms is destroying? Surely it would be an outrage for such an important work to be suppressed!'

Richarz shook his head. 'No, madam, it would be a scandal were these last degenerate scraps ever exposed to public scrutiny and ridicule.'

Still I protested, so that Richarz was finally forced to explain himself fully. 'Schumann is no longer the man you knew,' he said. 'The power of composition has left him, along with all his other faculties. He has even forgotten his own identity. Instead he has become a player in the drama he once dreamed of scoring. Yes, madam: he thinks he is Faust. He has visions of Helen meeting him here in this room.' Beside him, Peters gave an embarrassed cough. 'There you have it: the squalid truth of his condition.'

While still trying to absorb this extraordinary information, I heard Robert begin to speak once more. I stooped to listen.

'Helen!' he said.

'What do you want, Robert?'

'Music. More music.'

Now I understood. Schumann had often spoken of how he heard music dictated by angels. Brahms had come into his life as the embodiment of one such angel; here in Endenich, he had found another, born of fragmentary memories in his disintegrating mind. I went to the table and looked at the scribbled pages of music. I was saddened by what I saw: the most blatantly discordant, most hopelessly unmusical harmonizations one could imagine, in which all twelve notes of the chromatic scale were thrown upon the stave in equal measure, without any regard for the jarring cacophony that would result if such a random arrangement were ever to be played.

I went back to Schumann's bedside and asked him, 'Where does the music come from?'

'From Helen.'

No; it came more likely from Mephistopheles. I could see now why Brahms was right to destroy it.

Richarz said to me, 'We must let the patient rest. Do not inflame his hallucinations.'

Robert was lapsing back into unconsciousness. 'Did Helen visit you today?' I asked him.

Suddenly his eyes became focused. 'Yes,' he said clearly.

It chilled me. For a moment it was as if the dream were real: as if a ghostly visitor truly were the author of his strange pages.

Then the sedative reasserted its gentle power. His eyes rolled in their sockets, and soon he was sleeping. In his last days, Schumann was being granted the mercy of forgetting Clara, the children, and all the loves of his life.

It was time for me to leave. As Richarz and Peters escorted me from the room, I did not look round for a final glimpse of the sleeping patient. Better to remember him in happier times. I knew, as the carriage took me away from Endenich, that Schumann could have no more than weeks to live. Clara was finally summoned when death was certain, and it is said that he recognized her face before drawing his last breath.

That was three years ago. Brahms and Clara remain unmarried; Joachim will never understand my love for him. We are each a little closer to the grave. Yet still I wonder where it really came from: that strange, demonic music on Schumann's table; that hellish un-art of sheer chance. Richarz sought an answer as soon as Schumann's corpse grew cold, laying it naked on a slab and sawing open the skull, finding there only the same bloody pulp that harbours all our thoughts and dreams, of reason or of madness. Whatever Schumann saw and heard could not be scooped by the crude tools of science.

He imagined he was Faust: a creature of poetry and of destiny. He thought himself divine, when really he was damned. In his meaningless scribbles, whatever their source, was there perhaps a message and a warning to us all?

PREDESTINED

Sitting at his desk after the *Vicious Cycloids* talk, pondering its parade of coincidences masquerading as insight, John Ringer reminded himself that it isn't only literature professors who sometimes spout nonsense. He thought of Wolfgang Pauli, a colleague of Schrödinger in Zürich. When Pauli's first wife left him, he fell into an emotional crisis that took him to the door of a local shrink named Carl Jung. Together they hatched 'synchronicity': the idea that all coincidences are meaningful.

Pauli thought quantum theory implied a new kind of causality. Jung illustrated it by describing how he once dreamed about a kingfisher, then went for a walk and found a dead one. The future discovery, Jung argued, caused the prior dream.

Or else it was a random event, picked from a billion others merely because it proved what Jung wanted to believe: that everything has significance.

Ringer had fallen into the same seductive trap with the text message that had reappeared on his phone. *Call me: H.* Surely the only connection with Helen was the one in his head. Yet it was enough to make him think again about their first meeting in the university canteen, when she told him about Thomas Mann.

Their meal had ended; she had an appointment elsewhere. They exchanged phone numbers, and as soon as he watched her walk away with her book under her arm, Ringer decided to go to the library in search of a link between science and literature stronger than the respective role of TB clinics in the careers of Mann and Schrödinger. It would be an excuse for phoning her.

In the library, Ringer learned from Mann's biography that his first novel *Buddenbrooks* initially sold poorly. Then, after several months, a famous critic hailed it as a classic, it came out in a cut-price edition, and sold nearly ten thousand copies. Thanks to this lucky break, Mann at the age of twenty-six was suddenly a critical and commercial hit.

Ringer then read about *The Magic Mountain*, in which a young tuberculosis victim pines for a fellow patient – Clavdia Chauchat, a name like an esoteric pun – who resembles his former love. And another novel, *Lotte in Weimar*, about one of Goethe's lovers reminiscing in old age. After it came out, an unknown writer and certified lunatic claimed his own unpublished work had been plagiarized. These details had persisted in Ringer's memory, and now came back to him while he sat at his desk, toying with his Q-phone, wondering if he should try and locate the 'call trace' feature.

In the library, he had soon found himself gravitating to the familiar comforts of the physics section, where a biography of Werner Heisenberg caught his eye. For him too, chance played its part. Heisenberg originally planned on becoming a concert pianist; it was Niels Bohr who convinced him otherwise. In May 1925 Heisenberg discovered the version of quantum theory that established his reputation, and which Schrödinger soon challenged with his own rival theory. Later he headed the Nazi atom bomb project; and if Heisenberg's calculation of the required uranium had been as accurate as his performances of Bach, history might have taken a very different course.

It was while reading this that Ringer had found the connection he was looking for. As soon as he got back to his flat he rang Helen and told her about an idea that might be relevant to her thesis.

'Have you ever heard of the uncertainty principle?' he said.

'Of course. Everybody knows that whenever you observe something you alter it.'

'Yes, that's what everybody knows, and it's how Heisenberg originally interpreted his result. But it's wrong. You can measure electron spin, for instance, without changing it in any way. So Heisenberg and Bohr quickly came up with a more radical interpretation. Measuring something cannot alter it, because there's nothing there to alter. Measuring instead creates the thing being measured. An electron is everywhere or nowhere, until you look at it.'

'How strange.'

'And as a source for this idea, Heisenberg once cited

the nineteenth-century philosopher Fichte. So perhaps you'd better explain Fichte to me.'

They arranged to meet the following afternoon for coffee. Thus their affair – like *Doktor Faustus*, fascism and quantum theory – was predicated on German philosophy.

In the shabby surroundings of the Dolphin Cafe, Ringer learned that Johann Fichte was a proponent of something called 'transcendental idealism'. At the time this interested him less than the cut of Helen's blouse, but the gist was that reality is a creation of mind. If there were no consciousness in the universe, there'd be no universe. Fichte believed in a world of infinite possibility, with every act of human perception, at each instant of time, selecting a particular reality. A century later, this became a doctrine of quantum mechanics.

'Here's what I wonder,' Ringer told Helen, as he tried to stir some life into his grey-brown coffee while sunshine warmed the street beyond the cafe window, the two of them sitting intently opposite one another at a table whose cracked and faded plastic cover bore a crusty stain of dried ketchup. 'Suppose Heisenberg and the others had never read any philosophy. Suppose Kant was run over by a stagecoach when he was a kid, or Schopenhauer decided to throw himself out of a window. What then? Would we have ended up with the same quantum theory?'

Helen shrugged. 'Who knows?' It was a tacit acknowledgement that Ringer's scholarship was superfluous; their intellectual flirtation had gone far enough.

They were circling the point in time and space where they were destined to make love, and the transcendental orbit was becoming frustrating to two mere humans in need of warmth.

Ringer persisted. 'If *Buddenbrooks* had been a flop and Thomas Mann had never published another novel, there would only be a little hole in history that no one would ever notice. But if Schrödinger had failed to find his equation, can we be sure that someone else would eventually have discovered it?'

Helen wasn't listening. Rubbing the plastic tablecloth with her fingertip, she said suddenly, 'Are you a man without qualities?'

'What do you mean?'

'It's a book by Robert Musil,' she said. 'According to Musil, the perfect example of a man without qualities is a mathematician. Everyone can imagine what a poet or a soldier ought to look like. But not a mathematician. Nobody knows what he feels, how he behaves. He's a kind of ghost, a tangent to reality. When he appears to be eating a meal, or watching an opera, or taking a walk, what he's really doing is some other, secret activity inside his own head; one that's purely abstract, without any sound, colour, shape, texture.' She looked at him, and again it was with those eyes that during their first encounter the previous day had seemed to promise love. 'Is everything an abstraction to you?' she asked.

'No,' he said. 'Do you suppose I spend every waking moment thinking about equations?' In fact, the secret now in his head was abstract only to the extent that her body was still a matter of speculation beneath her lilac blouse.

'I can't imagine how your mind works,' she said. 'That fascinates me. What you do is so . . . romantic.'

'Physics?' Ringer wasn't used to hearing it described this way.

'Absolutely,' she said, leaning towards him over the table, close enough that he could smell her perfume. A loose lock of hair on her bare neck invited the correcting stroke of a finger. 'You physicists are always talking about beauty, harmony, elegance, symmetry. Artists gave up on those a long time ago. Nietzsche and Schopenhauer thought music was the ultimate truth; but by the 1920s, Musil could see how things were changing. Physicists, not composers, were the new heroes.'

'No one's ever called me a hero before.'

She blushed and looked down, shyly toying with her coffee cup. 'It's a figure of speech. I'm trying to state a cultural idea. Not very well, perhaps.'

They could have debated whether Beethoven and Einstein really had anything in common beyond a shared aversion to hair combs, but it was time to try and move beyond ideas. Ringer reached across the table and gently held her hand. 'I like you,' he said. She reddened further, her face still lowered.

'I'm not an easy person to be with,' she said. 'In a close way, I mean. If you're thinking of getting involved, I have to warn you it might not be wise.'

'Why?' The cafe was almost deserted, but an old woman at a nearby table was watching them with the casual indifference of one who's seen generations of lovers come and go.

'Never mind,' she said, looking up at him again. 'I'm trouble, that's all. Perhaps we should stick to philosophizing. It's safer.'

'Very well,' he said, 'if that's what you want.'

She noticed the old lady's scrutiny. 'Let's go for a walk,' she suggested. 'It's bright outside. I'd rather be in the park than here.'

They got up and left, and as they emerged into the sunlight, Ringer wondered if he should put his arm around her. The walk to the park, he noted, would take them in the direction of his flat.

Perhaps the entire universe is a mind: a commonplace notion nowadays; but in the early nineteenth century, a radical thought. For Fichte, the mind of God is in everyone. Similar notions led Schopenhauer to Eastern philosophy; Schrödinger and Bohr followed later. People highlight parallels between quantum theory and Buddhism, forgetting those similarities were built in from the outset.

In the park, the crocuses were out: purple, yellow and white beside the path to the boating lake. Helen and Ringer sat down on a wooden bench and watched the ducks. They held hands; they kissed.

What if it were all a dream in the mind of God? A simulation in a cosmic computer? Everyone has wondered things like this, in moments of euphoria, despair, or mere idleness. But suddenly Helen froze; she moved away and looked round towards the bushes behind the bench.

'What's wrong?' Ringer asked her.

She was listening to something. 'Can't you hear it?' He didn't know what she meant; she looked shocked and fearful. Then she said, 'There's a baby crying in there!'

The two of them stood up and peered among the branches; Helen was sure there must be an abandoned infant. At last, on the ground, almost completely hidden from view, Ringer saw a cat crouching suspiciously. It gave a childlike howl.

'There's your baby,' he said with a laugh. They sat down again.

'That was so silly of me,' she said apologetically. 'For a moment . . . No, never mind.'

'What?'

'I thought it needed me,' she said. 'That's all.'

He held her in his arms; they kissed again. This time, though, there was something false and automatic about the gesture. The two of them, Ringer sensed, were each thinking about completely different things; their embrace was a way of pretending otherwise, even though their orbits were still fixed by the same law that would bring them together in Ringer's flat not long afterwards, undressing one another on the floor. There, almost with a sense of disappointment, he would find the breasts he had not quite imagined; a mole close to her navel; the taste of her skin.

This was the recollection from which he was abruptly stirred now in his office by the ringing of his phone.

Might it be H? Putting the phone to his ear, he heard a male voice he didn't recognize, asking to speak to Professor Ringer.

'That's me.'

The accent at the other end was Scottish, the tone high and fluty; and from the ensuing burst of words Ringer caught only one: Craigcarron. This was the nuclear facility Ringer was shortly due to visit, invited by one of his former students – Don Chambers – who led the small research centre that worked independently alongside the ailing and soon to be decommissioned power plant.

'Is there a problem?' Ringer asked.

'Not at all, sir,' the caller insisted, his voice evoking some wild and windswept place that McDonald's and Starbucks had yet to reach. 'But I do hope I'm not disturbing you.'

'I didn't catch your name,' said Ringer.

'I am Findlay McCrone, church minister at Ardnahanish. I hear you'll be visiting Craigcarron, just down the road from us.'

Ringer's forthcoming trip was no secret; nevertheless he was surprised to learn it was such public knowledge. 'How did you get my number?'

'I really don't mean to bother you, but when Ena at the bakery heard from Moira that there was going to be a TV celebrity staying with Mrs Chambers, well, you can understand why the news was apt to circulate somewhat. Not that my parishioners are prone to gossip, mind . . . '

'Hang on,' said Ringer. 'Who's the TV celebrity?'

The minister gave a nervous laugh. 'Such modesty!' Then he continued his hurried explanation. 'I gave Craigcarron a call and asked if they could help arrange a public talk in Ardnahanish. The lady on the switchboard didn't quite get my drift but turned out to be a good friend of the McBrides, so next time I saw Jock I asked him to tell his son Dave to try and help, and now here I am, officially inviting you to give a lecture on black holes or particles, or whatever it is you talk about in that TV series of yours.'

'I don't have a TV series,' said Ringer.

There was a pause at the other end. 'No. I mean, you appear regularly on science programmes. Or so I'm told, though I don't actually look at the television much.'

'I'm not in any programmes,' Ringer said flatly. 'There's been a mistake.'

'Oh dear,' said the minister. 'How awkward.' Then his voice brightened. 'You are a physicist, though, aren't you? And if you should happen to be giving a talk at Craigcarron, perhaps I could arrange a coach trip for my parishioners. There's a very nice visitor centre, apparently.'

Ringer said, 'I'm giving a technical seminar, and it's not for the general public. I doubt your coach party would even understand the title: *Non-collapsible wave functions and hadron-hadron collisions.*' Ringer was simply showing off in the hope of making him go away.

'Hadron-hadron,' the minister began murmuring thoughtfully. 'Would that be a place up by Loch Connachie?'

'No,' said Ringer, 'it's something that happens in exploding stars. If any of your parishioners are interested in quantum field theory I can send them a copy of the relevant paper.'

By now it seemed he had succeeded in swatting Mr McCrone into submission. Then the minister said, 'Tell me, professor, do you believe in predestination?'

It was a strange question. 'Why do you ask?'

'I'm told that you physicists think everything is random. I even heard on the radio that there might be lots of parallel universes, and we're in this one completely by accident. Which is somewhat at odds with the revealed truth of scripture, would you not agree?'

Ringer, sensing the delicacy of the issue, thought it best to hide behind further technicality. 'Quantum theory is deterministic,' he said, 'to the extent that probabilities are fixed by boundary conditions, either in the past, or else perhaps in the future.'

'I see. Deterministic,' Mr McCrone echoed, ruminatively. 'Boundary conditions.' Ringer wondered if these might also happen to be places up by Loch Connachie. He said, 'You're a Presbyterian, then?'

'Not exactly.'

'No, I suppose not. But you evidently have a lot of ideas about where we all come from and where we're going. So you can see why my parishioners would find a lecture extremely interesting.'

Ringer reminded the minister that his talk was to be about elementary particles, not God.

'Of course,' said Mr McCrone. 'But I do still wonder if perhaps you could be tempted to pay us a visit in

Ardnahanish to speak about science in general. I can promise you a warm welcome.'

Ringer couldn't understand why the minister remained so keen on booking him, but the proposal began to sound tempting. He was due to spend four days at Craigcarron. If the weather proved bad he wouldn't even have hill walking as an excuse to get away now and again from the research station. So he accepted the minister's invitation as a way of punctuating his trip.

'Splendid!' said Mr McCrone. 'In fact, if the fifteenth is suitable for you, then it extricates me from an awkward situation. We were due to have a slideshow about ospreys, but unfortunately Archie has to take his wife to Inverness that day.'

So there was the deal. He was substitute for a bird-watcher.

'Just one thing,' said Ringer. 'Did you try texting me before you called?'

'No, but if you give me your address I can post details of how to find us.' Ringer gave what was asked, then said goodbye and hung up, wondering what he might have let himself in for.

Call me: H. It hadn't come from the minister; but was it connected with Ringer's trip? He could think of a dozen stories that might fit. Perhaps the true story was one he could not even imagine.

HARRY'S TALE

'How do you feel?'

It was a white-coated woman with jet-black hair who asked him this, standing beside the hospital bed with a clipboard in her hand.

'Who are you?' he said.

'My name is Dr Blake and I'm a consultant meta-neurologist.' She instructed him to gaze at the far wall and shone a tiny torchbeam into his helpless, flickering eye. 'Try to hold still please, Mr Dick.'

The name was unfamiliar. 'Is that who I am?' She began to inspect his other eye, wafting her clinically scented atmosphere across his face. 'What's my other name?'

Dr Blake switched off the torch and straightened herself. 'You're Harry Dick,' she said. 'You had an accident. Your wife can't be here with you yet, but she knows you're safe and well, and you'll see her soon. Can you remember her name?'

Harry tried a few guesses and eventually hit on Margaret.

'Well done!' said Dr Blake, making a note on her clip-board. While she scribbled, he looked around the room, trying to make sense of it all. There were few furnishings: an armchair for the unknown wife who was due to visit, a tilting table on wheels, a locker, a moveable screen.

'Do I have children?' he asked.

'Can you think of any?'

He couldn't; Dr Blake said his wife would supply all the relevant details. He remembered many things: what a hospital was, for example, or a doctor. Yet there were gaps in all the most important places, which he became aware of only at Dr Blake's bidding.

She said, 'What day is it today?'

He didn't know.

'It's Tuesday,' she told him. 'And it's ten past nine in the morning. Can you tell me what year it is?'

He offered several candidates until the flicker of Dr Blake's smooth, sternly attractive face finally guided him to the right answer. 'Excellent,' she said. 'And can you tell me the name of the First Minister?'

Now he was stumped. 'First Minister? What do you mean?'

'Can you tell me the name of the First Minister of Scotland?'

'Why?' he asked.

'Because it's a standard question we ask everyone with a head injury.'

Her comment merely added to Harry's confusion. He said, 'Do you know who the First Minister of Scotland is?'

'Of course I do.'

'And do you have a sore head?'

She wrote something down, then said, 'The First Minister is called John Fraser. Do you think you can remember that?'

'I'll do my best,' he told her. 'But what about the accident? What happened to me?'

'You were crossing the road and got hit by a car,' she said. 'You could easily have been killed. Better be more careful in future.'

Harry tried to picture it, but in his mind there was only a dark void where his past was meant to be. One small memory alone surfaced into consciousness. About to step into the road, he was carrying something in his hand.

'Do you recall your mother's name?' said Dr Blake. Again they went through the guessing game, ending with a tick on Dr Blake's clipboard that denoted either his success or her ultimate boredom. 'Father?'

The reconstruction of Harry's family tree was an exercise in arbitrariness. Suddenly a name came to him. 'Thomas Mann,' he said.

'What?'

'Might have been a relative. Or a First Minister. Or somebody famous.'

'I've never heard of him,' said Dr Blake. 'Interesting though; the name sounds symbolic. Thomas could be from John Thomas; which would give us Penis Man.'

Harry wondered who else in his family might be no

more than a phallic symbol. 'Why can I remember some things and not others?'

Dr Blake sat down on the edge of the bed, placing the crisp outline of her thigh not far from Harry's idle fingers. 'Let me try to put it in simple, layman's terms,' she said. 'Memories, Harry, are somewhat like pencils.'

'Like pencils?' he parroted. So far, he was with her completely.

'Yes,' she said. 'And our heads are full of them.'

'Like a pencil case?'

She didn't appreciate this interjection. 'One must never push a scientific analogy too far,' she warned, then resumed her idiot's guide to metaneurology. 'You see, it isn't only the pencils themselves that constitute our memories, but also the way they're arranged.'

Clearly Harry's pencil case had been badly jumbled. Perhaps he'd even been left an HB short of a full set.

'When you look at the end of the pencil,' Dr Blake enthused, 'you see a small hexagonal shape.'

'Or circular,' he suggested.

'Actually in the case of the human brain it's neither,' she said dismissively. 'The point is . . .'

'The other end of the pencil?'

'No, Harry. The point is that the smooth end of the pencil . . .'

'The one opposite the point?'

'Yes, that end, is quite small. But when you turn the pencil sideways, it looks long and straight.'

'And hard,' he contributed, while Dr Blake's eyes narrowed beneath her sleek brows.

'Interesting,' she said, then made a note on her clip-board.

'I see you use a ballpoint,' Harry observed.

She looked up. 'Yes, why shouldn't I? Pencils are only an analogy, remember?'

She made him promise not to interrupt any more, then told him that the end of the pencil – the antipoint, so to speak – represented a memory's trigger, while the shaft (as they eventually agreed to call it) was the memory itself. 'For example,' she said, 'I once read about a French writer who tasted a piece of cake after dipping it in his tea, and immediately it made him think of his childhood.'

'Flaubert,' Harry announced proudly, the name leaping forth out of nowhere, to his considerable delight, proving that his memory was returning by leaps and bounds.

'Very well, Flow-Bear, if that's what you want to call him,' said Dr Blake. 'For him, the cake was the end of the pencil: the trigger.'

'So memories are like guns?' Harry asked.

'No, pencils.'

'And what about cakes?'

'They're triggers. When Flow-Bear tasted one, it became the end of a pencil in his head. Then Flow-Bear could turn the pencil, inspect it from another angle, and retrieve the entire memory. It was all there in his brain, but the problem was finding that pencil among the others.'

'I see,' said Harry. 'So he took the pencil and started writing a book with it.' In Dr Blake's hands, the very frontiers of metaneurology were a piece of tea-sodden cake in Flow-Bear's kitchen. Unfortunately, however, Harry's own pencil box was in a complete mess.

'Your mind is still in the dark, Harry, and you're grabbing those pencils at random, mixing them up like a child. You're drawing strange, swirling scribbles. But if we gaze carefully enough at those infantile efforts, we may be able to unlock the meaning that must lie within them.'

It was good to know he was being looked after by an expert. He said, 'Shall I tell you more about Flow-Bear and Penis Man?'

'No,' Dr Blake instructed firmly, standing up again and straightening out the few creases that had dared intrude upon her crisp white medical coat. 'By telling me, you'd only reinforce the false memories.'

Harry gave a start. 'False? You honestly think my own memories could deceive me?'

Dr Blake lowered her voice. 'Harry,' she said, in the earnest tone medical practitioners are trained to use when delivering bad news. 'We still need to do a few more tests to confirm it, but it appears you have AMD.'

'What does that mean?'

'AMD is a name covering a collection of symptoms whose cause we frankly still don't understand. It involves altered states of consciousness characterized by hallucination or false memories. And you've already offered me at least two false memories, with your Penis Man and

Flow-Bear. So if all the tests for other conditions turn out negative, we'll have to conclude you have AMD.'

'And how will you be able to eliminate AMD from the list of possibilities, assuming I don't happen to have it?'

Dr Blake couldn't help smiling at Harry's difficulty in fathoming the methods of modern medical science. 'The only way to eliminate AMD is by finding a problem we can explain with some other cause,' she clarified. 'Now, I've been looking at the cranial endograms: all the results are consistent with the CTM scan and the dinoxene analysis. You're in the clear, Harry. Everything's negative.'

'That's great.'

'In other words,' she continued solemnly, 'we must conclude you're AMD-positive. We'll have to keep you in for a while.'

He wasn't going to put up with this. 'If all the tests are negative, then how can you conclude I'm positive?'

'Didn't you do maths at school? Two negatives make a positive – everyone knows that. There's clearly something wrong with you, and AMD is the only remaining possibility.'

Dr Blake was sympathetic. She said she'd seen this sort of thing countless times. Somebody feels perfectly healthy; there's absolutely nothing wrong with them. Then a minor irritation arises; a sore leg, dizziness, an inconspicuous mole. They see their GP, get a few tests done. The next thing they know, they've got a life-threatening illness.

'You're very lucky, Harry.' Dr Blake placed a hand on his arm; a gesture no doubt calculated to appear emotionally meaningful. 'You've probably had AMD for months. That's how you got yourself run over; walking into the road, not looking at the traffic. But at least it means we've been able to diagnose you. You could have gone on living with this for years, without you or anybody else knowing.'

'Can you cure it?'

'No,' said Dr Blake, 'but you're a valuable addition to our statistics. You can help us with some experiments, and we can maybe get to the bottom of this strange new condition. I'm sure you must have read about it in the newspapers – I've even given a few interviews.'

Harry had no recollection. He asked her to outline the symptoms.

'There are many,' she told him. 'Though no single patient ever exhibits more than a handful. Do you have any stiffness in your limbs?'

'No.'

'Blurred vision?'

'No.'

'Irritability?'

'Only when irritated.'

'I see,' said Dr Blake. 'Well, that's all perfectly consistent with acausal AMD. Now, have you been feeling depressed recently?'

'I can't remember.'

'Hmm,' said Dr Blake, 'I suppose not. But would you

like to take a guess? Had you begun writing poetry, perhaps?'

'I told you, I can't remember.' Except that it was a book he was carrying, when he came out into the street and stepped onto the busy road.

Dr Blake was continuing her search for symptoms. 'Itchiness while urinating?'

'Don't know.'

'Loss of appetite?'

'Doubt it.'

'Inappropriate desires?'

'What are they?' he asked. Dr Blake told him to imagine he was standing on a high bridge. Did he want to jump from it? Did he ever feel a devilish impulse to thrust his hand into a burning fire, or hit a stranger for no reason?

'I don't think so.'

Dr Blake suggested several other inappropriate desires, the list growing more and more detailed and elaborate in response to Harry's negative answers.

'You go into an off-licence and buy a bottle of wine,' she said. 'The person behind the counter is watching a small portable television and hasn't noticed you. Are you tempted to walk out without paying?'

'No,' he told her. 'I'd be caught on the security video. I'm an honest man, not a professional criminal. At least I think I am.'

'Very well,' she continued, unperturbed. 'You pay for the wine and walk out into the street. An expensive car is parked nearby and no one is around. Though you have no intention of doing it, do you think of smashing the bottle over the car?'

'Yes,' he replied. 'I do now. But only because you made me think of it.'

'So we've found two symptoms of AMD.'

'What do you mean?'

'One is a tendency to lie – everyone has inappropriate desires from time to time – and the other is the spontaneous creation of false memories, produced without the intention of deceiving anyone except perhaps yourself.'

Dr Blake started trying to tell him that as well as pencils, the human brain also contains tubes of paint which sometimes get trodden on, squirt their contents all over the place and totally spoil the picture, but Harry was having none of it. 'Why do you keep insisting the few memories I have are false? Why won't you trust my own judgement about what's real in my life and what isn't?'

'I'm sorry, Harry,' she said. 'A person with AMD simply cannot be trusted. Everything you say, to me or to yourself, has to be treated with suspicion.' Then she added, 'Don't worry, you'll learn to live with this. There are thousands like you – I'll make sure you're given details of the AMD support group before you're discharged. Try to think of it not so much as a disability, more as a new opportunity. A lifestyle option. It takes time to adjust, but believe me, you'll get there.'

Then she glanced at her watch, scribbled another note on her clipboard, and went out, leaving Harry to ponder his strange predicament.

He had been carrying a book in his hand, and he was about to cross a road. Perhaps the book had something to do with Thomas Mann, or was even by him, which was why the name had come into his head. Or was it a false memory?

He tried to remember what his wife Margaret looked like. All he could come up with was a fruit shop and a display of melons.

Then he noticed a woman standing beside his bed. 'Are you Margaret?' he asked her.

'I don't think so,' she said. She was wearing a hospital dressing gown, and Harry realized she must be another patient. 'Good dream?'

Harry didn't know what she meant.

'You were out of it,' she explained. 'I've been standing here for at least ten minutes watching you.'

Harry was puzzled. Surely only a moment had passed since Dr Blake left the room?

'Your eyes were open and it looked like you were mumbling to yourself,' his visitor told him. 'At one point you stared straight through me and said something about the square root of minus one. I didn't understand a word of it, but it was quite entertaining.'

Dr Blake had mentioned altered states of consciousness: here was the evidence. He wondered how long it had lasted. 'What's the time?' he asked.

The visitor shrugged. 'I don't know. Evening, I suppose.'

'And what day is it?'

'Thursday or Friday, I think. Maybe Monday. Mind if I sit down?' She drew up the bedside chair. 'You're AMD, aren't you? Me too.'

'Are you sure it isn't still Tuesday?' said Harry. 'Dr Blake told me it was Tuesday.'

'And you believed her?'

'Yes, why shouldn't I?'

She shook her head. 'Don't trust anything Dr Blake tells you.' From the pocket of her dressing gown she took a crumpled scrap of paper and smoothed it out. 'One of the cleaners left a newspaper in my room by mistake. This article was in it.' She handed it to him.

Unlocking A Medical Mystery

Ever felt you might be losing your marbles? Relax, you're probably only showing signs of stress, tiredness or age, according to leading expert Dr Sharon Blake. But if you start remembering things that never happened, you could be a victim of Anomalous Memory Disorder.

'First let's dismiss all those clichés about designer illness,' says Blake, who – as head of a new privately funded meta-neurology unit in northern Scotland – is a world authority on the condition. 'When first diagnosed in the US,' explains attractive 41-year-old Dr Blake, 'cases were mainly professionals with high-powered careers. Hence the notion that this was a disorder somehow brought on by an affluent lifestyle.' The comely doctor explodes. 'Poppycock!' she declares. 'This is a condition that can affect anyone.'

In fact, says Dr Blake, AMD had already been predicted as a theoretical possibility, and had even been named and studied, before the first patient – a dentist in Milwaukee – came to light. Since then there have been thousands more in every country of the world.

'There are AMD cases in Europe, Asia, Africa,' Sharon Blake warns. 'I've seen reports of AMD being found in the rainforests of New Guinea. This is a worldwide epidemic.' An outbreak typically begins with the victim experiencing a flash of memory that is vivid, detailed, yet completely false. A place that never existed. A name or face that seems important but cannot be recognized.

'Throughout all human history there have been cases of AMD,' says Dr Blake. 'They have given rise to tales of reincarnation, telepathy or second sight. Nostradamus was almost certainly a victim of AMD,' she adds. 'He showed many of the classic symptoms, including unusual dietary preferences.'

Rather than prophecies of the future, says Blake, the visions of Nostradamus were recollections of a fictitious past he could not explain except by means of obscure verses that have puzzled generations, until now. Composer Robert Schumann and philosopher Friedrich Nietzsche were also victims, according to Dr Blake. It even seems that Sigmund Freud, the father of psychoanalysis, may have been a mild case, basing some of his theories on patients who never lived. Ironically, says Blake, one of those theories was that people invent false memories to satisfy subconscious needs.

'That view is totally discredited,' says Blake. 'We now know it was Freud who was deceived, and the reasons were organic.'

Dr Blake and her colleagues have gathered strong evidence showing AMD to be related to chemicals called neurotransmitters. These send signals between brain cells, enabling memories to form or be recalled. With characteristic aplomb, the vivacious Dr Blake puts it in everyday terms. Memories, she says, are like pencils: they last a long time but need regular sharpening. With the aid of several free-hand sketches, Dr Blake clearly shows how bright red neuroactive hexagons of epiphremanine erase relative percentages of dark blue serotonin in a bimodal distribution of standard deviation.

'So what we really need,' Blake concludes, 'is a blank sheet on which to start afresh.'

Dr Blake is doing this by studying a small group of patients diagnosed with AMD following bouts of amnesia. Unable to separate real memories from false ones, these unlucky people offer hope to the thousands who must do battle each day with an endless deluge of junk memory. Various drugs are being trialled, with promising results.

The good news, Dr Blake says reassuringly, is that AMD is not a degenerative condition, and many live with it for years without even noticing any problem. But where does it come from in the first place?

'I hear wild scare stories that you can get AMD from spending too much time watching television, playing computer games or using mobile phones. There is no evidence for this,' says Dr Blake. Other environmental factors being studied include food colourings and agricultural organophosphates. 'We just don't know what causes AMD,' says Dr Blake. 'But my advice is to eat plenty of fresh fruit and vegetables and get regular exercise.' It clearly works for her, and the raven-haired medic will set male viewers' hearts fluttering next year when she fronts a four-part TV documentary taking a serious look at the history of mental illness, titled *Loonies*.

Harry handed it back to his companion.

'So now you know why you're here,' she said. 'You're part of Dr Blake's experiment. Whatever she tells you is probably her way of seeding a false memory, so she can see what it grows into.'

'And what name have they given you, in this so-called experiment?' Harry asked.

'Clara.'

'What's your other name?'

'I don't have one. When I was found, someone decided I was Clara, so Clara it is.'

'When you were found?' Harry asked incredulously. 'What do you mean?'

She explained that some time ago, in a wretched and confused condition, she was brought to the hospital by police unable to find any evidence of her identity. She had been walking in the surrounding hills, with little protection against the weather, and had become lost. 'At least that's what they tell me; though I don't remember any of it.'

'Have your family come here yet?' he asked her.

Clara shook her head. Nobody had come looking for her. 'Then I saw the newspaper article,' she said, 'after the cleaner left it by mistake. If it really was a mistake. And I understood why Dr Blake is so keen for me to be kept in isolation. She probably knows everything about me, but she's waiting to see what false memories I come up with.'

Harry was shocked by what he was hearing. 'Why don't you discharge yourself, or call the police?'

Clara shook her head gently. 'There must have been things I needed to forget. Everything in life has a purpose.' Then she turned her head towards the door, as if afraid that someone might come in and find her. 'I'd better go,' she said, and without any further comment got up and left the room, closing the door after her.

Harry was still puzzling over the newspaper article when he heard a knock. He thought it must be Clara again, but immediately the door was opened by a new female visitor of indeterminate age and uninspiring appearance, with long carrot-coloured hair and a purple dress that radiated an air of ethnic poverty.

'Hello,' he said to her. 'Are you Margaret at last?' He quietly hoped she wasn't.

She came and stood at the end of his bed. 'Priscilla Morgan,' she said, extending a bangled hand he couldn't possibly shake unless he had arms like a gibbon's. 'Writing therapist.' She retracted her hand with a metallic jangle.

'What a busy day I'm having,' Harry said patiently. 'Did you bump into Clara in the corridor?' Priscilla didn't know what he was talking about, so Harry explained, without mentioning the article.

'I didn't see anyone,' said Priscilla, and Harry realized he must have had another lapse of consciousness. 'Anyway, I don't think patients are supposed to go around chatting to each other without permission. Dr Blake is very particular about the sort of things that can safely be said to people with AMD. It has to be done properly, gradually. Otherwise it's like giving a gallon of water to someone dying of thirst: the shock could be lethal.'

All Harry knew was that Dr Blake wanted to feed him information as part of her experiment. And this curious creature at the foot of his bed was apparently meant to do some of the feeding.

'Are you really a writing therapist?' he asked her. 'Or has Dr Blake made that up?'

Priscilla gave a laugh, then with an irritating scrape drew up the chair that had somehow moved back across the floor in the moment since Clara's visit. 'Dr Blake thinks I might be able to help you. I'm the health trust's writer in residence.'

'You mean you actually choose to live here?'

Priscilla laughed again, jangling as her shoulders trembled. Harry couldn't be sure whether this noise came from her excessive jewellery or her internal workings. 'My job is to help patients put their experiences into words,' she said. 'Some of the pieces get published in a special magazine – the spring issue's got a really lovely poem sequence about hip replacement.'

So far, this latest therapy proposal excited Harry about as much as a course of suppositories. He said, 'How can anyone expect me to write about my experiences when I can't remember any of them?'

'That's all right,' said Priscilla, 'writing doesn't have to come from real events.' She spoke on the subject with the disagreeable animation of a specialist.

'What sort of things do you write?' Harry asked, then soon wished he hadn't, as it was an invitation for a lecture.

'I do short stories, primarily,' she said. 'I've had seventeen published to date. So you see, I really am a genuine writer.'

'But not a poet, novelist, or any other kind with its own job title?'

'No,' she laughed, in the casually dismissive way Harry had already begun to loathe. 'You could say I'm something in between. The short story is a neglected medium, and a good one is the hardest thing in the world to write.'

'I've no doubt it is,' Harry agreed. 'Which is perhaps why it's so neglected. But you're also a therapist?'

Priscilla shrugged, jangled, and then – still exuding an unhealthy interest in the mechanics of her career – explained. 'The therapy aspect is merely part of the job while I'm doing the residency here. The only way to write short stories for a living these days is to do stints like this: it's not like the old times when the Board of Literature subsidized everything. Free market and all that. But it's so interesting! I've worked in schools, prisons, day-care centres. I was even writer in residence on an oil rig. Now that really was fun!' She leaned towards him and gave him a hearty nudge he could have done without.

'Yes,' Harry agreed, 'writing short stories in the middle of the ocean must be quite exhilarating. And do you draw on experience?'

'Sometimes,' she told him, then began to explain the plot of a three-page tale (*Gash* magazine, Issue 4) in which an old woman looks out of her kitchen window. 'That woman was me, really. When I'm older. And also my aunt, who died last year. But the whole point, you see, is the moment when she notices the wilting hydrangea and it brings everything back. We call that sort of thing an epiphany.'

'That's good to know,' said Harry, feeling as humbled and bewildered by this technical secret as he had been by Dr Blake's dinoxene analysis. In the hands of someone like Priscilla, a hydrangea could, it seemed, hold the key to the entire human condition, if only you knew how to understand its meaning. And with seventeen published stories under her belt, it was clear that Priscilla was as much an expert in her field as Dr Blake was in hers.

Of those seventeen stories, Priscilla soon, for Harry's benefit, had outlined four. She'd reached one in which an oil worker has gone home to his wife for the weekend and finds a postcard from his son on the kitchen table. Kitchens, Harry realized, were a recurring motif in the Priscilla Morgan oeuvre.

'Was the oil worker someone you met on the rig?' he asked with as much interest as he could muster.

'Actually he's a mixture of three or four people. And also my English teacher at school, Mr Michaels.'

Harry deduced that when Priscilla said she only 'sometimes' drew on experience she was being unduly modest. In fact it appeared her creative budget was substantially overdrawn, given the number of living souls she could cram into a single fictitious character.

'I might even use you one day,' she told him playfully, as if he should be any more flattered by such attention than by his appearing as a case study in Dr Blake's next conference talk.

'Would you use my name?' Harry asked her.

'Of course not. It would be quite wrong to use real names. I only use the essence of a person.'

'My name was quite possibly invented by Dr Blake,' he told her, 'so as far as I'm concerned, you can do what you like with it. As for my "essence", whatever that is, I think I'd prefer it to be left alone.'

Priscilla said she thought Harry Dick would be a good name for a fictional character; preferably one of a symbolic or possibly humorous kind.

'Have you ever heard of someone called Thomas Mann?' he asked.

Priscilla pensively put a finger to her lips before shaking her head. 'No, I don't recognize the name. Why?'

'When it first came back to me I thought he must be a relative. But now I think he may have been a writer, in which case you ought to know about him.'

'Reading other writers isn't an important part of the creative process,' she said, 'except to the extent that you need to be aware of the market. When I did my MA in creative writing three years ago we only read one novel during the entire course, and that was so as to practise turning it into a film script.'

'I think Thomas Mann may have lived quite a long time ago,' Harry added.

'Then I would definitely have heard of him if he was any good,' said Priscilla. 'So I can only assume he wasn't.'

Was she telling the truth? Harry had no way of deciding. In Dr Blake's regime, truth and falsehood had been replaced by new categories: the things he was meant to know, and those he wasn't.

Priscilla said, 'While we're on the subject of names, you don't happen to know who the First Minister is, do you?'

The remark was made in a calculatedly off-hand way. Harry could easily imagine the list of tick-boxes Priscilla would later complete for Dr Blake's benefit. He thought hard. 'Now then . . . is it . . . Gordon Robinson?'

A frozen smile of indecision hovered on Priscilla's lips. Then she said animatedly, 'Well done, Harry. You see how much you can remember, though you don't even realize it!'

She stood up and fetched the wheeled table, bringing it to Harry's bed, then cranked him into a more upright position. For a moment he thought he might be about to get some food; but next she dumped her capacious handbag on the tabletop and said, 'I have a suggestion to make.' She rummaged in the bag and pulled out a large amount of paper, a pen, and an assortment of objects including a broken toy car, a stone, an old key, a cheap ring. Harry looked at all this rubbish she had strewn before him, waiting for some explanation, but none came.

'Do writing therapists habitually carry around items like these?' he eventually asked her, wondering if such detritus was the equivalent of a thermometer and stethoscope, or that little torch with which Dr Blake had probed his flickering eye half an hour or three days ago.

'I want you to look at these objects,' Priscilla instructed. 'Let your mind relax, let it wander freely. Pick anything that interests you, and write whatever comes into your head. It could be a story, a poem, anything.'

'About this stuff from your handbag?'

'Yes,' she said earnestly. 'I often do this exercise with my writing groups, and it's amazing what comes out of it.'

'It's certainly amazing what comes out of your handbag,' said Harry. 'Haven't you got a book in there I could read? I'd even settle for one of your seventeen stories.'

Priscilla shook her head. 'Dr Blake expressly forbids it. Now, see what you can come up with, and I'll collect it later.'

In this way Dr Blake would obtain some more data for her research project, Priscilla would get a few lines of verbiage to put in the hospital magazine, and Harry would be kept harmlessly occupied. The useless junk on the table made him feel anything but relaxed.

She could sense his unease. 'Don't worry, Harry. I know there's nothing more soul-destroying than the sight of a blank page.'

He would have put 'writing therapist' higher on the list of depressing sights, but already Priscilla was making him take hold of the pen. 'Write anything,' she said. 'Anything at all. Don't worry about art or inspiration. Remember, it's only therapy.'

Then she picked up her handbag and jangled to the door, promising to come back in a day or two to see how he was getting on. Once she was gone he stared at the white, empty page, finding it a lot easier on the eye than her purple dress.

Richer by far than her collection of objects was this clean sheet of paper. It was like a field of snow; like mountain crests or the caps of breaking waves. It offered Harry's mind some welcome relief after the strange sensation of waking up – it seemed no more than a few minutes ago – in a world he was unable to understand.

How long had he been here? Why did he not feel hungry, or in need of the toilet? Were these things attended to during phases of altered awareness? He wondered how much of his life was becoming lost to his other self: the one Clara saw, mumbling and staring into space.

He was about to cross a road, he reminded himself, and there was something in his hand. A book. But what was it, and why did it mean more to him than the traffic he ignored? As he tried to recreate its weight and appearance, Harry instead saw only the unpolluted page before him. An eternal whiteness. A dumb blankness, full of meaning.

FROM *PROFESSOR FAUST*
by Heinrich Behring*

A promising young scientist was travelling, just before Christmas 1925, from the city of Zürich where he was employed, to a rest clinic at Arosa, on a three weeks' visit.

It was not the first time he had made this journey; on previous occasions, however, he had not travelled alone. Instead of his wife beside him on the railway carriage's leather seat, there now lay a book, scarcely opened, brought in case of boredom, but which instead had proved merely to aggravate the condition our traveller hoped to avoid.

Since the route could offer him only the modest pleasure of recognition, the scientist had chosen instead to think of the woman he was due to meet. He had written to her in Vienna; she had replied to his work address, perfuming her promises in a letter that now served as bookmark, jutting licentiously from the volume beside

* English translation by Celia Carter. Cromwell Press, British Democratic Republic, 1954

him. As the train rocked and jolted towards the enchanted mountains of his destination, our hopeful traveller sought to recreate mentally the shape and texture, not of the landscape that enveloped him, but of his former lover, whom he had not slept with for more than a decade.

We call him young; the word, though, has a meaning that is relative. Such relativities, moreover, had become as fashionable, and as facile, as the latest show tune or hemline, thanks to Einstein, only eight years older than our hero, yet long hailed as a genius throughout the world.

We call him promising; this too is a blade that cuts straight to the ambitious heart, since it is another way of saying that at the age of thirty-eight he had yet to make his mark upon the world. He was, to be sure, a renowned authority on his particular area of specialization; the theory of colour perception initiated by Goethe. His publications, though, as the English say, had 'hardly set the world on fire'.

We could damn him yet further were it our purpose to be ironic. Fame, however, lay but a short step away as Erwin Schrödinger – for such is our hero's name – gratefully alighted at his station, there to be greeted from among the small throng of thickly clad seasonal tourists by a waiting driver who was heartily bellowing steam from his mouth into the cold air and cheerfully clapping his gloved hands, and who recognized his appointed passenger at once, having been instructed by Dr Schwarzkopf to look out for a gentleman whose round glasses, noble features and lofty brow were a mark of greater distinction than Professor Schrödinger's eccentrically humble dress.

The driver, cordially announcing himself, swiftly took care of the professor's luggage, loading the suitcases into the back of a handsome black car parked in the forecourt outside, an object of admiration for two small boys who stood staring at it in the chill breeze. It was only when Schrödinger climbed into the back seat and saw the driver glance round at him that the scientist suddenly realized his error.

'Why, I left my book on the train!'

It had been there beside him throughout the entire journey; and it was not the loss of the book that Schrödinger found alarming, but rather of the letter it contained.

'Shall I go and inform the station master, sir?' the driver asked. Already they could hear the train puffing away.

'It is of no consequence,' Schrödinger told him. 'The book has my name and address on a note inside; if anyone cares to return it, they will have no difficulty locating the owner.'

Such forgetfulness was an ill omen. The letter, should it fall into the wrong hands, might prove compromising. The world may not know his name, but any traveller on the line could now discover, merely by flicking the pages of a mislaid novel, that Zürich University had among its faculty members a professor of theoretical physics who chose to spend Christmas not with his wife, but with a woman 'eager to rekindle passions that are dormant but not spent'. Zürich was Schrödinger's first professorship; was it also to be his last?

Love affairs were habitual and accepted among his circle; but bourgeois approval does not extend to behaviour one reads about in a newspaper. Even if it did not destroy his career, it would surely harm it, were he to enter public consciousness in such a laughably undignified way.

Once more, therefore, our hero ignored the familiar surroundings during the final stage of his journey. With his wife Anny he had been to Arosa three times previously: first for a rest cure that lasted nine months until his lungs, displayed on Dr Schwarzkopf's X-ray plates, were declared clear of tuberculous shadows; and then during the next two Christmases, when he and Anny came here on holiday. Now, in this fourth year, Schrödinger was to be joined by another woman; and he had no reason to suppose that Schwarzkopf or anybody else would object. Unless, that is, the matter were to find its way into the casual morning reading of office clerks and typists, delivery boys and shop workers, who expected better of their social superiors, and who must never be allowed to think that the fashionable, exclusive clinics dotting their country's mountains were in fact devoted less to the curing of disease than to satisfying well-heeled clients' needs for affection.

This last section of his travels was consequently a time of painful reflection for Schrödinger, whose real reason for coming here was in any case not sex, which he enjoyed well enough with several lovers in Zürich, but rather the creative energy that sex alone could provide.

He had come to Arosa to work on a problem of physics, far removed from what Schwarzkopf called 'the flatland', the world below, where daily concerns are as detrimental to the brain as foul air is to the respiratory system.

Schrödinger had come in order to solve a mystery brought to the world's attention by Einstein, who twenty years ago proposed that light, though traditionally thought a wave phenomenon, behaves in some cases as if composed of particles. Now a young Frenchman named De Broglie had suggested, conversely, that every piece of matter, from a loose thread on Schrödinger's coat that he picked at, to the steep yet barely noticed mountain road the car ascended, might consist of particles that can be considered waves. How should the motion of those waves be described?

The solution would be enough to bring fame; but for Schrödinger, there could be no solution without sexual fuel. His wife had long ago stopped supplying it; their childless union was one of comfort and convenience. Anny preferred the company of Schrödinger's friend and colleague Hermann Weyl, and this was an arrangement that could suit everyone (for Weyl's wife had her own lover too), just as long as none of it went beyond the individuals concerned.

Our affairs, though, send out waves; and it is very hard to guess where those treacherous undulations might finally break. Already, a scented love letter, jammed inside a novel, was making its steady way to Chur, there to be chuckled over, perhaps, by a corpulent porter who would at last have something to chat about, other than his back problems. Schrödinger, fidgeting in the car's ample rear seat, was being delivered just as helplessly, and now almost reluctantly, to Dr Schwarzkopf's lofty sanatorium.

Everything, after all, comes down to chance. The letter might fall into the wrong hands, and a succession of other accidents could then follow that would wreck his ambitions. He might be disgraced, yet rise again; for is history not full of great men who defy ruin? Only the other day, he recalled, he was speaking to someone who had attended a National Socialist rally in Berlin. Adolf Hitler took the stage, cheered by a thousand disaffected workers, though he was not long out of prison. Who knows where fortune can take a man's career?

Some, of course, are less lucky. As the car swerved round a precipitous bend, offering Schrödinger a sudden and unwelcome view of the hillside beneath them, he thought of how his earliest plans had been thwarted when, as a nineteen-year-old, preparing to study in Vienna, he anticipated working with the famous Ludwig Boltzmann. Yet only a few weeks before Schrödinger entered the university, Boltzmann committed suicide.

Boltzmann knew all about the power of chance. The entropy of the universe increases, he reckoned, because a random fluctuation once made that entropy small. Clocks run forwards, people grow old and die – or else hang themselves, like Boltzmann, while on holiday – because of a mere flicker, distant and insignificant. Had it been otherwise, then time would run backwards, or not at all.

What if the car were to skid now? A sudden bursting of a tyre, or an unexpected goat in the middle of the road, and then our hero would be no more, his name surviving only on some forty or so research papers soon destined to fade from expert view. Not even a son to bear his name into the future; and as for Anny, she would soon find someone else. All it would take would be a tiny accident, as easy as forgetting a book on a train – as absurd as the slip of an author's pen – and Erwin Schrödinger would be dead. The driver too, come to that; though what could the future possibly hold for him?

As a student in Vienna, Schrödinger heard countless stories about dear, fat little Professor Boltzmann, so sorely missed. A man who oscillated between boundless energy and despair, and whose greatest pleasure outside physics was playing the piano. Instead of Boltzmann, it was his successor Fritz Hasenöhrl who became Schrödinger's supervisor; another man cheated by fate. In 1904, two years before Schrödinger entered the university, Hasenöhrl published a paper showing that if heat were trapped inside a hollow container, then the weight of the container would be increased. If Hasenöhrl had made a simple modification to his formula it would have become $E=mc^2$, which Einstein published the following year.

Hasenöhrl was a kind, generous man, Schrödinger now recalled. A good friend, a perfect teacher, and perhaps therefore an imperfect scientist, concerned too much for other people, and with too great a sense of honour. When he was blown up on the Italian front, it was as if Schrödinger had lost a member of his own family.

During all these thoughts, the driver was sometimes chatting. Schrödinger wished he would shut up and concentrate on the road. Having evidently been up and down it many times, the driver felt no need to take care.

'I understand you're a physicist, sir?' the driver asked, turning his head enough for Schrödinger to see the man's profile as he gazed casually at right angles to their direction of travel.

'That is correct,' Schrödinger replied.

'What do you think of Einstein, then?'

These days, even a driver wanted to know about relativity, having caught a whiff of Einstein's fame from the daily newspapers. At a station kiosk, we might add, before mounting his train, Schrödinger had seen for sale a popular guide to relativity, written for the benefit of just such a person as the man he was now speaking to.

'Einstein formerly held the professorial chair I now occupy,' Schrödinger said with an air of ostentation quite lost on the driver. 'Then he became a celebrity and went to Berlin instead. As for relativity, I find it highly persuasive, but still not conclusively proved.'

'What about that eclipse, then?' the driver countered. He remembered some front-page photograph a few years ago of a blackened sun which, according to the headline writer, had changed the world.

'Science, like history, is never as simple as journalists would have us believe,' Schrödinger told him, and this silenced the driver, who left his passenger once more to reflect on the mislaid love letter and its possible implications. His own friends would not be shocked – colleagues like Weyl and Debye, whose adventures were far more outrageous than his. Nor would Anny be surprised. Since his lover's husband was a public figure, though, the affair could be a matter of wider interest. Schrödinger might find himself drawn into scandal, destined to be remembered only as 'the other man'. And he had not even slept with her for ten years!

'You think he's wrong, then?' the driver suddenly asked, swivelling his head once more, which only added to Schrödinger's annoyance. 'Einstein, I mean. I've heard there's experts reckon he must have made a mistake. Can't be too careful with the circumcised, can we?' He took a bend too sharply, sending Schrödinger sliding towards the window before pulling clear.

It was true, some doubted Einstein's work. Lennard was the most vociferous, citing Hasenöhrl's paper as evidence that Einstein's discoveries were pre-empted by Aryans. Now there were plans to conduct a mountain-top experiment that could finally disprove relativity. Schrödinger was keen to see it performed.

'Science is a complicated business,' he told the driver dismissively. 'Politics only makes it even more complicated. Hence I avoid politics altogether.'

They might have pursued this philosophical discourse further, but were now approaching the Villa Herzen. Perched on a snow-covered slope, its steep roof sporting long icicles, the clinic came into view as they rounded the last bend, and soon the driver was pulling up before the entrance. It might be better to call the place a hotel, such was its overall appearance of comfort, were it not for the almost incidental affinity of sickness that the guests shared among themselves, providing a common culture around which all life inside the Villa Herzen could slowly revolve. Though they came from Germany, France or Britain, the guests found in tuberculosis and its dialects a lingua franca whose vocabulary they could exchange, while taking the air from their balconies, as easily as a nod of greeting.

A few of them, like Schrödinger, came back as visitors after they were cured. Most, however, were never cured; their stays extended into lifetimes measured, by those left down below, as barely a few months, but which in the other timescale appropriate to these morbid altitudes, possessed the idleness of years. If any mountain-top experiment were thought necessary to demonstrate the plasticity of time, it was surely enough to come here; and perhaps even to seek out – in the company of some patrolling, crisply uniformed nurse – those grey faces haunting the more secure and quarantined sectors of the Villa Herzen, in an annexe to the east, and to see in the eyes of those now-hidden guests, whose former places in the well-appointed dining room remained ominously empty, how an extra day or second of life, if grasped for with sufficient desperation, can seem like an eternity.

A porter was attending to the luggage now, while a male nurse welcomed Schrödinger and escorted him inside, into the panelled lobby with its guns and antlers hanging on the wall, and its blazing fire giving much-needed warmth. Nothing had changed since last Christmas, Schrödinger noted, when he was here with Anny. Even the seasonal decorations were the same, as if in this isolated, timeless place there were only a single Christmas, re-enacted perpetually for the benefit of patients in whom a single, classical pathology was itself repeated and multiplied.

He was invited to sign the register, laid open on the heavy walnut desk. Leaning over it, Schrödinger quickly glanced at the other entries on the page, noting that his lover's name was not there, and he decided that it might be best on this occasion to omit his own name from official record. He was about to offer an excuse for not signing when a bellboy approached, bearing on a silver tray a letter that had arrived that morning for the professor. Schrödinger took it, and knew before opening it what its message must be. Her husband's plans had changed, she wrote, and she was no longer able to come to Arosa. Schrödinger read the note swiftly before burying it in his pocket, telling himself this turn of events was probably for the best. But he left the register unsigned in any case, since a new interruption now came to distract him.

'Herr Professor, how wonderful to see you again!' Bearded, portly Dr Schwarzkopf, director of the establishment, was approaching with outstretched arms. 'I must say, sir, that you are looking very well indeed.' And as he shook Schrödinger firmly by the hand, the doctor began to scrutinize his former patient's face, as if perhaps expecting to find hectic spots upon it. 'No shortness of breath?' Schwarzkopf enquired brusquely. Schrödinger shook his head. 'And the sputum, I take it, is clean? Good, good! You will certainly enjoy a peaceful Christmas with us, professor.'

Schwarzkopf turned and noticed behind him a colleague, standing in the dining-room doorway, whom Schrödinger had observed already but did not recognize. A lean man with a cunning look, he approached at Schwarzkopf's bidding.

'Professor, allow me to introduce Dr Hinze, who has come to us recently from the Burghölzli hospital.'

Schrödinger knew of the place, which was in Zürich. 'That's a mental institution, is it not?' Schrödinger asked, offering the new doctor his hand and finding Hinze's grasp to be as cool and firm as a coiled snake.

'My position there was temporary,' Hinze explained, his voice soft and somewhat rasping. 'I've decided on a change of field.'

'I see,' said Schrödinger. 'From lunatics to consumptives: an intriguing leap.'

Dr Schwarzkopf, sensing some impropriety in the remark, intervened gently. 'Dr Hinze's expertise adds a new dimension to our regimen of care, since we can now offer our patients psychoanalysis. It's advertised in our prospectus. And you know, I even think one or two of our newest arrivals may have been attracted more by that, than by the fresh air!' Schrödinger, though, showed little interest in pursuing the topic further, and so Schwarzkopf suggested that perhaps he would like to go to his room to freshen up.

'Is it the same room as before?' Schrödinger asked.

'Unfortunately not,' Schwarzkopf told him. 'I had expected your usual room to be vacated in time for your arrival; however, its occupant has rallied, and may even remain with us for a few more weeks. Which is, of course, excellent news; though clearly something of an inconvenience for yourself, Herr Professor.'

Schrödinger disliked being placed in the position of regretting that a patient had not managed to die soon enough for him to enjoy the view he was accustomed to. 'Logistical problems are not my concern,' he said loftily. 'If you will have me shown to my room now, I can find out if it is suitable.'

'Of course, of course,' Schwarzkopf said obsequiously. 'Hans, take the professor to number thirty-four.' The bellboy began to lead the way, carrying Schrödinger's two suitcases. 'And, professor,' Schwarzkopf added, 'I do hope that you will join us in the restaurant for dinner.'

'I should be delighted,' Schrödinger told him, then followed the bellboy to the lift, whose cage lay open in readiness. The youth closed it, and a moment later they began to ascend, carried with much heavy whirring to the first floor.

'Tell me, lad,' Schrödinger asked, as they emerged. 'What's the gossip on Dr Hinze?'

'I don't know what you mean, sir,' said the bellboy, setting off along the corridor and soon arriving at number thirty-four, where the key was in the lock.

'Come now,' said Schrödinger, following him into the room. 'I'm sure there must be many stories about this new psychoanalyst whom Schwarzkopf has employed. Is he a fraud, or a genius?'

Illuminated by a shrouded electric bulb, the room was much like the one Schrödinger was used to, where he and Anny had been accommodated during their previous visits. There were twin beds, narrow and firm, neither of which was likely, Schrödinger reflected sadly, to see much action this Christmas. The balcony – such an essential feature of the treatment he recalled receiving during his nine months here – looked out across the valley, and although it was now too overcast for him to assess the view properly, he anticipated the sort that would console any doomed consumptive for the freezing cold he must endure in the supposed interest of his own health.

Schrödinger brought out some coins from his pocket as a tip. 'We all know what psychoanalysts are obsessed with,' he said with a knowing wink to the bellboy. 'Tell me, are there any pretty young patients here for him?'

The bellboy weighed the coins in his hand and found them sufficient. 'There's the one they call the Invisible Girl,' he replied. 'They say she's Dr Hinze's special patient. She isn't consumptive at all, though. I don't expect you'll see much of her – no one does.' He closed his hand, then slid the coins into the narrow pocket of his neatly tailored trousers. Schrödinger guessed that more was required, and was prepared to bring out his wallet in order to find a bank-note. But the bellboy, as if struck by a sudden pang of conscience wholly inappropriate to his occupation, said, 'It's not my place to discuss the guests.' Then he turned on his heels and went out of the room, leaving Schrödinger to puzzle over the mysterious Invisible Girl, whom he imagined to be adequately attractive and conveniently vulnerable.

He thought of her as he opened the suitcases and began to unpack; but very quickly his thoughts moved to other spheres. There was his lover, whom he was not after all to see. Schrödinger's Christmas was genuinely to be the solitary one he had described to Anny when he told her of his need to work on De Broglie waves.

He thought of the seminar he had given at the university a few weeks previously, describing De Broglie's idea that all particles are associated with waves. Debye had remarked that if there are waves, then there must be an equation describing how they move. And this was Schrödinger's problem. If he could solve it, who knows, it might make his name. One day Einstein, sitting in the back of a car, might see his driver turn to him and say, 'What do you make of this new fellow Schrödinger?'

He opened the oak wardrobe's heavy door and began to hang his shirts. De Broglie's formula was so simple – that was its beauty and its power. A particle of momentum p has an associated wavelength λ. Multiply the two together, and you always obtain the same magical number, Planck's constant h. The yellow light issuing from the electric bulb, and casting a sickly hue upon the walls and ceiling of the room, had a wavelength λ, and hence a corresponding momentum p. Each quantum of light carried a tiny, irreplaceable amount of weight from the bulb; each of these raindrops of luminescence exerted an infinitesimal pressure on the surface – be it carpet, washbasin or bedside chair – where it was absorbed.

The electric current producing this light consisted of moving electrons, of momentum p', let us say. And by De Broglie's formula, these electrons also had a wavelength, λ'. Are light quanta and electrons really little bundles of travelling waves? Schrödinger knew this could not be so. Or are the particles we observe merely passengers, riding on waves that represent a deeper reality? For Schrödinger, the idea was attractive.

There was a heavy red curtain drawn across part of the wall behind a desk. He went and drew back the curtain, finding a door whose smooth knob he tried, supposing it to be a cupboard. But the door was locked, and the keyhole was covered by a wooden flap rendered immoveable by several coats of the same glossy white paint that had been used to smother the rest of the door, which now appeared purposeless and inconvenient.

He tugged the thick velvet curtain back in place and decided to wash and change before dinner. Already he had made some progress with Debye's suggestion about finding a wave equation; the difficulty, however, lay in the fact that neither Schrödinger nor anyone else in the world knew what those waves really were. It was like following the tracks of an unknown beast.

If electrons are waves, then these waves must fold themselves around atoms. Yet Schrödinger had tried this calculation, and found the waves were apt to become caustics, like the deformed images produced when light reflects from the curved edge of a coffee cup onto the fluid's dark surface. He chose a clean shirt and began to put it on, checking his appearance in the long mirror beside the dressing table.

A new vision of nature was emerging, which in the last year or two had come to be called quantum mechanics. Schrödinger had seen a popular book about relativity at the railway station; how long would it be before he would see one on quantum mechanics? And would his own name appear in it? Already there were many contenders. Bohr and others had tried to develop a theory of 'probability waves', but found it wanting. Whatever De Broglie waves are, they are certainly not waves of probability. And now Bohr's young disciple Heisenberg had developed some obscure mathematical game – 'matrix mechanics' – with which he thought he could win the prize.

Such were the idle thoughts of our hero as he prepared himself for dinner. We called him young and promising; however, the reader has now had ample time, and has been presented with considerable evidence, to conclude that Schrödinger, quite to the contrary, saw himself in imminent danger of being eclipsed and forgotten. Soon he would be forty; and a physicist who has not found fame by that age might as well abandon hope. It was against such a background that he had recently decided to compose his own philosophical testament; a manuscript he had then filed away in case his reputation should ever rise high enough for it to become publishable. The questions he asked in it were simple. 'Do I exist? Does the world truly exist? Will I survive bodily death?' For his answers, Schrödinger had turned to the Eastern philosophy he knew from Schopenhauer: to Brahman, the being of pure thought which is everything, and Maya, the illusory world we must pass beyond.

We think we are surrounded by objects made of particles of matter; yet these are Maya. Everything, Schrödinger felt sure, consists of waves, and all that seems solid amounts to little more than evanescent bubbles, dancing like white shreds of foam on ocean crests.

It was with these thoughts that Schrödinger readied himself for dinner. Straightening his tie one last time before the mirror, he went out along the corridor, then downstairs to the dining room.

GHOSTS

John Ringer steered his car off the deserted main road, past a huge sign showing Annie Atom; the jovial, kilted mascot of Craigcarron visitor centre. The nuclear power station gleamed brightly in winter sunshine as Ringer approached. Far out to sea – beyond the smooth, enormous geometry of the plant – soaring gulls were sunlit specks like stars in daylight. It would be a pleasure working here, thought Ringer.

He came to another sign. Annie Atom directed tourists to the right; Ringer took the alternative route marked *Authorized Vehicles Only*. Soon he reached a barrier where two armed guards scrutinized his face when he wound down his window.

'I'm here to see Don Chambers,' he confirmed for them as they compared his nervous expression with the picture on their clipboard, then they waved him through after radioing to check. The barrier swung up; he drove inside, following a sign that veered him away from the vast reactor hall towards the simpler prefab units of the research centre. Soon he was sitting inside a bland, white-painted waiting room of a kind found in any industrial estate, holding a cup of tea provided by the receptionist. Don Chambers was still in a meeting.

Ringer was to give a talk next day to Don's small research group; this was the excuse for his visit. But Don had hinted to him on the phone that there was another topic he wanted to discuss. Ringer guessed he was looking for a new job, now that the nuclear plant was due to close.

Don had been his student some years before; the most important lesson he'd learned during his postgraduate studies, he once told Ringer, was that academic life was not for him. Instead he'd chosen this lonely place, with only seals and engineers for company, a receptionist the wrong side of fifty, and a hefty salary by way of compensation. It would be something of a climbdown coming back to work in academia, assuming Ringer could even swing it.

While he waited, Ringer perused the magazines and journals on the coffee table but saw nothing of interest. As the minutes dragged, he wished he'd brought the book that lay in his suitcase in the boot of his car.

It was the cycloids talk that had prompted him to buy it: E. T. A. Hoffmann's *The Life and Opinions of Tomcat Murr*. According to the lecturer, this was the inspiration for Schumann's piano suite *Kreisleriana*. And from what Ringer had read so far, it was very odd indeed.

Johannes Kreisler, a musician, is writing his autobiography. But his pet cat Murr mixes up all the pages and writes his own life story on the reverse sheets. So the novel consists of two parallel narratives, Kreisler's and

Murr's, intercutting randomly. It was one of Franz Kafka's favourite novels; and Ringer could see why Schumann too was so impressed, given that the composer's own divided self ultimately landed him in a lunatic asylum.

If Ringer had come across it years ago in the library, his first phone call to Helen could have gone differently. 'I've been thinking about your thesis,' he might have said. 'Tell me, have you ever heard of Schrödinger's cat?'

He hears her laughing. 'Of course,' she says. 'Everybody knows the cat in the box is neither dead or alive until the moment you open the lid and look inside.'

'Yes,' he tells her, 'that's what everybody knows. But the point Schrödinger was making was a lot more subtle than something Berkeley had already said a long time previously. Have you read Hoffmann's *Tomcat Murr*?'

'Certainly,' she says.

'Then you know the book describes two parallel stories: two conflicting realities. And that's what happened when Schrödinger found the wave equation.'

Why did he need to rerun the past? If their first conversation had been any different, would the rest of their story be altered in any way? The people who know all about the uncertainty principle and Schrödinger's cat from countless popular books and TV programmes also know about something called the butterfly effect, which says that a gnat's fart in Angola can alter the history of the world. What they don't always appreciate is that the theory of dynamical systems – which perhaps includes world history – also allows for things called attractors:

destinations you will inevitably reach, as long as you come anywhere within range.

He and Helen were circling such an attractor when they sat together in the Dolphin Cafe. They were still circling it when they walked to the park; when she came to his flat, and they made love on the floor. Perhaps her eventual disappearance from his life was another, greater attractor.

All this, though, was simply a way of passing the long minutes until Don Chambers came out of his meeting. Ringer saw the prim receptionist look up at him from time to time over her half-moon spectacles, as if making sure he hadn't died yet. He decided that by way of preparation for the other talk he was due to give – for Mr McCrone's parishioners in Ardnahanish – it might be worth pursuing the alternative history that could have begun with a conversation about Murr and Kreisler.

So now, once more, we are in the quaintly tatty Dolphin Cafe, where Helen's eyes tease Ringer's thoughts as he lectures her.

'Back in 1925, people wanted to know if everything is made of particles, or else waves,' he says. 'In the spring of that year, Heisenberg came up with matrix mechanics: a theory of particles making random quantum jumps. Fame beckoned. Then a few months later, this unknown outsider Schrödinger says it's all waves, and he's found the equation showing how they change smoothly and predictably over time. Two completely different interpretations of nature: two parallel stories.'

'Which one's right?' she says.

'Both.'

Helen laughs. 'In that case you're either a romantic like Hoffmann, or else a postmodernist.'

Ringer shakes his head. 'I'm no postmodernist. The issue is how you interpret nature, and those two men – Heisenberg and Schrödinger – offered contradictory interpretations. It turns out they're mathematically equivalent – Dirac soon proved this. Both theories make the same experimental predictions, and which you use is like choosing between long division and a pocket calculator. But people don't just want to calculate; they want to understand how the world really works.'

Helen looks down at her hands on the table top. Her fingertips are almost touching his. This is a moment he enjoys replaying. 'If you're not a postmodernist,' she says, 'I suppose you must be a romantic.'

Perhaps she was right. Watching the receptionist typing at her computer, Ringer imagined telling the parishioners of Ardnahanish how Niels Bohr summoned Schrödinger and Heisenberg to Copenhagen in 1926 so they could sort out their differences. Eventually Bohr proposed a compromise that E. T. A. Hoffmann might have felt perfectly comfortable with.

Schrödinger's wave functions change predictably just as long as they remain unobserved; but as soon as a measurement is made, the waves mysteriously 'collapse' in one of Heisenberg's quantum jumps. Thus an electron is everywhere and nowhere, until it interacts, leaving its footprint on the universe. This is known as the Copenhagen Interpretation; and once Bohr got used to the idea that two conflicting stories can both be true, he decided the world is made not of waves or particles, but of things that can be either according to taste.

Schrödinger never accepted Bohr's compromise; he ridiculed it by means of his famous imaginary cat, trapped in a box alongside a vial of poison gas that will be released if struck by an electron. Since the electron is everywhere and nowhere, the cat is both dead and alive, until the box is opened.

Where did Schrödinger get the idea for his schizophrenic cat? Perhaps he was a fan of *Tomcat Murr*, thought Ringer; then he heard footsteps approaching, looked round and saw Don Chambers striding in his direction with outstretched hand.

Ringer put down his teacup and got up to greet him. 'You're looking well,' he told Don; and it was true. Don had always been the outdoor type; and here in northern Scotland the abundance of fresh air and lack of human contact had rendered his features more chiselled than ever. The suit and tie were mere concessions to the meeting he'd just attended; muddy Gore-tex was his natural attire.

Don's handshake was like accidentally slipping one's fingers inside a piece of industrial machinery. 'How's life?' he asked chummily. Fine, Ringer told him. As they asked about each other's wives and kids, Ringer saw no indication of a man whose career was in peril. Then, with the introductory pleasantries disposed of, Don suggested they go to his office and talk. Ringer followed him there.

'Take a seat,' Don offered, closing the door in a way that suddenly and inexplicably made Ringer feel like a junior employee being treated nicely as a prelude to the sack. If Don wasn't in trouble, perhaps Ringer was. Don sat himself at the other side of a desk whose neatness showed he really had left academic life far behind. Then he got straight to the point. 'I'd better fill you in on a few changes happening around here. I think you know about the decommissioning of the plant, and the sell-off. The good news is that the research facility is staying operational.'

'I'm glad you won't be out of a job.'

Don smiled at Ringer's comment, making him understand how naive it was. *If only you knew*, was the look on his young, weathered face.

Don said, 'I can't tell you too much at this stage about the buy-out.'

'Of course.'

'But I wanted to let you know that representatives from the Rosier Corporation will be attending your talk. So I thought it'd be a good idea to run through a few of your findings beforehand.'

Don had a copy of Ringer's paper on his desk. He began flicking through it. 'There's an element here of, let's say, speculation.'

'Yes, an element.'

'To begin with, there's your claim that gravitational effects might influence wave-function collapse.'

'Penrose says similar things,' Ringer replied, realizing this appeal to authority was an indication of the way

Don's unexpectedly business-like manner had rendered him immediately defensive.

'You go further,' said Don. 'You imagine a wave function unable to collapse. That's a bizarre claim. Are you honestly telling me you could open a box and find Schrödinger's cat alive and dead at the same time?'

'I don't know the extent to which decoherence would be disrupted,' said Ringer. 'But if the gravitational field were strong enough, and if the cat could stand the tidal forces, then I think the answer might be yes.'

Don gave a matey chuckle whose undercurrent was one of unmistakable derision. 'Fortunately our visitors aren't philosophers,' he said, leafing through Ringer's paper like an end-of-year examiner intent on failing a troublesome candidate. 'So I don't expect we'll find ourselves getting into any discussion of quantum metaphysics when you deliver your talk. It's real-life science we do here at Craigcarron, not armchair theorizing.' Now he'd found the part he was looking for. 'Let's talk numbers,' he said, inspecting the page on his desk whose offending words he now pinned with an accusatory forefinger. 'Here, for instance, at the end of section five. *Non-collapsible wave functions could exhibit themselves at energies as low as 500EeV.*'

'According to my estimates,' said Ringer, 'it's quite possible.'

Don shifted in his chair. 'Under the new research plans, we need to allow for energies of 1000EeV.'

Ringer couldn't help laughing. 'How in God's name do you intend to do that? I thought you were meant to be doing "real-life science", Don. Is this corporation of yours going to build a particle accelerator stretching from here to the moon?'

Now Don wasn't smiling. 'I can't discuss technical details. The array will peak at 1000EeV. So maybe we'd better think about how you reached your estimate.'

Ringer realized his mouth had fallen open. He closed it, but the gesture only added to the sense of unreality. 'You're telling me this little research station of yours, in a corner of Scotland that nobody's ever heard of, will have the most powerful particle accelerator in the world?'

Don shook his head. 'It's not an accelerator; and by no means will it be the biggest. It'll be part of a network.'

A network? What was he talking about?

Don pensively rubbed his hands, making a dry and unappealing sound. His blue eyes shone. 'I only wish I could tell you all I know,' he said, with a shaft of candour that briefly resurrected something of the younger man Ringer had known. 'Boy, you'd love this stuff.'

'What stuff? Why can't you tell me?'

Don looked down again at the paper on his desk. 'We're talking highest-level classification here. The commercial, military, political aspects are all enormous.' When he paused, it was for effect. Ringer was meant to be impressed that his former student had done so well for himself. Then Don sat back in his chair. 'It's all about harnessing vacuum energy.'

This wasn't the first time Ringer had heard of such a thing. But on previous occasions, the suggestions had come in hand-scrawled letters from cranks. 'You can't tap the energy of empty space,' he reminded Don.

'It uses leaves of nickel-tantalum alloy. The surfaces have to be perfectly reflecting, with a geometry accurate to one part in fifty million.'

'Ah, so it's all done with mirrors,' said Ringer. 'Well, I hope they do a better job on this than they did with Hubble.'

Don didn't appreciate the sarcasm. 'Vacuum energy is the biggest technological advance since the electric motor or the steam engine. A group in Texas managed a gain of 50GeV.'

'Let's see,' said Ringer, 'with an output like that you'd only need a few million such devices to power a light bulb.'

'Please,' said Don, 'don't be frivolous. I had to go through all kinds of hoops to get clearance to discuss this with you. I've had to sign God knows how many pieces of paper, telling me what I can and can't share with you about the project. Last week I was sitting round a desk with the EU technology commissioner, a government minister and the head of one of the biggest communications companies in the United States. They're all taking vacuum energy very seriously indeed; but if you aren't prepared to, then you can go back out to your car right now and drive home, and we'll never say another word about it.'

His eyes now were like ice. He had the passionate, vacant look of a true believer; an ideologue.

'Tell me more,' Ringer said softly.

Then Don explained how the idea went back to the 1940s, and the discovery that empty space is in effect teeming with elementary particles, virtual, fleeting and evanescent. Thousands of shiny nickel-tantalum leaves in an American laboratory had apparently plundered a tiny portion of energy from these particles before they could disappear. Though the effect was minuscule, its potential impact was so enormous that the experiment was immediately cloaked in secrecy. A paper was published, stating that no energy release had been measured. This was merely to prevent rival nations from attempting to repeat what now was being covertly scaled up.

'How much will it all cost?' Ringer asked.

'So far, something like thirty million dollars has been committed to our part of it.'

It sounded a depressingly familiar story. Get politicians and businessmen interested in a flaky idea – be it Star Wars, cold fusion or the Millennium Dome – and soon there's so much money riding on it that no one is prepared to admit it's a turkey.

Don said, 'Power generation is still decades away – but there's another application we're working on right now that could prove even more significant. When vacuum energy is drawn from the nickel-tantalum array, negative energy remains trapped between the leaves. If two separate arrays are in an entangled quantum state, tapping one produces a corresponding change in the other. Do it carefully enough and you have a linked pair of quantum computers. So vacuum energy could provide the perfect communication technology: error-free and totally secure. I've seen it for myself. They sent a recording of piano music across a distance of ten metres; the reception was excellent.'

'What was the piano piece?' asked Ringer. 'Schumann, by any chance?'

'I don't know,' said Don. 'I'm not a fan of that classical stuff. Anyway, the hope now is to get the same effect at a more practical scale.'

'I can see why. Half a ton of mirrors strapped to your ear would look a lot less stylish than a mobile phone.'

Don's imperviousness to irony was further evidence of the vertical career trajectory he'd followed. 'The biggest problem is setting up the quantum entanglement in the first place,' he continued. 'You could say we're in the same situation as Logie Baird, trying to make television work using spinning discs. What we're looking for is a quantum equivalent of the cathode ray tube.'

'Any ideas?'

'Lots,' said Don. 'The technical issues are largely to do with heat control.'

'And what if your hot bubble of negative energy caught between some mirrors should happen to inflate at the speed of light and eat up the world?'

'According to our calculations, that won't happen.'

'I hope you've double-checked your calculations,' said Ringer.

'We have,' said Don. 'In a full-scale array, we have to allow for virtual particles going inadvertently on-shell at energies up to 1000EeV.'

'You mean, if somebody happened to let a speck of dust drift between those mirrors?'

'Contamination is one possibility; imperfect geometry is another. We really don't think such an energy surge could ever happen; it's the sort of hypothetical scenario one merely has to make allowances for.'

'That's good to know,' said Ringer. 'Even a very small chance of destroying the solar system is the sort of thing I'd prefer to insure against.'

'The important thing is what this technology could do,' said Don. 'Imagine a global network of identical arrays: entangled quantum computers communicating instantaneously. It'll make the Internet look like pigeon post.'

Ringer was unimpressed. 'The Internet already looks like pigeon post. At least pigeons are fast. And what catchy acronym have they dreamed up for this new network?'

'Casimir Entanglement Transfer Instrument,' Don announced. 'CETI for short. Once it's fully operational it'll revolutionize telecommunications. You've heard of Q-phones?'

'My wife bought me one,' Ringer told him. 'And I'll probably need another PhD before I can figure out how to use it. Either that, or I need to be twenty years younger.' Then Ringer remembered the text message. *Call me: H.* Did someone else know about CETI? Were they trying to tell him something?

'As you realize,' said Don, 'Q stands for quantum.'

'That's only a sales gimmick.'

'Initially, yes,' he agreed. 'But everyone knows that quantum computation is the future. Q-phones are already being produced that will be compatible with the CETI network once it's up and running. Let me see your phone, I'll tell you if it's a P-Quad.'

Ringer didn't feel like entering into some laddish tech-talk that would only give Don another opportunity to look smart. Don might even trace the text message in Ringer's phone and find it came from some spook in his own research station. Ringer wanted to get there first, as soon as he could wade through a user manual fatter than his Hoffmann novel, and even harder to follow. 'Never mind about my phone,' he said, keeping it in his pocket. 'When is the great changeover due to happen?' Ringer was fully confident it would never occur.

'I can't discuss that,' said Don. 'But I want you to appreciate that this is the future, John. The smartest people have already given up on superstrings and black holes: they're doing vacuum energy now; only they aren't allowed to publish it. Haven't you noticed how quiet some of the big names have become in the last year or two? Sure, they maybe do a popular science book or a magazine article, but where's their research? The best brains know that TV appearances don't win Nobel Prizes. No; the smart guys have gone inside the wire.'

'Free, I presume, from inconveniences like peer review.'

Don leaned forward, conspiratorially, in a gesture that only made him look even more like a time-share salesman. 'My advice to you, John, is to come in too. Do it now. Get in on the ground floor. Believe me, this is the biggest thing since the Manhattan Project.'

'If you're not careful,' said Ringer, 'it could also make the biggest bang in fourteen billion years.'

Don sat back and shook his head. 'The technology is perfectly safe. Do you honestly think the world's leading scientific institutions would give this the go-ahead if there were any danger?'

Behind Don, through the slatted blind of the office window, Ringer could see the dome of the nuclear reactor. 'I suppose not,' he said.

'I want you to be part of this,' Don told him. 'I want you to be with me, not against me. That's why I've worked so hard to bring you here. That's why you'll be giving a talk in front of some of the most senior executives on the project.' He glanced down at Ringer's research paper, still open on his desk. 'And that's why we need to discuss this. Section five: *Non-collapsible wave functions could exhibit themselves at energies as low as 500EeV*. A bit like saying motor cars will never go faster than a walking man, don't you think?'

'No,' said Ringer. 'More like warning that if you pump energies higher and higher, you might one day bump into some new physics you never expected. There could be grave risks if you run your machine at the level you're talking about.' Then he added, 'Fortunately, I'm totally convinced that your trick with mirrors will never work, and the people of Scotland can sleep safely in their beds.'

Don shrugged. 'Fine. Your talk's cancelled.'

'What?'

'Well, I'm hardly going to let you air groundless quibbles like these in front of our biggest financial backers. They're not specialists in the field; they aren't equipped to separate airy speculation from hard science.'

'Ideal backers, then,' Ringer said sourly.

'It appears our meeting is at an end.' Don stood up. Ringer remained seated.

'Are you serious?' Ringer asked him.

'Absolutely. I know you can be trusted to keep this conversation completely secret. Naturally, any attempt on your part to divulge what you've learned here would be severely dealt with. I'm willing to reconsider if you change your mind; but unless we can discuss the errors in your paper in a free and candid way, I'm afraid we can't pursue any kind of collaboration. Nor will I allow you to express unsubstantiated hypotheses that could undermine the progress we're making here.'

It wasn't from being Ringer's PhD student that Don had learned to talk this way. He'd obviously sat round too many tables, with too many suit-wearers accustomed to getting whatever they wanted.

Ringer stood up too. 'I'll think about it.'

'Call me tomorrow,' he said curtly.

Ringer added, 'Under the circumstances, I'd better turn down your offer of accommodation. If you don't mind, I'll go and find myself a bed and breakfast for the night.'

'I'm sorry to hear that,' Don said stiffly. 'If you change your mind and decide to work with us on the project, naturally you'll be most welcome at my home. Susan would love to see you again.'

She and Don were young sweethearts when Ringer first knew them. He wondered how she felt about the way her husband had changed. She probably didn't even know.

'Give her my regards,' he said. 'Goodbye, Don. I'll call tomorrow.'

Don went to open the office door. 'And remember,' he said. 'Not a word about this to anyone. I've already risked a great deal for your sake, John. Don't let me down.'

'I won't,' Ringer promised, then said he'd find his own way out. As Ringer walked along the corridor, he didn't look back. All he heard was the closing of Don's door again, as he retreated into the safety of his office.

The receptionist made Ringer sign several forms before releasing him; and when he got back in his car and drove to the gate, the two armed guards didn't bother with their clipboard this time, but instead made him get out while they searched both Ringer and the car. He wondered if this little piece of theatre was Don's idea, meant to intimidate him in a way that Don himself had been unable to manage.

Soon, though, Ringer was driving along the main road again, in winter sunshine whose long shadows heralded daylight's early end at such northerly latitudes. He was trying to make sense of everything Don had said, and just as urgently trying to find a place to stay. Craigcarron itself was a characterless village serving only as the plant's dormitory. Ringer thought it best to put some distance between himself and Don, and so drove in the opposite direction, expecting to see a B&B sign at any moment. A quarter of an hour later, he'd counted only sheep on the moorland beside him, and seeing a turn-off for Ardnahanish, figured that if all else failed he could at least throw himself on the charity of Findlay McCrone. So Ringer headed inland, as the sign directed. The sea – a thin grey line in his rear-view mirror – was soon out of sight, and the rugged moors grew rapidly more mountainous, with snow piled thickly on rocky peaks. It was still the middle of the afternoon, but the light was already fading.

He thought about the vacuum energy device. At best it sounded like wishful thinking by over-eager scientists; at worst, it reminded Ringer of countless hoaxes that have fooled gullible investors and governments over the years. Don had staked his career on a glorified perpetual motion machine. And it wasn't even meant to generate electricity – what Don proposed instead was a quantum computer.

Suppose Don was right, though; and suppose too, that his vast array of mirrors were one day to be intruded upon by a stray housefly or forgotten strand of hair, creating the sudden enormous energy surge he anticipated. Would there be any real danger? A thousand exa-electron-volts is no worse than the energy of a falling rock. Concentrate that at a point, however, and you get particles ten times more energetic than anything ever seen in nature.

What might happen? Ringer had already given a possible answer in the paper left lying on Don's desk. At such uncharted energies, quantum theory itself might be altered.

With his puzzle about a cat, Schrödinger's aim had been to reveal the absurdity of Bohr's Copenhagen compromise. Yet many have seen Schrödinger's parable as anything but absurd. That was the view taken by Hugh Everett when in 1957 he proposed what became called the 'many worlds' interpretation of quantum mechanics.

When the box is opened, the universe splits in two: there is a world in which the cat survives, and another in which it is dead. Which is real depends only on your frame of reference; like seeing a train in motion or at rest according to your own velocity. The forking paths of nature are then part of a greater labyrinth in which every possibility is actual; a multiverse of parallel worlds. Everett came up with the idea in his PhD thesis; it was the only thing he ever published. He went to work at the Pentagon and pursued the rest of his career behind closed doors – leading to amusing suggestions that he was involved in attempts to make parallel universes interact with each other in the hope of steering our world into one where the Russian Revolution never happened. More realistically, Everett's idea provides a way of understanding quantum computation.

To speed up a calculation, several computers can be made to do it simultaneously in parallel. A quantum computer would do the same thing, except there would be one machine effectively working in many parallel universes. The hard part is ensuring that nothing disturbs it before the calculation is finished and the wave function of possibilities collapses, gently returning an answer to the universe we live in. Don Chambers appeared to think this problem could be solved using his new vacuum array.

What if the waves should refuse to collapse when required? At very high energies they might prove stubborn, vacillating, recalcitrant. Drive the vacuum array hard enough, and the particles trapped between its mirrored faces could then be cats that never decide which world they're meant to be in: that of the living, or of the dead. These orphaned shreds of matter would be neither real nor virtual. If Ringer's troublesome section five were right, then Don's computer would not know which universe to send its output to. Nor could its users even be sure which world they'd started out from. If Ringer's fears were justified, then Don's immaculate hall of mirrors would be a device not for global communication, but for universal confusion. Its trapped, rebounding particles would be ghosts and vampires, oscillating eternally between one universe and the next, bridging worlds and confounding them.

What would it take, to lead to disaster? A glimpse inside the mirrors, perhaps. A lifting of the lid by a foolish trainee; the inadvertent tumbling of a screwdriver in a shaft, or the pulling of a lever that wiser men would have left unpulled. A flash as someone vaporizes in the heat; and another flash as Craigcarron becomes another Craigcarron, Scotland becomes another Scotland, the world becomes another world. No one would even notice at first. For all we know, it might already have happened.

We would all be like Schrödinger's cat: an unresolved mixture of possibilities, in a box from which no power of heaven or earth could ever free us. It might take no more than a poor alignment of those nickel-tantalum mirrors to cause the fatal leak of doubt. Then once it spread, there would be no more truth or falsehood; no fact or fiction. No; the earth – instead of being swallowed by a black hole, or pulverized into the quark consommé of physicists' eternal dread – would have suffered a more terrible misfortune; the greatest, most laughable fate of all. Don's hellish contraption – if such a thing could even be envisaged beyond the dreams of madmen – would have turned the planet, perhaps the very cosmos itself, into make-believe; into a joke, which God alone might laugh at, were he not instead to weep at mankind's folly. Just as well then, that people like Don, and the EU technology commissioner, and countless heads of industry, were merely pumping money into the clever light-show of a fairground huckster. Just as well, that none of this could ever happen.

Would that make a good performance for the parishioners of Ardnahanish? No, thought Ringer, they'd probably prefer birdwatching. He was approaching the place now and could see its feeble huddle in the valley beneath the hill his vehicle clung to; a village swathed in smoke and mist condensed upon it like a shroud, the grey vapour tainting the air of a few houses, a church, a pub. Streetlights glowed, a score or two like dying orange stars, enough to bind the little town in all the sickly light it needed. It looked an uninviting place; one you'd only visit if a guidebook said you must.

As he drove down and entered it, a brown tourist sign immediately caught his attention. Burgh House Hotel, up a road to the right, might lift him back out of the despondent valley. He imagined better views, a decent restaurant. A woman was walking on the pavement; Ringer slowed, wound down his window and called to her.

'Is it far to the hotel?' he asked.

She was wearing a thick coat, carried a shopping bag, and looked puzzled.

'The Burgh House Hotel,' he said. 'Is it far?'

'Closed three year ago,' she said bluntly, as though he ought to have known.

'But there's a sign,' he said, pointing.

'Aye, well nobody thought to take it down. Place was meant for winter sports. Skiing and the like. But there's no skiing round here. Never enough snow, or not the right kind. That's why the hotel closed. They've made it a mental hospital now, so I wouldn't drive up there if I were you.'

It appeared Ringer would have to take his chances here in the village. The way things were looking, he feared he might end up on a pew of Mr McCrone's church. 'Thanks,' he said to her; but she was already walking on. He parked and began his search on foot. The village pub – the Pepperpot – looked the obvious place to start; but it wasn't open yet, and Ringer hoped for something a little more domestic. Some kind old lady who'd cook him a decent breakfast in the morning, while he decided what to tell Don.

In the dying daylight, he walked up and down Ardnahanish's main street and its adjoining lanes. Though the village was far from any obvious tourist route, there were a few houses offering B&B. He rang the bell of one.

The lady who answered looked to be in her seventies, friendly in appearance, her unkempt hair and broad smile giving her a reassuringly relaxed look.

'I don't normally get anyone wanting a room this time of year,' she said apologetically. 'But I can make one up for you.' She invited Ringer inside and showed him the house: photographs of children and grandchildren on every available surface. The room would be fine, once the bed was made.

'I'll come back in an hour,' he said.

'It'll be ready before, if you like. You can wait here and I'll make you a pot of tea.' She didn't want to lose a customer.

'Don't worry, I'll be back.' He'd decided he might as well use the time to exhaust the village's every possibility. The pub would be opening soon, and he'd need a meal. 'See you in an hour,' he told her.

'All right,' she said, showing him out. 'I hope so.'

He went back to the main street. There were a couple of shops, but their displays of tinned peas and cornflake boxes didn't attract him. He wondered if he should try looking for Mr McCrone.

Then suddenly he saw her. A figure in the corner of his eye, making him turn his head to look. A woman, walking swiftly, already reaching the other side of the road and disappearing round a corner before he could fully comprehend.

At once he pursued her, going to the lane she'd followed, ready to discover there someone who, on fuller inspection, would bear only a passing resemblance to the person he was sure he had just seen. Ringer was surprised by what he found. The lane was a cul-de-sac lacking any sign of life. Almost as soon as she had appeared out of empty space, Helen had vanished back into it.

HARRY'S TALE

'Interesting,' Priscilla Morgan was saying as she examined Harry's completed pages.

'And you're telling me I was scribbling this stuff only a few minutes ago?' Harry asked her.

She looked at him over the page she held and gave a nod that shook her carrot-coloured hair. 'I couldn't stop you,' she said. 'You were writing like a demon and didn't even seem to notice me watching you. Then all at once you snapped out of it.'

Harry remembered nothing; but at least he had now carried out the creative writing exercise Priscilla demanded of him.

'What's it like?' Harry asked. 'Any good?'

She was swiftly scanning his work with the look of someone who did this kind of thing a great deal, and only when paid for it. 'Intriguing,' she said.

'Is the therapy working?'

'What do you mean?'

'Is there any indication to you, as a professional in the field, that this will help improve my condition?'

'It's not that sort of therapy, Harry.'

'Not the sort that cures anything?'

'No.'

'Then what sort is it?'

'It's writing therapy. That's all it is. It's meant to make you feel better about yourself.'

The exercise had instead made Harry feel considerably worse, having proved to him beyond doubt that something very strange was going on in his brain.

'I can't find any mention of the objects I gave you,' she said, leafing through pages whose contents were completely unknown to him. 'The key, for instance. It came from an old jewellery box belonging to my mother.' Then she began to describe the role it had played in one or two of her seventeen published stories. 'And what about the ring?'

'I expect it's in there somewhere,' said Harry.

'There's a character named John Ringer,' Priscilla told him. 'But I'd call that cheating. Still, as long as you're writing something, we shouldn't complain. And you certainly have a fertile mind. You know, Harry, all you need is a feel for language, character, setting and plot, and you could even turn out to be a decent writer.'

Harry thanked her for this compliment, but said that creative writing appealed to him no more than the thought of training to be a consultant metaneurologist. Skilled and specialized fields should be left to those willing to give up all their time and energy to doing the job properly. Though without having actually seen any of Priscilla's seventeen published stories, Harry still couldn't be sure she wasn't merely an actress performing a role of

Dr Blake's scripting. And even if he were to read Priscilla's stories, he probably still wouldn't be able to decide.

She said, 'Might John Ringer be someone you once knew?'

'I can't remember.'

'No, I suppose not. Sounds symbolic, though. Loops and circles. Does it "ring a bell"?'

They were back to Flow-Bear and Penis Man. Yes, Harry decided, Dr Blake must be pulling the strings. Maybe that was why Priscilla kept jangling so much whenever she moved.

'And what about Schrödinger?' she said.

'Who?'

'Another name in your tale. Is he real?'

Harry wasn't listening; he had suddenly recalled walking out of a shop with a book in his hand, preparing to cross the road. Schrödinger was a name from the book; he felt sure of it.

'It's an anagram of "chord singer",' Priscilla noticed. 'Could that be significant?'

'I suppose so,' said Harry.

Then, feigning sudden insight, she cried, 'Hang on. Isn't Schrödinger the name of the First Minister?'

'No,' Harry replied confidently. 'The First Minister is Alexander Macintyre.'

'Oh yes,' she nodded, 'that's right, of course.' And with equal implausibility she added, 'By the way, do you remember the seventh article of the Constitution?'

Harry admitted he had no idea what she was talking about.

'The articles?' she said incredulously. 'Didn't you recite them at school?'

The change of topic was forced in a way that showed Dr Blake's ever-guiding hand; it was another step in her experiment of strategically fertilizing Harry's memories in order to see how they blossomed. But now that they had arrived at the nation's constitution, Priscilla spoke with a conviction he was sure could not be falsified, even if she really were the author of seventeen published short stories. 'Go on,' said Harry, 'remind me.'

'It is the duty of every citizen,' she began, 'to uphold the Constitution and its articles, except where this may be contrary to the security of the Republic.'

Even as she spoke, Harry found himself dimly recalling a distant classroom scene. Wearing short trousers and needing to go to the toilet, he was standing to attention with all the other children, reading aloud what was written on the blackboard while the teacher (a stern woman in a tartan skirt) rapped each word with a wooden pointer.

'Why yes,' he said, 'I think I remember.'

He noticed Priscilla jotting something down in a notepad she'd brought from her pocket. She only gave this therapy because she had to, until her next writing residency came along; but he was grateful for the little spark she'd set glowing in his mind. He started remembering other things too. A boy standing at the front of the class, about to be beaten for misbehaving. Above him, on the wall, the sombre black-and-white photo-graph of a balding man, kindly yet terrifying. Vernon Shaw.

'Was there ever a First Minister called Vernon Shaw?' he asked Priscilla.

'No,' she said. 'He was leader of the Party.'

'Which party?'

'The one that kicked out the Germans and ran this country until fifteen years ago.' Then she added disarm-ingly, 'I'm probably not meant to tell you that.' She made another note, and Harry wondered if he'd just been given a false memory.

He said, 'Will Margaret be here soon?'

'Who?'

'My wife.'

'I wasn't aware you had one. You'd better ask Dr Blake about that when you next see her.'

'And when will that be?'

She shrugged. 'I don't know. But she sees you every day, doesn't she?'

Harry tried to work out when the doctor had last vis-ited, going back through meals and bowel movements, the cycles of waking and sleeping, and even allowing for time lost to the trance-like state in which he must have produced his story about a chord singer. 'I don't think I've seen Dr Blake for at least a week,' he said.

Priscilla smiled. 'You've been here three days, Harry. Your sense of time must be affected by AMD. I've heard it can make a second seem a lifetime, or a lifetime like a second.'

Harry was startled. 'Just as well that in my case it's the former.'

Then she resumed her cursory inspection of his writing, having presumably by now reached the next part of her own pre-rehearsed script. 'I see a few recognizable scraps of reality here, but much of it is evidently invented. For example, you mention a writer . . .'

'Flow-Bear?'

'No, Thomas Mann.'

'I might have known.'

'You even cite particular books by this imaginary author. That does show a certain flair, Harry.'

He could feel himself blushing with pride.

'Though on the other hand,' she said, 'writing about writers is best avoided. I'm sure if you think hard enough you'll find a memory of being treated badly as a child – that's more promising ground.'

Again he saw the boy about to be beaten, his arms outstretched, palms held upward, as Miss Flynn raised the leather belt in readiness. Whether real or fabricated, the memory was becoming stronger.

She continued, 'You say in your story that Thomas Mann wrote a book called *Doctor Faustus*. I bet you were thinking of Goethe's *Faust*.'

'Was there a real writer called Goethe?'

'Certainly,' said Priscilla. 'I'm no expert on all that classic stuff – none of it's relevant any more and the attitudes are so dated – but I do remember a film about one of Goethe's love affairs, based on a novel; it was very popular during the Time of Restructuring. Now what was it called . . . ?' She thought hard, or pretended to, the effort appearing as great as the one that had brought the Constitution back to Harry. '*The Angel Returns*,' she declared. 'That was a lovely film – it had Grace Rutherford as the old woman, and Audrey Milbank as the young one in flashback. There's a beautiful scene where she first meets Goethe . . .'

Harry's mind wandered as Priscilla gave what sounded suspiciously like a period-costume version of one of her own short stories. There was no kitchen sink or oil rig, but it nevertheless climaxed in the same obligatory epiphany that brought a tear to Priscilla's eye, followed by a loud jangling as she wiped her cheek dry. All he wanted to know was how this bit of genuine information had filtered itself, by way of AMD and a bump on the head, into his own tale about an invented writer.

'Who wrote *The Angel Returns*?' he asked.

Again Priscilla thought hard, doubtless trying to repeat in her mind the experience of sitting in a darkened cinema, watching the credits roll and waiting for the part saying *Based on a story by* . . . Or else it was simply taking her a while to remember what Dr Blake had instructed her to say.

'Heinrich Behring,' she announced at last. 'Silly of me to forget. He was really famous – a hero of the old times.'

Perhaps Harry was only being fed misinformation; yet as soon as he heard the name, he felt sure of its authenticity. He could even see it on the cover of a book. It was the one he held as he prepared to cross the road, failing to see the car that hit him.

Priscilla said, 'I think the old woman was called Bettina. But *The Angel Returns* isn't only about her and Goethe. If I remember correctly, it's also about her friendship with a composer.'

'A real composer?'

'Yes,' she said. 'It might have been Schubert.'

To Harry this definitely sounded false. Shoe-Bird. It was too close to Flow-Bear to be anything but the same sort of misplaced pencil Dr Blake had warned him about.

'He went mad,' said Priscilla.

'Who?'

'The composer. Bettina went to visit him in an asylum. I think it might have been based on a true story. It wasn't Schubert, though.' She was gazing at the pages in her hand as she tried to remember. Suddenly she cried out, 'Here it is: Schumann!'

Shoe Man, Penis Man. Was Dr Blake – by way of Priscilla – trying to explore the symbolic meaning of Harry's dreamworld by throwing in a few dreams of her own? Plenty of men in them, that was for sure.

'Look, Harry, you mention Schumann in your story about John Ringer.' She held the page under his nose, but all he saw was a swimming blur on which his eyes were unable to focus. 'And here . . .' she leafed through the pages again. 'One of the books Thomas Mann is supposed to have written: something about Goethe's lover. I think we're starting to see where you got your inspiration, Harry. Your Thomas Mann is a fictional version of Heinrich Behring. And I've thought of something else. I'm sure Behring wrote a novel called *Professor Faust*! So that's where you got *Doctor Faustus* from. Incidentally, you've spelled Doctor with a *k*.'

Such infuriating attention to detail revealed her as genuinely being the writer she claimed. In her analysis, Thomas Mann and his imaginary oeuvre fell rapidly to shreds: a fragile collage of half-remembered facts. As she gathered up Harry's completed pages for further inspection, he found himself seeing even more vividly the scene as he emerged from a bookshop, carrying a copy of *Professor Faust* and hardly looking as he stepped into the road. Both his hands, he now remembered, were full. What was in the other?

'I'll be off now,' Priscilla was saying. 'No need for me to suggest another writing exercise; you're doing perfectly well as it is, thanks to AMD. I almost wish I could catch it too. You know, some people reckon it comes from mobile phones.'

That was it: a phone in one hand, *Professor Faust* in the other. Priscilla went out, and the scene continued to assemble itself in Harry's mind like a scene from a movie. Yet each time he played it, the weakness of its details became more manifest. Was the book in his right hand or his left? Each was equally plausible, equally untrustworthy. Harry realized that the memory was probably false, its components seeded by Priscilla.

She had left more blank paper for him. He stared at it, soon losing himself in the snowy expanse. He wanted to get out of bed but found himself unable to move; instead the whiteness grew, spreading beyond the pages, filling his entire field of view so that at first he was startled, then understood that such hallucinations must be a normal aspect of his condition. Snow was falling all around him. He shivered as he watched the flakes descend.

On his outstretched arm, white powdered jewels began to heap themselves, glistening over his frosted limb. Through the tumbling curtain of icy crystals he could see the wasteland that surrounded him. A harsh breeze stung his cheeks as he discerned a barbed-wire fence, picked out amidst the swirling snowfall by the play of a searchlight, to the fearfully resonant accompaniment of a barking guard dog. It was all becoming clearer to him, this terrible whiteness. On the hard ground lay a line of frozen corpses awaiting burial.

He blinked, and woke to see the pages filled.

A NATURAL EXPLANATION

Ringer stood looking down the lane where Helen had disappeared. No, he couldn't have seen a ghost; such things do not exist. Surely it was a woman who only resembled Helen, and who had retreated into one of the houses lining the cul-de-sac.

He heard a male voice behind him.

'Can I help you?'

Ringer turned and saw a short man in minister's garb; a thin, elderly fellow with a mottled scalp. Ringer guessed at once who it must be.

'Mr McCrone?' he asked.

'I am he,' the minister confirmed. 'Have we met?'

Ringer introduced himself.

'Professor Ringer! What a surprise!' They shook hands. 'Well now, I wasn't expecting you until tomorrow. I hope there hasn't been a mix-up.'

Ringer told him he'd decided to stay here in Ardnahanish, rather than at Craigcarron. The minister looked concerned. 'I have to tell you,' he said solemnly, 'that our church funds are very meagre, and only extend to your speaking fee. I'm so sorry we can't undertake to pay your accommodation costs.'

Ringer was glad he hadn't thrown himself onto Mr McCrone's charity after all; but once he assured the minister he wouldn't be claiming expenses, Mr McCrone's face brightened and he was keen to find out where Ringer was staying. 'Ah, Mrs Moffat,' he said when Ringer told him. 'You'll be well looked after.'

The night was gathering. 'Are there any guesthouses in this street?' asked Ringer, pointing down the lane.

'There's Mrs McFarland at number eight; she takes guests. Has one at the moment, I believe.'

'A woman?'

'That'd be right, I think.' The minister spoke with the air of one who knows all, and worries only about whom he shares it with. 'Have you seen the kirk?' he said, changing the subject.

'The church? Yes, quite impressive, from the outside.'

'Why not come and have a wee look at the interior?' he suggested. It was an invitation Ringer was in no position to refuse, so they walked there together, and the minister unlocked a side door.

'It dates from the middle of the nineteenth century,' Mr McCrone explained, switching on the lights as Ringer followed him inside. 'Not long after the Disruption.' Then he gazed up at a Victorian stained-glass window, presumably wishing Ringer to do the same, though the window, against the darkness outside, seemed to Ringer no more than an indecipherable jumble of lead outlines and mud-coloured panes. The minister looked round at him. 'I take it you've heard of the Disruption of 1843? No, perhaps not. It was when the General Assembly of the Church of Scotland fell into grievous disharmony. Many ministers resigned their livings and formed the Free Church of Scotland.'

'Which is different from the Church of Scotland?'

'Oh yes.'

'And what about the Episcopalians?' Ringer had heard the name but had no idea what it meant.

'Never mind about them,' said Mr McCrone.

'But at least you all follow the same God.'

Mr McCrone smiled sweetly. 'Yes. And since there is one true God, there can only be one true church that worships Him correctly. To a physicist such as yourself, the arithmetic must be pretty straightforward.'

All Ringer could discern was a process of division. 'I'd better go now,' he said, glancing at his watch. 'I promised Mrs Moffat I'd return within the hour, and I'd like to unpack.'

'Of course,' the minister said. 'I'd invite you to my own home for dinner, but unfortunately my wife has trouble with her wrist. I believe the Pepperpot does good bar snacks, very reasonable. I don't go there myself, you understand. Shall I show you the way?'

'No need,' Ringer told him. To be lost in a village as small as Ardnahanish would require the navigational ineptitude of a shopping trolley. He said goodbye and after only a short walk arrived back at his B&B.

'Your room's ready,' Mrs Moffat told him; but before allowing him upstairs to settle in, she ran through the breakfast options. 'Full Scottish?' she said. He told her that'd be just fine. 'You do like black pudding, then?'

Yes, said Ringer, he liked anything.

'Because you see, a lot of people don't, if they're not from here and don't know what it is. And if they do know what it is, they like it even less. And sausages?'

Great, said Ringer.

'I have some that are a wee bit spicy; would you mind that?'

The spicier the better, he told her, his foot by now on the third step of the thickly carpeted staircase.

'Or do you prefer sliced?' Now she'd got him. 'To links, I mean.' It was like being in a replay of Mr McCrone's guide to northern religions. She said, 'Which would you like? I've got Lorne sausages – the square sliced ones – and I've got links.'

'Can I have both?' Ringer thought it safest to remain agnostic.

'Of course!' she said. 'Or you can always have kippers if you prefer.'

'No,' he said, treading hopefully onto the fourth creaking step. 'Just the full Scottish breakfast.'

'Beans?'

'The works.' Fortunately there was only one variety of bean in these parts. The same went for the mushrooms and bacon she offered; and by now Ringer was starving, though he wouldn't get to see any of it until tomorrow. Then before he could escape they embarked on the egg possibilities, of which there were many. After that, the tea versus coffee dilemma seemed positively pedestrian.

He'd hit the sixth step by the time he was finally released from Mrs Moffat's kindly attentions.

'My, you do have a big appetite,' she said. 'I hope I remember it all in the morning.'

At last he was free. He reached his room feeling as though he hadn't eaten for a week. He wondered if the Pepperpot would live up to Mr McCrone's praise.

Ringer closed the door, switched on the table lamp, kicked off his shoes and lay down on the bed. It was like the boudoir of a septuagenarian with a fondness for pink; which of course was exactly what it was. He was in Mrs Moffat's bedroom, and apart from her having cleared the wardrobe and chest of drawers, it looked as though she might roll in at any moment, perhaps to double-check the breakfast schedule before hauling herself into bed beside him.

Ringer stared at the ceiling and heard the rumble of his own stomach. He thought of Don at Craigcarron, with his tale of free energy. It was crazy; but imagining seeing Helen was crazy too. Ringer needed to recalculate the energy limit in his paper. Make it higher, and Don would be happy. Then Ringer could join the research project and find out exactly what was going on.

He reached into his pocket and brought out his Q-phone. He still hadn't even figured out how to store numbers on it; instead he began keying the digits, then heard the ringing tone. He pictured the phone at the other end, in his own home. But nobody was there; perhaps she'd taken the kids out. He heard the answerphone; his own voice inviting him to leave a message.

Ten thousand years of technology and this is what you get: a fancy way of talking to yourself.

'Hello, it's me,' he said to the waiting silence. 'Everything's fine. I got here without a hitch. Bye.'

He hung up, and the two parts of his life disconnected once more. On the answerphone he could now lie dormant. The machine would be flashing its greeting when the three of them got back from the bowling alley or pizzeria they'd gone to. As for Ringer's Q-phone, its screen was flashing a load of useless data about length of call, baud rate, estimated cost, and other stuff that might mean something to an engineer but was really only there so that the device could lay claim to more features than its competitors.

Then on the screen there was a cartoon of an envelope flying through the air. A new text message had arrived. *Call me: Ha.*

So it wasn't about Helen after all. Was it a marketing campaign, perhaps? Some lousy teaser that would eventually tell him to phone a building society? Or was the caller unable to complete the message; constantly interrupted by a suspicious onlooker? A mole at Craigcarron, trying to tell him something.

The philosopher Leibniz believed everything happens for a reason. There must be a reason for the text messages; also a reason why Ringer thought he saw Helen again, here in Ardnahanish of all places. A reason why they met in the first place, talked about Thomas Mann and Schrödinger, began an affair. If everything has a reason, then life makes sense.

There was a knock on the door; a voice calling to him from outside. 'Hello? I just wanted to check – did you say poached or fried?'

'Fried eggs, please.'

She creaked away across the landing as Ringer keyed through his Q-phone's endlessly ramifying menus, trying to work out where the messages had come from, or when they had been sent. It might even be a single message that he still hadn't discovered how to display in its entirety.

Must there be a reason for everything? When Schrödinger and Heisenberg found their two varieties of quantum mechanics it looked like the answer could be no. An atom emits a photon. Why? No reason, it just does. Things happen, it's all random. If mobile phones were one day to be powered by quantum computers, such chance events might be the sort of thing everyone would have to get used to.

A knock again. 'Did I show you how to use the shower?'

'I'll figure it out.'

'You need to pull the string quite hard.'

Perhaps he should simply invite her in. She was probably missing her bed. As she padded away, Ringer sat up and decided to look again at the energy calculation. His workbook was in the suitcase, lying beside Hoffmann's *Tomcat Murr* on folded clothes. He went and fetched the small notebook, expecting at any moment to hear the heavy tread of Mrs Moffat's slippered feet coming once more to disturb him, then settled himself in the bedroom's only armchair.

If Don's vacuum array could truly reach the energies he anticipated, it might prevent wave functions from collapsing. An electron could be everywhere and nowhere, even after it was observed. Don's proposed quantum computer could then be in two different states at once; it might give the answers 'yes' and 'no', and both would be true. This was the kind of snag even Don's financial backers could understand. The vacuum array, if Ringer's fears were justified, might entangle parallel realities, making each inconsistent.

What would such a world be like? It would be hell – an irrational place where everything becomes true and hence meaningless; a place where no possibility, however monstrous, is denied. Perhaps the kind of place where Ringer could bump into Helen in the street.

But no, it wasn't her. The coincidence of finding her here would be simply too astounding. There was no reason for Ringer to think he had somehow been jolted into another universe by Don's conjuring trick with tantalum mirrors. The machine would never work; Ringer need only modify his research paper in a form that would be palatable to Don, and then he could learn exactly what was happening at Craigcarron.

And so he recalculated. Twenty minutes were all it took to convince him that certain plausible guesses could be substituted for various others, yielding an answer Don Chambers would be happy with. In fact Ringer was able to raise the safety threshold a long way. The vacuum array would have to produce a thousand times more energy than expected before any problem could arise. He'd tell Don tomorrow.

Ringer closed his eyes, feeling weary after all the strange experiences of the day. Then his eyes blinked open – he thought there'd been a flash of lightning. He got up and went to the window, but there was no rain or wind outside. Beyond some houses, he could see part of the Pepperpot, lit up now and evidently ready for business. It was time for dinner.

He got ready to go out, putting on his shoes and coat and slipping the notebook into his pocket so that he could review the calculation over a pint of beer. In the other coat pocket he put *Tomcat Murr*. Then he went downstairs, where Mrs Moffat naturally decided to make an appearance.

'Will you be needing dinner?' she asked. The combinatorial possibilities of its menu would probably have kept Ringer detained for a week and a half, so he quickly told her he was going out.

'You could try the Pepperpot,' she suggested as he made for the door. 'Don't worry if you're late back; I never lock up. And for the morning, was it tea or coffee you said . . . ?'

'Coffee,' he called over his shoulder, almost breaking into a trot. His hunger couldn't stand another round of hypothetical choices. He went swiftly to the Pepperpot, which looked a pleasant enough place once he was inside. There was a stone-floored bar where a couple of men stood with the silent, mournful look of regulars; and a doorway marked *Dining Area*, which Ringer passed through at once. The room beyond had pine furniture and a smell of disinfectant, and a single customer who sat alone with her back to him. He immediately knew who she was.

This was the woman who had gone down the lane to her B&B; the one who looked like Helen. From behind, it was an easy mistake. Now he could set his mind at ease.

She was reading the menu as he approached. 'Good evening,' he said politely. She turned, and as soon as he saw her face, her expression changed, registering the shock she must have witnessed in his own.

It was Helen. Older now, her hair different, her features subtly matured, and with something indefinably altered in her appearance that time alone could not account for. Yet it was her.

'I don't believe it!' he could hear himself saying. Still she made no comment, as if she somehow hadn't recognized him. 'It's me,' he said. 'John.'

Her eyes scrutinized him with a mixture of suspicion and embarrassment. 'Forgive me for being rude,' she said at last, 'but you'll have to remind me where we've met.'

'Please, Helen,' he said, 'don't do this.'

'My name's not Helen,' she said curtly. 'I'm afraid you've made a mistake.' She turned to look at her menu again, and he stood there feeling rising indignation at her charade, though he was determined not to show it.

'I know it's been a long time,' Ringer said to the back of her lowered head. 'But your memory can't really be so bad.'

She looked round again. 'I'm sorry, I'm not the person you think I am. We've never met, and I'd like to have a quiet meal.'

A young girl came in, wearing the unflattering white blouse of a waitress. 'Sit anywhere you like,' she told Ringer, 'I'll be with you in a moment.' Then she asked her other customer if she was ready to order.

'I need another minute or two.'

The waitress looked at both of them, sensed the tension hanging in the air, and went back out.

Even more incredible than seeing Helen again was the possibility that Ringer might have made a ghastly mistake. The resemblance was so perfect. She was stroking the menu pensively with her thumb, then pushed a lock of hair behind her ear in a gesture he recognized.

'Do you even have a birthmark on your back, just like Helen? Are you allergic to cats?'

She turned round again. 'Who are you?' she said. 'What do you want?' Her anger was tinged with fear.

'I'm sorry . . . I didn't mean . . .' The confusion was becoming overwhelming. 'Seeing you is such a surprise . . .'

She was staring at him as though he were a madman. 'My name is Laura,' she said firmly. 'I don't know anything about your friend.' She paused, then suddenly her face brightened as a smile broke through at the corner of her mouth. 'Wait a minute. This is some kind of stunt, isn't it?' She looked up towards some small coloured spotlights in the corner of the room, as if suspecting a hidden camera. 'Did the guys on the newsdesk put you up to this?' But when she saw his unwillingness to share the joke, her smile faded. 'Well,' she said, 'however the trick works, I'm very impressed by your mind-reading skills. But now I'd really like to have a peaceful dinner on my own. I've had a long day, and it's very nice of you to talk to me, but I'm honestly not in the mood for conversation.'

'This isn't a trick or a chat-up,' he told her. 'I don't understand it any more than you.' While she pondered her menu again, studying it only as a way of avoiding Ringer, he said, 'Do the guys on the newsdesk know how much you hate garlic?'

'What the hell is this?' she snapped. 'I don't know you, I don't know why you're pestering me like this, and I want you to leave me alone.'

The waitress came in again. There was a burly man with her, and they stood silently watching as Laura turned away. It was time for Ringer to leave. 'I'm very sorry,' he said, addressing himself to the three of them. He walked out and found himself in the cold street, feeling foolish and humiliated.

Was it really Helen? She must have got herself a new career as a journalist, judging by her comment about the newsdesk. She'd changed her hair, and her name, and now she was pretending she didn't know him.

Or else the resemblance to a woman he hadn't seen for years existed only in his head. He had imposed himself on a stranger and scared the daylights out of her, acting like a deranged stalker.

He needed to think, and he needed a meal. Mrs Moffat would have to cook dinner for him after all.

When he got back and opened the door she came straight away to see who it was. 'No food at the Pepperpot tonight,' he told her, trying to sound pleasant while inside he was seething.

'That's unusual,' said Mrs Moffat. 'Well, have something here instead.'

The dining-room door was open; she switched on the light and invited him to sit down at the table. Knick-knacks and memorabilia cluttered every shelf and surface; glass animals and porcelain figures competing for space with family photographs.

Though Ringer's mind was elsewhere, Mrs Moffat proved to be a good cook, feeding him so heartily that his anger began to dissipate. 'Stay here and watch television if you like,' she said to him when the meal was finished.

'No, I need a walk before bed,' he told her, lifting his coat from the dining chair where he had draped it.

'All right,' she said. 'Goodnight, then. And for your breakfast, was it slice or links you wanted?'

'Either please, Mrs Moffat.' If he was going to get back to the Pepperpot before closing time he had better avoid the sausage issue altogether.

'Have both,' she said with matronly generosity, offering what in any case he had requested earlier, then she waddled to the kitchen while Ringer buttoned his thick coat and headed for the front door.

It was a frosty night, the moon was nearly full, and silvery breath billowed around Ringer's face as he walked back to the pub, cautiously looking through the window from the other side of the road. Laura was still there, at the same table, talking to an elderly couple who must have decided to join her. So much for the quiet meal she wanted, Ringer thought. He crossed the street, remaining careful not to be seen, and observed as he came closer that Laura was taking notes while the couple spoke. She really was a journalist. The waitress appeared from the far end of the room, and Ringer moved clear of the window's warm glow. He couldn't go inside: he would have to wait.

Along the street from the pub was an old fountain with benches beside it. Ringer went and sat on one, but it was so cold he thought he might freeze before Laura ever came out. So instead he stood at the Victorian fountain, completely dry, whose smooth bowl of polished granite bore an inscription round its edge that he read from sheer idleness. *What meanest thou, O sleeper? Arise, call upon thy God.*

He waited, and he shivered. Thirty or forty minutes must have passed until at last he saw Laura coming out of the Pepperpot, alone. He'd had time to work out his approach, and now she was walking in his direction.

'Excuse me, Laura.' She gave a start when she saw him. He would have to win her confidence before she turned and fled. 'If you're looking for a news story,' he said, 'I might have one for you.'

In the gloom, he could see her eyes narrowing. 'What kind of story?'

'About Craigcarron,' he told her.

'The nuclear plant? What about it? This hasn't got anything to do with your friend Helen, I hope.'

Ringer shook his head. 'To be honest, I only made that up as a way of talking to you.'

She burst into laughter. 'I guessed as much.' The laugh faded again. 'But how did you know about my birthmark? Or the cat allergy?'

'I suppose they were lucky guesses,' Ringer said with a shrug. 'Lots of people have birthmarks and allergies. Was I right about your star sign?'

'I don't recall your mentioning it,' she said.

'I'm sure I did. Scorpio, I reckon.'

'As a matter of fact you're wrong,' she said lightly. 'So it seems you're not such a mind-reader after all.'

No, Helen was Capricorn.

'Well, let's forget about chat-ups,' she said. 'I forgive you for the little faux pas in the pub. But right now we're freezing, and unless you give me some idea what your story is, I'm afraid I'll have to give you the brush-off for the second time tonight.'

She meant it. She was on the point of walking away and leaving.

'They're developing new technology at Craigcarron,' said Ringer. 'There could be enormous risks.'

Now she was interested. 'Tell me more.'

'I can't. If you like, I can explain how I've calculated the dangers. But not here.'

Her face once more registered a succession of doubts. 'Give me your number and I'll call you tomorrow,' she said.

'No, this can't wait. I'm going to Craigcarron first thing in the morning, and if there's to be any discussion between us it has to be now.' She looked as if she was about to go. 'I'm taking a big gamble talking to you like this. There are powerful players involved.'

Still she was hesitant. 'Give me your number,' she repeated.

'No, I'll only talk about this face-to-face, tonight. There's too much at stake – far more than my career. If you don't want this story, I'll find someone who does.'

At last he'd won her. 'Very well,' she said. 'Let's go to my guesthouse before we both get hypothermia. I'll give you half an hour there to convince me you aren't a lunatic, and then I'll throw you out. Deal?'

'It's a deal,' he said. 'Let's go.'

They went to the lane he'd first seen her go down, arriving at a B&B which, once he followed her inside, looked less lived-in than Mrs Moffat's, more like a genuine hotel: the kind of place where a real journalist might choose to stay. She directed him to a small lounge whose tastefully co-ordinated decor was perfectly anonymous, free of personal items or any trace of identity.

'We won't be disturbed here,' she said. 'I'm the only guest.' She sat down on the sofa, backing away slightly when Ringer placed himself there too. Though the two of them were at opposite ends, their knees almost touched. 'Now,' she said, 'tell me about Craigcarron.'

Don had warned him not to talk about the project; but it was the only way he could be with Laura. 'They're developing a new kind of machine,' he said, and began describing what little he knew about the delicate arrangement of tantalum mirrors that would supposedly harness the energy of empty space.

'What's this machine meant to do?' she asked.

'They're trying to make a quantum computer – a device whose information is stored in elementary particles.'

'Where's the danger?'

'It's a little hard to explain,' he told her.

'I'm all ears,' she said, opening her handbag to retrieve a small reporter's notepad wedged inside. When she flicked it open, Ringer saw a page scrawled incomprehensibly in shorthand. 'OK, tell me whatever I need to know about quantum computers. And make it simple enough for a journalist to understand.'

Ringer had an idea. Reaching inside his coat pocket, he took out the novel he'd put there earlier. 'Have you ever read this?' he asked, showing her E. T. A. Hoffmann's *The Life and Opinions of Tomcat Murr.*

'I've never heard of it,' she said; though Helen had.

'Didn't you study German literature?'

She looked puzzled, then suspicious. 'Please, no more mind-reading tricks.'

'It's a novel about a musician called Kreisler,' he told her. 'His pet cat writes a totally different story and mixes up the pages. So it's a very jumbled novel – two stories at once, and you can't tell which one's real.'

'So?'

'Quantum computers are a bit like that,' he said. 'And they also involve a story about a cat.'

She looked at her watch. 'You've got twenty minutes to tell me it,' she said. 'Then you're out, remember?'

It was the tale he'd told her double, in another life. Ringer had described to Helen how Schrödinger went to an Alpine sanatorium in 1925 and discovered the equation that instantly lifted him from obscurity to fame. Now he told it to Laura. 'Think of the Schrödinger equation as a machine for writing stories,' he said. 'You put in certain boundary conditions: the main characters, for example, or the beginnings of a plot. There's a musician called Kreisler; his friend gives him a cat called Murr. Imagine all the different stories that might follow from that outline. There are infinitely many, of course. Try to imagine a book that somehow contains them all.'

'It'd have to be a big book,' said Laura.

'The Schrödinger equation gives a way of working out every single one of them, and the big book is called the quantum wave function.' Ringer was still holding *Tomcat Murr* in his hands. 'Pretend this is more than simply the novel Hoffmann actually wrote and published. Think of it instead as the Big Book: the wave function containing every possible story of Kreisler and Murr. Now I open the book; equivalent to making an observation of the system.' Ringer chose a page at random. 'Out of all the possible stories, I've selected one in particular.' He read – silently to himself – the first words he found:

Approaching Master Abraham's house, Kreisler saw his own double, his own Self walking beside him. Stricken with terror, he burst inside the cottage and sank into a chair, gasping and deathly pale.

The words made Ringer shiver; it seemed an uncanny coincidence. The passage was about a man seeing his doppelgänger, and here beside him on the sofa was Helen's double – her reinvented self. He decided to read out a later paragraph:

Master Abraham stepped outside, and straight away there appeared another Master Abraham standing beside him in the lamplight. Kreisler saw that it was an effect produced by a curved mirror.

There was the simple explanation of Kreisler's ghost. But what about Helen's?

She saw him lingering pensively over the page. 'Twelve minutes,' she reminded him.

He said, 'Out of all the possible stories in the Big Book, my observation selects just one. This is called a quantum jump. Bohr explained it by saying that as soon as you take the tiniest peek, the Big Book disappears – the wave function collapses – leaving you with a single story. An electron has so many parallel narratives that it can be anywhere, until the moment it is observed and its particular story – its location – is fixed. Schrödinger never liked the idea, which is why he invented his own story about a cat in a box that is neither alive nor dead until, like the opening of a book, the box's lid is lifted.'

For the first time, Laura jotted something in her notepad. 'Wait a moment,' she said. 'All these analogies and metaphors are mixing me up. Is Schrödinger's cat equal to your Big Book; or is the cat a character in the book?'

'That's a good question,' he told her. 'In fact it's what physicists have been arguing about for the last eighty years. Is the wave function a real object, or is it a description of reality? A book can be either.'

She checked her watch again. 'You've got ten minutes to start making sense, then I'm going to bed.'

Ringer said, 'For many years, physicists have been trying to create a Big Book that would simulate interesting problems: a quantum computer. Most books, of course, deal with pretty mundane things like falling in love or creating a perfect soufflé. But if you could find the right boundary conditions – the right cast of characters – and if you could find a way of preventing anyone from looking inside the pages too soon and making it all collapse, then you could conjure up a Big Book that could do any calculation you like – it could simulate any system you chose. If it was big enough, it could simulate the universe itself.'

Time was running out, and Ringer got the feeling from Laura's facial expression and lack of note-taking that his story wasn't the kind of thing journalists find exciting.

'This is all very well,' she said, 'but what are the dangers?'

'At the sort of energy envisaged by the people at Craigcarron, it may not be possible to make the Big Book settle on a single story. It could remain trapped in several different contradictory ones.'

'Sounds just like this Hoffmann novel,' she said. 'So apart from making people's heads hurt, where's the problem?'

'The difference,' said Ringer, 'is that *Tomcat Murr* is a fictional story, made up a long time ago by somebody whose only purpose was to amuse his audience. My Big Book is an analogy for something that's perfectly real – something you can make predictions with. My Big Book is the kind of thing that tells you: go to such and such a place at such and such a time, and this is exactly what you'll see. And you go there, and you see it, just like the Big Book said. We physicists call that "reality", and it has little to do with tricksy novels.'

As Ringer's voice rose, he caught a renewed glimpse of Laura's earlier fear, when he had first accosted her in the Pepperpot. He calmed himself, realizing he had become agitated because the memory that lingered in his mind was of the infuriating talk he had attended not long ago at the university – *Vicious Cycloids* – with its facile relativism, its denial of objective certainty, its intellectual game-playing. Life, he reminded himself, is not a narrative, not a story we can interpret however we choose. If it were, we would be free to deny the Holocaust, the Big Bang, our own existence. What was at stake, Ringer knew, was the very thing that made the science he lived for meaningful, the same crucial ingredient that ensured *Vicious Cycloids* would always be no more than a form of entertainment, like a novel or a symphony, whose only criteria were those of personal or collective taste. That crucial ingredient was truth. Fact and logic were in peril, and Ringer was gripped by the heady thought that it might be his personal duty to protect them.

'As far as I can gather,' he continued, 'the people at Craigcarron are involved in plans to set up a network of quantum computers, communicating through a mechanism called entanglement. Let's suppose one of these computers produces a non-collapsible wave function corresponding to a high-energy photon. This photon could do lots of things – its Big Book is pretty enormous. It might get quickly absorbed by the tantalum mirror, in which case its story ends abruptly. Or perhaps it collides with a stray oxygen molecule that didn't get evacuated properly from the machine, causing some other little sub-plot. It might even leak out through a crack in the device, enter the body of a worker and create a free radical inside his liver that eventually gives him cancer. If the wave function is prevented from collapsing, then perhaps – who knows – all of these mutually contradictory events will occur together.

'The problem could be replicated in every other device in the network. Nobody knows exactly what this damned photon is supposed to be doing: there are two copies of the same particle, then four, eight. Soon there might be billions of phantom particles breeding and proliferating.'

Laura looked sceptical. 'How do I know this tale isn't simply another way of chatting up somebody who happens to look like an old flame of yours?

Ringer shook his head. 'I admit this is all purely speculative – my fears are probably groundless. What's more important is that a great deal of public money is going to be pumped into Craigcarron to create a device that will never work. There's your story. But tell me, please, is there any chance you and Helen could be related? Lost sisters, perhaps?'

'Forget it,' she said emphatically. 'It's a crazy coincidence, nothing more. You obviously don't like coincidences – I expect they don't fit in with your rational scheme of things. Well, life's full of them, and today you hit one.' Her voice softened. 'I take it you and Helen were pretty close. It must have been quite a shock, seeing me and thinking it was her. How long is it since you saw her?'

He added it up and was almost surprised. 'Twenty years,' he said.

'People can change a lot in such a long time.'

'I know,' said Ringer. 'Something reminded me of Helen recently, and since then it's been like a chain of coincidences, one after another. Seeing you is just the latest of them.'

'Except that I probably don't look much like her at all,' she said. 'Was she a journalist too, by any chance?'

'No,' said Ringer. 'She studied literature, and was a big fan of Thomas Mann. Though when I eventually tried reading his books I found them terribly boring. That's the trouble with literature; it's totally subjective. Like a love affair. Helen was in love with Mann, but over the years I've come across lots of people – intelligent critics who know about these things – who reckon he never deserved the reputation he got. I wouldn't know; all I can say is that I'm glad I'm not a literary critic. You could spend your entire life in a bad marriage, infatuated with an author who's completely worthless.'

'Not like physics?'

'No,' said Ringer, 'not like physics. Take away all the subjectivity – all the emotion, if you want to call it that – and what you're left with is truth or falsehood.'

'And no room for coincidence,' Laura added. 'Forgive me, but it sounds like you physicists might still be missing part of the picture.' Then she directed her gaze to the book he still held. 'Mind if I take a look?'

He passed it to her.

'Let me check I've got it right,' she said. 'This book is meant to contain everything that could possibly happen.' She opened it. 'And now I've chosen one possibility that becomes real.'

'I think you're getting the hang of quantum theory,' Ringer told her. She was looking at the page she'd chosen, reading silently. 'Found anything interesting?' he asked.

'Oh, not really.'

'You can borrow it if you like,' he offered. It would be a way of ensuring a further meeting.

'All right, I will.' She put it into her handbag. 'And thanks for the lecture. But now it's getting late.'

'Is my information any use to you?'

'Perhaps,' she said cryptically. Then she explained. 'I'm investigating a new privately funded hospital not far from here. I've heard rumours about it.' Ringer recalled the sign he'd seen for Burgh House. 'Lots of people round here have been getting jobs at it,' she continued, 'but so far there are hardly any patients. Looks more like some kind of work-creation scheme. Very convenient, now that the power station – the area's main employer – is being decommissioned.'

'Don't you know about the buy-out?' he said. 'Some outfit called the Rosier Corporation is taking over the plant; that's why the research station is going into quantum computing.'

Laura pursed her lips and nodded thoughtfully. 'Even more interesting,' she said. 'Big money's being ploughed into the hospital. There may not be enough patients to fill it yet, but perhaps somebody expects there will be. There have been health problems in these parts for decades; high rates of lung cancer and leukaemia, almost certainly due to Craigcarron. Now there are reports of mental problems too. Depression and suicide have increased, as well as schizophrenia and premature Alzheimer's. Some researchers in Edinburgh think they've identified a new brain condition causing false memories. Could be bigger than BSE.'

'Somebody told me Burgh House is a mental hospital,' he said.

'It might be. Or else that's a way of deterring the public. Given all these new changes at Craigcarron, I wonder if there could be some connection. The locals are tight-lipped, but I do know a great deal of work was done on converting the old hotel. Contractors were blasting out bits of the surrounding mountainside for months. Why? Have they got some kind of office block hidden underneath their empty little health centre in the middle of nowhere? And why all the security? Try driving up there and you soon come to a checkpoint.'

'What do you think's going on?' asked Ringer.

'That's what I intend to find out,' she said. 'I'm going to Burgh House tomorrow. If I can't bluff my way past the roadblock I'll scramble up the hillside, but one way or another I'm going to get in there to see for myself.'

'I'll be going to Craigcarron,' he reminded her. 'I might be able to find out something for you.'

'Let's meet tomorrow night,' she suggested. 'How about dinner at the Pepperpot?'

'Sounds good,' said Ringer. Then she got to her feet as an indication that his time was up. Leading him to the front door, she shook hands with him in a cool, professional way; and as she reached for the latch on the door, Ringer became aware for the first time of something he hadn't fully registered earlier while she was taking notes. Unlike Helen, Laura was right-handed. In fact, so much about her was different from Helen that he felt a fool to have been persuaded by the unreliable evidence of facial appearance alone. This woman was Laura; the chance resemblance meant nothing outside Ringer's own mind. He was determined to help her.

'We both need plenty of sleep,' she said, showing him out. 'We've got a big day tomorrow, and work to be done.'

HARRY'S TALE

A dark-haired woman was at his bedside. 'Hello, Harry,' she said. For a moment he wondered if she might be his wife; but as he looked at the elegant white-coated medic he realized it must be Dr Blake. He felt as though he hadn't seen her for weeks.

'How are we today?' she asked.

'I don't know.'

She raised an eyebrow. 'Is it such a difficult question?'

It was. While Harry searched vainly for an answer, Dr Blake made a note on her clipboard.

She said, 'Can you tell me the name of the First Minister?'

'Donald Davie.'

She jotted it down, then asked, 'Can you remember what I told you yesterday about the tortoise and the hare?'

'I didn't see you yesterday,' he said. 'When will my wife come and get me out of here?'

'You'll see her soon, but you must be patient. It's only been four days since you were admitted.' He was sure Dr Blake was lying. He'd been here long enough to count at least a fortnight's worth of hospital meals. He'd even begun hiding bits of food under his pillow as a way of keeping track. But whenever he looked under the pillow, the scraps were gone. If he said anything about it to Dr Blake she'd only tell him it was a false memory caused by AMD; but he knew the truth. Dr Blake didn't want him to have any awareness of time. It would spoil her experiment.

'Have you been trying to remember your life before you came here?' Dr Blake asked.

Three memories had come to him: a prison camp in a snowstorm, a school lesson about the Constitution, and walking out of a bookshop with *Professor Faust* in one hand and a mobile phone in the other. All, he felt sure, were false.

'It's very hard to remember anything,' he said.

'That's perfectly normal,' she told him. 'Your mind needs rest in order to heal; AMD often brings about a state of apathy and inertia that is really the brain's way of protecting itself, like immobilizing a broken limb. By not trying to remember, not trying to understand, you can save your energy for the more important process of neural restructuring . . .'

'Time of Restructuring,' he interjected.

Dr Blake pursed her lips thoughtfully. 'What can you tell me about the Time of Restructuring?'

'Vernon Shaw,' he said. 'Heinrich Behring.'

She made a further note on her clipboard. 'Who were they?'

'Vernon Shaw was General Secretary of the British Communist Party. Heinrich Behring was a famous author whose novel *The Angel Returns* was made into a film.'

'Do you recall seeing it?' she asked.

'It was in black and white, and everybody stood up for the national anthem at the end.'

'Can you sing the national anthem for me?'

He hummed the tune but couldn't remember the words until he got to *we'll keep the Red Flag flying here*.

'That's fine, Harry,' she said, then brought out a little torch from her pocket, sat down on the edge of his bed and shone the beam into his right eye. 'Very good,' she said soothingly as she tugged his eyelid.

'What can you see?'

She gave no reply; merely switched off the torch, returned it to her pocket as she stood up, then said, 'Priscilla Morgan showed me what you've been writing.' She described to him the latest instalment of a story about someone called John Ringer that he had no recollection of having written. 'As far as I can tell,' she said, 'it bears no relation to fact, except perhaps in one or two places. Some of the characters resemble real people, almost in the manner of a dream.'

Priscilla had already explained this to him. 'Penis Man is based on Heinrich Behring,' he said.

'Perhaps,' Dr Blake replied. 'In any case, it gives us a good idea of how the AMD mind attempts to construct an alternative reality. I hope you'll continue with it.' She lifted a page on her clipboard. 'Now, let's see if you have any new symptoms to report. Fainting fits?'

'No.'

'Dizziness?'

'Only if I move too abruptly.'

'Any pains outside your body?'

This gave Harry pause for thought. 'I'm not entirely sure I understand what you mean.'

'Oh well,' she said casually, 'that means the symptom hasn't occurred. Blurring of vision?'

'Hang on,' he said. 'Do some people with AMD get pains outside their own bodies?'

Dr Blake nodded brusquely. 'Blurred vision?' she repeated, preparing to make a tick on her sheet if necessary.

'Yes,' he said. 'But these external pains . . . what do they feel like?'

Dr Blake looked at him quizzically. 'I suppose they feel like any other pain.'

'Stabbing?' he asked. 'Throbbing? Dull? Nagging?'

'I expect so.'

'Except that they come from outside?'

'That's right, Harry.' To a clinician, the most exotic and extreme experiences that humanity has to offer can become ticks or blanks on a piece of paper.

'How can you have a pain outside your body?'

She said, 'How can you have one in your foot or your stomach, when really we know they're all inside our heads?'

'Might I, for example, develop a sore chair?'

'I believe such things were reported by a patient in southern Italy,' she told him calmly.

'And when that patient went out for a walk, did the pain go with him, or stay in the chair?'

'It went with him,' she said. 'It was in his wheelchair.'

Harry tried again. 'Let's say I was to become afflicted by a sore window.'

'A window pain, Harry?' She gave a patronizing laugh.

'Yes, suppose I was to start feeling pain in that window over there. Would the pain get stronger or weaker depending how far I moved from it? If I went wandering around the hospital and got lost, could I use my window pain as a homing device?'

'I've no idea,' she said dismissively. 'If the symptom occurs then perhaps we'll find out. Premonitions?' Harry realized she must be moving on in her list of symptoms. 'Do you find yourself remembering things before they happen?'

'Don't tell me your Italian fellow in a wheelchair developed second sight.'

'I believe it's only a theoretical symptom that hasn't yet been reported,' she said. 'There's always a first time.'

Harry was still having too much trouble recalling the past, he explained, to worry much about what was yet to come. Dr Blake looked up from her checklist.

'But you do know what's going to happen to John Ringer and Laura, don't you?' she said.

'I can't even remember writing about them. And besides, they're made up.'

'Are they?' she asked. 'Can you be sure of that?'

It was Dr Blake who had described Harry's tale as an alternative reality; but ever since Clara had shown him the newspaper article about Dr Blake's experiment, Harry had known that whatever Dr Blake told him was open to doubt.

She said, 'Your writing is a form of dream activity. That's why you forget it as soon as you stop; it's as if you're waking up. But unlike ordinary dreams, your periods of altered consciousness have their own consistent logic. You become another person. You're even able to get out of bed and take exercise.'

Harry was surprised. His AMD alter-ego was in better physical shape than he was. 'When I'm in these trances, do I speak?'

'Sometimes, though you tend to be morose, petulant and uncommunicative. Priscilla finds this consistent with your new-found literary vocation. But what about when you're asleep?' she asked him. 'Which person are you then?'

'How am I supposed to know that?' Harry asked helplessly.

'Do you recall any dreams?'

'I think I had one last night.'

'A genuine dream?'

'I can't be sure,' he said.

'Do you have sexual dreams?' she enquired blandly.

'Not last night. It was about submarines, I think.'

'That sounds sexual to me,' she said authoritatively. 'And when you have sexual dreams, do they ever include me?'

'Is this for your checklist?'

'I need to know these things, Harry. As part of your treatment.'

There was no treatment; Harry knew this. He told Dr Blake he had not had any sexual dreams about her, and she almost looked disappointed.

'Have you ever dreamt about me at all?' she asked.

'Not that I'm aware of.'

This gave her a grain of hope. 'We mustn't dismiss the possibility that your dreams about me have all been forgotten, perhaps selectively so. I've had very few AMD patients, male or female, who did not at some stage dream they were having sex with me, or watching me have sex with someone else. It seems almost symptomatic, but I need to get further data on this before I can definitely add it to the list. Harry, I want you to pay very careful attention to your dreams, and note what happens when I appear in them.'

Then she looked at her clipboard again, and asked, 'Do you ever dream that you're awake?'

'Yes, always.'

'Never that you're asleep?'

'Not that I can recall.'

She continued, 'Do you ever dream that you're somebody or something else? You know, a patient in Argentina recently dreamed she was a fruit bat.'

'What's it like to be a fruit bat?'

Dr Blake didn't know. 'The journal paper reported only the content of the dream, Harry, not what it was like to have it.'

'When the woman woke up, could she remember what it was like to be a bat?'

'I don't think so, Harry. Since she had AMD she wasn't very good at remembering anything, and if she thought she knew what it was like to be a bat she was almost certainly wrong. She only knew what it would feel like for a human with AMD to believe she once dreamt she felt like a bat, which hardly counts, really.' Then Dr Blake asked him, 'Do you ever doubt that you're awake? Right now, I mean. Are you completely comfortable with the notion that you're fully conscious, Harry, or do you feel as if you might be dreaming?'

She was quite serious. He said, 'Are there AMD patients who can't tell when they're awake?'

'Certainly,' said Dr Blake. 'So let's try and suppose, for the sake of argument, that you're dreaming all this, right now.'

It was not hard. 'It would be so much better if this were a dream,' he said.

'Well, Harry, if we agree you're dreaming, we can see that you lied to me earlier. And lying, we have found, is one of your most persistent symptoms.'

'When did I lie?'

'You said you never dream about me. Yet here I am before you.'

'Yes, but I'm awake!'

'Only for the sake of argument, Harry. Did you lie to me about anything else? Premonitions, perhaps?'

'No, I honestly don't know what you're going to say next.'

'You mean you're powerless to control your dreams?'

'Isn't everybody?'

'Dreams are the work of the imagination, Harry. If you don't control your own thoughts, then who does? You've been dreaming about me quite a lot, haven't you?'

His mouth had become quite dry – a result of his medication, perhaps, or else something to do with the way she had allowed her hand to brush his arm; the way she was leaning closer to the bed, so that he could smell what must have been a combination of liquid from an expensive bottle and vapour from her own smooth body, mingled with a clinical aura of pathological cleanliness.

Or else he only imagined it. She was standing clear of him again, absorbed by the checklist that summed up his irrational existence. She made a note, then directed her cool gaze at him once more.

'I want you to realize that AMD can affect a person's judgement and perceptions in quite a profound way. If you were to leave hospital right now, you'd be a danger to yourself and others.'

'Am I still supposed to be dreaming this?'

'What?'

'For the sake of argument.'

'I've no idea what you mean.'

'You told me I was dreaming, only a moment ago.'

'No I didn't.'

'You did! You wanted to know if I have sexual dreams about you.'

She looked flustered. 'I never said anything of the kind. Is this a lie, Harry, or a false memory?'

'Sorry,' he said meekly.

'You can see what I mean about being a danger to yourself. We even have to be careful about who you see while you're here.'

'What about your other patient Clara?' Harry asked. 'Can I meet her? We could exchange false memories.'

Dr Blake looked momentarily surprised. 'We don't have any patient named Clara,' she said calmly. 'Now, Harry, when you wake up . . .'

'I am awake.'

'Yes, I mean, when you next wake up after you've had some sleep, I want you to try and remember your dream in as much detail as possible.'

'What if I don't have one?'

'I'm sure you'll think of something,' she assured him. She clicked her pen and returned it to her breast pocket, then walked to the door. As she reached it, she turned and said, in what was clearly meant to be a casual manner, 'By the way, that journalist woman – Laura – did she ever say anything to you about possible causes of AMD?'

'No,' Harry replied. 'According to you, Laura is a fictional character. And I'm not dreaming any of this.'

'Good, Harry,' she said. 'Very good.'

ENLIGHTENMENT

Ringer presented himself in Mrs Moffat's dining room at half past eight precisely and settled himself at the table. 'Here you are,' his landlady declared as she came and deposited in front of him a large and steaming bowl of porridge.

Laura had as good as warned him. There were mental problems round here: premature Alzheimer's, and a strange new condition causing false memories. Laura would be going up to Burgh House later to find out more; and Ringer could only hope she'd have a better breakfast in her stomach than the 'full Scottish' in front of him, which contained none of those countless varieties of sausage Mrs Moffat had kept going on about, but instead amounted to this single bowl of congealing wallpaper paste looking slightly less nutritious and appetizing than the place mat it stood on. But in the presence of a sick woman, Ringer felt the need to be tactful. He could always eat the place mat.

'Everything all right?' Mrs Moffat asked, her plump mass sensing the uneasiness her guest now exuded.

'Fine,' he told her.

'I only put in a wee bit of salt,' she assured him. 'There's sugar on the table as well, if you need any.'

Neither additive appeared likely to turn the over-heated baby food she'd presented him with into a fair substitute for the promised fry-up. So great was his disappointment, his nose was even beginning to hallucinate the smoky tang of bacon.

'Now,' she said, 'I'll go and get on with the rest of your breakfast.' This comment lifted his spirits. 'You wanted slice and links together, didn't you? I hope you'll have room for it all after your porridge.'

That smell of bacon was genuine; Mrs Moffat's boiled oats could go to fill a few cracks in the brickwork where they belonged. 'Actually,' Ringer called out to her as she went to the kitchen, 'I didn't ask for porridge yesterday.'

She came back. 'Did you not? I was sure you did. Well, why did you not say so?' She chuckled as she lifted the bowl. 'Really, there's no need to be polite, you know.'

She went away, and when she returned she was carrying a pot of coffee and a mug. 'You still want coffee, I take it?' she asked teasingly. 'Haven't changed your mind about that, have you?' She'd evidently decided it was Ringer's memory at fault, not hers.

'Do you know anything about Burgh House?' he asked.

Her brow furrowed. 'Hospital up the hill? What about it?'

'I hear they've been doing a lot of work there. Looks like they're expecting to be busy.'

'I wouldn't know about that,' she said, going back to the kitchen.

Ringer couldn't tell if she was being evasive, or else genuinely didn't know. He chose not to raise the matter again when she returned to the table a few minutes later bearing a heaving plate of calories greasy enough to see him through the day. Crisp lean bacon; two kinds of sausage as promised; a glistening egg that ran when he pricked its golden yolk, smothering the tasty triangle that Mrs Moffat called a 'potato scone'. This was another item Ringer had never asked for, but he didn't mind. Soft brown mushrooms and a fried tomato filled the remaining square inches of plate, and Mrs Moffat left him to gobble it all down.

Afterwards, finishing his coffee, Ringer brought out his Q-phone and called Don, who sounded cautious when he first heard Ringer's voice, unsure if his former supervisor had chosen to join the project after all.

'You were right,' Ringer told him. 'I checked my calculation and found the mistake. Now I can raise the safety limit by three orders of magnitude.'

Ringer could detect a sigh of relief at the other end. 'That's great, John. I'll see you later, and we can discuss this in more detail. I can't think of any other contentious issues in your paper; but you do realize we've got some top people with us today, and we don't want any gaffes.'

Ringer told Don there was nothing to worry about, and they fixed a time to meet. Then as Ringer hung up, another cartoon envelope made its way across the phone's display screen. He read the new message. *Call me: Harry*. So he had a name at last. Now all Ringer needed to know was why Harry kept pestering him.

He got up from the table as Mrs Moffat came back. 'Everything all right?' she asked.

'Wonderful,' he told her. 'It'll last me all day. I'm going to Craigcarron.'

'My Jim worked twenty years there,' she said, starting to clear the table. 'Been gone nearly five.' She lifted the empty plate. 'We thought the cancer might be from his work, but they said it wasn't a kind he could get that way. The company looked after us very well, so they did. But that's all going now.'

She smiled; an old lady's look of stoical resignation, or of apathy. Ringer took his leave and went up to his room to get ready for what lay ahead.

He was going inside the wire. He'd made his pact with the devil; now Don would open the gate and show him the secret of his mirrored machine. At another door stood Laura. For the sake of one he would betray the other.

Soon he was prepared. Wrapped in his winter coat he went back downstairs and stepped out into the cold morning air, puffing grey swirls of breath as he went to his car and found it sugared with a fine layer of frost. Once he got it going he trundled along the main street and saw Ardnahanish properly by daylight for the first time, finding it a prettier place than he'd first thought. Again he saw the brown sign at the end of the village, pointing uphill to Burgh House Hotel.

Ringer decided to follow it, turning left and finding himself ascending a steep, wide road that looked newly upgraded. Soon the trees gave way to barren scrub, the views lengthened, his ears popped. Winding up around a bend that took him onto the mountain's far side, he got a glimpse of the distant hospital; a group of buildings standing in complete solitude. And coming up quickly ahead, a lowered barrier painted red and white, and a roadside hut from which a uniformed guard was emerging.

Ringer came to a halt and wound down his window. 'I'm looking for the hotel,' he said.

'Did you follow the sign from Ardnahanish?' The security guard was plump, cheerful and evidently starved of conversation in his little hut, where pop music crackled from a portable radio. 'I do wish they'd get rid of that notice. We keep telling them.'

'Telling them what?' asked Ringer, playing dumb.

'Hotel closed a long while back. It's a private clinic now. I'm afraid you'll have to turn back.'

'What a pity,' said Ringer. 'Any idea where I might be able to find a place for the night?'

'Best try Ardnahanish or Craigcarron.' While the guard began to give directions, Ringer got out of his car to listen.

'Turn right at the junction?' Ringer parroted, glancing around to try and take in whatever details he could. In the hut, a newspaper lay open, a walkie-talkie rested beside it. Further up the road, a minibus was reaching the main hospital building, disappearing into what was probably an underground car park.

The friendly guard was continuing his suggestions. 'It's a wee bit past the pub,' he was saying. 'Might get a room there.'

From the abandoned walkie-talkie, Ringer heard a voice. 'Five seconds.'

'Thanks,' he said to the guard, then nodded towards the hospital. 'Big place.'

'Aye it's . . .'

Ringer didn't hear the rest of the sentence. Suddenly the ground was trembling, his body was shuddering as a sickeningly deep vibration took hold of his limbs, his stomach, his head. Then almost as soon as it began, the earthquake was over.

'Shouldn't take you long to get there,' the guard was saying, as if nothing had happened. 'Now I'll let you be getting on your way.'

Ringer turned to get back into his car and was instantly gripped by nausea. His legs buckled; he grabbed the car to support himself.

'Are you all right there?' The concerned guard helped steady him.

'I don't know what came over me.' Ringer was able to regain his balance now. He had almost passed out.

'I expect it's the altitude. Quite a few people get sick up here, though you wouldn't think it's high enough. Just as well we've got a hospital, eh?' He gave a chummy laugh as Ringer sat down in the driver's seat and wiped his forehead with the back of his hand.

'Did you feel the ground shake a moment ago?' Ringer asked.

'Last time the earth moved for me was my honeymoon,' the guard said with a chuckle. 'Maybe they're still doing some blasting and it gave you a turn. I don't notice these things. I'm used to them.'

By now Ringer had recovered fully. 'Where do they do the blasting? Is there a quarry?'

'Oh, I don't know anything about it. I'm just the fellow that moves the barrier up and down for all the lorries that come this way. But I'll need to get on to them again about that old hotel sign in Ardnahanish. Why can't they just put up one that says Burgh House Hospital instead, then everybody'd know what's up here?'

'Good idea,' said Ringer. Clearly he wasn't going to get any more information; the guard knew even less than Ringer. At least Laura wouldn't have too much trouble bluffing her way past him. Ringer thanked him and waved goodbye as he turned the car and headed back downhill. At the bottom of the road he swung away from Ardnahanish and towards the coast, in the direction of Craigcarron.

Half an hour later he was once more in the foyer of the research centre, where the same middle-aged receptionist he had seen the previous day was beautifully turned out for the benefit of no one except perhaps the top people Don had promised would be visiting.

She said Don was still in a meeting. 'You could go to the library,' she suggested, pointing along the corridor. 'It'll give you something to read while you wait.'

It sounded a good idea, and Ringer went as instructed, turning right at the end of the corridor. This brought him to another long row of anonymous-looking doors, sickly and forbidding in the artificial illumination, all of them identical and unmarked. The place evidently didn't cater for strangers; and Ringer couldn't quite remember which door was supposed to be the library. He opened one he thought to be correct.

What he saw inside surprised him. Differing totally in character from the rest of the research centre, it was a small room of a sort that might be found in an old-fashioned hotel. It had plain white walls, a narrow bed, wooden furnishings. A man in an antiquated suit stood with his back to Ringer. Beyond him, a woman whose face was obscured sat cross-legged on the floor.

Silently and with infinite haste, Ringer closed the door. They hadn't even noticed him. The startling image remained imprinted on his mind as he tried to decide which door to try next. Then the receptionist came crisply round the corner.

'Can't find it?' she said. Ringer shook his head. 'Here you are.' She went and reached for the same door handle he'd only just released. Her perfumed hand stretched out to it, making her white blouse taut as she opened the door to the room where the couple were having their strange meeting.

But it was a library after all. A bigger place, conventionally modern in appearance, with rows of technical books, and racks with the latest journals neatly placed for inspection. Ringer was stunned.

'Are you feeling unwell?' he heard the receptionist say, with the same concern the hospital security guard had shown. Yet Ringer was not nauseous now; only bewildered.

'I'm fine,' he said, and walked in. It really was a library; and yet he'd seen something completely different, with his own duplicitous eyes, only a moment earlier. The hallucination had been every bit as vivid and detailed as the reality that replaced it.

'I'll leave you here,' she said, closing the door as she departed. How could Ringer's own mind have played such a powerful trick? Was he developing the brain condition Laura had mentioned?

Hesitantly he went to the rack, lifted one of the research journals and opened it. His vision was normal; the text made about as much sense as scientific papers ever do. There was no indication of anything unusual, except that his palms were moist with perspiration. This, he knew, was only because of the shock of what he had just witnessed, and the awareness that the same illusion might occur again.

He put the journal back in its place, lifted another. Ringer was too distracted to read, and it was only when he picked the fourth or fifth from the rack that his attention became suddenly more focussed, thanks to the sudden falling of several pages. A previous user had inadvertently left some papers tucked inside the journal; they fluttered loose and dropped around Ringer's feet. He stooped to pick them up, and as he tried to restore them to order, he saw at the top of the first page: *Top Secret. Approved responses: media and public enquiries.* Ringer only had time to glance through the contents, but the three-page memo was enough to convince him Laura was right. There was a connection between Craigcarron and the region's health problems.

The fourth fallen page was even more significant. It was a map of a building; a skeletal plan with the abstract, utopian quality all such blueprints possess. Figures were sketched in; pinmen brought to frozen life only as a means of displaying the vast inhuman scale of the project they served. At the very bottom of the proposed structure, occupying its most infernal level – far below ground as a precaution, Ringer guessed, against accidental blast – a tiny shaded person unwittingly stood, arm upraised in hope, beside a huge tapering cylinder lying horizontally on the floor and moored like a captured beast. It bore the legend *Vacuum Array*.

Ringer heard the door opening. Hurriedly he stuffed the pages into his pocket, then saw Don entering, beaming as he extended his hand for Ringer to shake. 'Feeling better after a good night's rest, I take it?'

'Absolutely,' Ringer replied, trying not to tremble. Don led him out, saying they should go to his office.

'Today I can tell you a little more about the project,' Don said as they reached his door. He ushered Ringer inside, offering the same chair in which yesterday he'd made Ringer feel like an errant schoolboy. Don positioned himself once more behind his desk.

It was time for the initiation; yet Ringer was still too dazed to savour the moment as fully as he would have liked.

'I have to be very careful what I say,' Don began. 'As you're not yet officially part of the project, there are certain aspects I'm not at liberty to discuss. However, I've been cleared to explain some of the technicalities.'

Don took a pen and began sketching on a scrap of paper. 'Here are the reflecting surfaces of the vacuum array,' he said, aiming his penpoint at a row of gently curving lines he'd drawn, like nested parentheses. These, Ringer reasoned, would fill the great torpedo marked on the plan in his pocket. 'Between some of the surfaces, we insert low-pressure acetone vapour.' Don drew in hatching to illustrate this; and a jagged line depicting the next ingredient. 'An electric current is discharged between the plates. And we find that the spark energy is greater than the input.' Then he said, 'You look pale, John. Anything wrong?'

Ringer told him again that he was fine; but he was unnerved and distracted. Mistrustful of his own senses, Ringer also found himself questioning the resistance he'd felt yesterday to Don's extraordinary claims. To his array of mirrors, Don had added only some vaporized nail-varnish remover; the kind the receptionist might use tonight, preparing for a solitary bed. But as Don spoke of the proposed device, Ringer became increasingly persuaded that it could really work.

'The process arises from the Casimir effect,' said Don. 'We're effectively harnessing the energy of the quantum vacuum between the reflecting plates.'

'That energy is negative,' Ringer objected.

'Sure,' said Don. 'Gravitational energy is negative too; and people have been using that for millennia.'

Ringer felt suddenly stumped, though they were conducting a discussion at a level barely above what a first-year physics student ought to know. This was stuff Ringer had learned long ago, yet it was all hazy now, fuzzy and hard to recall. Don was blinding him with science of a kind which, he assured Ringer, everyone else understood perfectly.

'This is how the mass of the mirrors is converted,' said Don, scribbling a formula. 'You can easily get the rate by solving the Schrödinger equation. The wave function is where quantum information is encoded, and by tuning the nickel-tantalum leaves appropriately, the device becomes capable of computation.'

Don's sketch was starting to become cluttered, though he appeared happy with it. 'Of course, I haven't drawn this to anything like the true scale. You ought to see it . . .'

Ringer blurted, 'You mean this has already been built?'

Don fell silent. He stopped sketching. 'Forgive me; I'm not able to discuss that.'

But it was suddenly clear that he was describing an existing machine. The blueprint was a reality. Ringer asked him, 'Have you got this thing running here now?'

Don's eyes were steady and unblinking. 'I can assure you no vacuum array is currently operational at Craigcarron.' Ringer was left guessing where the patiently drawn plan in his pocket had been turned into concrete and steel.

'Have you already reached the sort of energies we talked about yesterday?' Ringer asked.

Don remained evasive. 'I can't go into operational details, John. But yes, the quantum computer we envisage could peak at 1000EeV.'

Then all Ringer's fears were unfounded after all. The machine was running safely, touching summits possibly unseen since the Big Bang. The world was unharmed. The mistake Ringer had found in his calculation was genuine.

'I know this all sounds a little like science fiction,' Don admitted. 'But just think how it must have been when Volta put some bits of metal in salt water and invented the battery. The vacuum array is so simple and elegant, the strangest thing is that nobody thought of it sooner.'

Ringer's nausea began returning. The ground wasn't shaking this time, but his stomach was heaving, making him feel as if he might be about to vomit. There was a family photograph on Don's desk, and Ringer hoped that by fixing his attention on it he could suppress his sickness.

'John, do you want a glass of water?'

Perhaps scatter-brained Mrs Moffat should have fried that egg a little longer. In Ringer's imagination, its yolk now oozed with multiplying salmonella. Or else, thanks to her disordered mind, she'd possibly managed to put some dreadful extra ingredient in his breakfast. There she was, in her kitchen, gleefully tipping dishwasher powder into Ringer's coffee, and taking from a dog's red plastic feeding bowl the triangular object she'd called a 'potato scone'.

'John, please!'

The room was swirling; Ringer tried to stand, but instead found himself collapsing to the floor. He clutched at the edge of Don's desk as everything became engulfed in whiteness.

Then the receptionist was saying something to him. He'd been out for a minute or two, apparently. Ringer lay stretched on the office carpet, and the receptionist was putting a pile of books under his feet.

'Just need to get the blood back to your head,' she told him. 'Feel better now?'

Don looked down at his stricken colleague with a dismay that was not wholly insincere. 'Too bad we'll have to cancel your talk,' he said. 'Let me go and check something.'

Don went out, leaving Ringer in the care of the receptionist who now assumed a pleasantly maternal air. Her scented bosom hovered in Ringer's field of view as she scrutinized his face.

'Shall I call a doctor?' she asked.

She moved aside as Ringer sat up. The nausea and dizziness were gone. His fainting fit was as transitory and inexplicable as the hallucination that had presaged it.

'I'm fine now,' he said, as she helped him to his feet. 'Thanks.'

Don returned, holding a glass of water, and told the receptionist she could leave. Then he said to Ringer, 'Although you can't give your presentation, the visitors would still like a chat with you, if you're feeling up to it.'

Ringer said he was, and after taking some sips, he followed Don out along the corridor to a conference room whose door stood open. Two men in expensive-looking suits sat at a smoked-glass table, leafing through documents.

'This is John Ringer,' Don announced. They stood to greet him.

'I'm Mike,' said one, shaking Ringer's hand.

'Dave,' said the other. Both were immaculately groomed, spoke with American accents, and had the suntanned look of men who didn't do a lot of physics.

Don stood waiting for some kind of cue. 'Thanks,' Mike said to him eventually. 'We'll dialogue later.' Evidently surprised by his abrupt dismissal, Don turned and went out, closing the door behind him.

They invited Ringer to sit down opposite them. Though their features were dissimilar, they looked as though they could have come from the same school, yacht club or religious sect.

'We don't intend to beat the bunker . . .' Mike began.

'Or leave you at the dog track,' Dave added.

'No,' said Mike, 'what we want to do, John, is bowl straight down the middle. We're talking wave functions, right?'

Ringer nodded, not quite sure of anything.

'Quantum wave functions,' Mike continued.

'Schrödinger's cat,' said Dave.

'The waves of the future, you might say. Thing is, John, we aren't physicists. We're not calculating men. No, we're good-old, down-to-earth businessmen, that's what we are.'

'Entrepreneurs, if you will.'

'Impresarios, even. We're the men who turn your ideas into everybody's money. And that's good.' Mike sat back. 'First thing I want to know is: can we trust Don?'

Mike and Dave stared at Ringer with faces whose calmness indicated that nothing much rode on his answer except a man's career.

'Yes,' he said.

'Good,' said Mike. 'Second thing is: can we trust you?'

The same calm faces this time; but with an added gleam in Mike's eye, reminiscent of the oozing yolk in Ringer's breakfast.

'Yes,' Ringer said again.

'Excellent,' Mike beamed, smoothing the table with his palm. Two of his fingers bore heavy gold rings.

Now it was Dave's turn. 'We don't know much about computers,' he said.

'Not much at all,' Mike echoed.

'But we do know that a few kids in the sixties made themselves into billionaires because while their friends were playing guitars and screwing chicks, they were doing electronics in their garage.'

Mike was nodding sagely.

'And we know something else about computers,' said

Dave. 'Which is that they get faster every year, and have more memory. It's . . . what do you call it?'

'Moore's Law?' Ringer suggested.

'Right,' said Mike. 'Moore's Law. Computers get better and better all the time.' He gave a rhetorical shrug, raising his outstretched palms. 'Can't go on, can it? Has to be a limit. And what is that limit?'

A general pause while Ringer tried to figure out if they wanted him to answer, until Dave said, 'Speed of light. The c in mc^2. God's own natural speed limit. Can't send information faster than that.'

Mike stepped in again. 'Unless . . .'

Another pause. Ringer had no intention of helping them out this time, and eventually Mike continued. 'Unless the speed limit can be broken.'

'Wave functions,' Dave chorused.

'Instantaneous transmission of quantum information,' Mike intoned. 'Entangled states, many-worlds theory, superstrings and higher dimensionality.' Mike stopped to draw breath. 'We want you to explain it all to us.'

Dave grew earnest. 'We're not physicists,' he reminded Ringer, somewhat redundantly. 'But we know a good idea when we see one.'

'And we think you're a good idea,' Mike drawled. Then the two of them sat back, staring at Ringer like he was a piece of meat in a shop window.

'So tell us about it,' said Dave. 'From what I hear, you think the vacuum array is going to do more than anyone bargained for.'

'Non-collapsible wave functions at 500EeV,' Mike recited, quoting the contentious gist of Ringer's paper.

Ringer was surprised they knew about it. 'Did Don . . . ?'

'We have our sources,' Mike said with a knowing wink. 'We may not be physicists, but we do our research.'

They wanted Ringer to describe exactly what would happen when the vacuum array reached its energy limit. They said he should pull no punches; they wanted a full and frank discussion. 'Nothing is ruled out,' said Mike. 'Everything is ruled in.'

Ringer wasn't sure if there was any language all three of them could understand. There was surely no point trying to go through technical details. Since they were businessmen, all they wanted was answers, preferably in the affirmative. But as he pondered the problem, Ringer felt the room begin to sway.

'Give us everything you've got,' Mike was saying, his face beginning to rotate and distort. Ringer could feel himself trembling; he wondered if these two men would suddenly turn out to be another hallucination. Then they came back into focus.

'Tell us what these non-collapsible wave functions of yours might do to the vacuum array,' Mike continued. 'Obviously we aren't specialists, but we're intelligent, educated men, just like yourself. I majored in business administration.'

'I did international politics,' Dave added.

'So you see, we're perfectly able to deal with logical reasoning. And we want to hear the facts, John.'

Ringer hoped mental concentration would be enough to save him from another swooning fit. 'You've heard of a prism, haven't you?'

'Sure,' they both agreed.

'What we call white is really a mixture of every possible colour. A prism bends each wavelength by a different amount, splitting them up.' Ringer's head ached, but he was determined to get to the end of this meeting without fainting. 'Like light, matter is associated with waves. Their mixture is not one of colour, but of possibilities.'

His interrogators, becoming stationary as he regained control of his eyes, stared blankly at him.

'We realize you aren't feeling too good today,' said Mike. 'So let's make this as short as we can.'

'Think of the vacuum array as a kind of prism,' Ringer said, his dizziness abating. 'And think of the quantum wave function as being like white light containing every possibility, each of which is a different colour. You have a red life, say; this is the one that has happened, and is happening. But there's also a blue one, a green one – even infrared and ultraviolet lives you could have led. The mirrors of the vacuum array, if the energy were to tip high enough – perhaps very high indeed – might make us all . . . technicolour.'

Dave nodded pensively. Mike said, 'Is this how we'll be able to talk to God? And what about telepathy? You know, we're putting a lot of funding into speculative science. The ideas may be long shots, but the potential reward is simply too great to ignore. Levitation, time travel; the Rosier Corporation keeps an open mind about everything.' He tapped the table with the point of his finger. 'That's why we're so much better than all these government agencies who insist an idea has to be already proved before they'll even give it a chance.'

Dave intervened. 'John, will vacuum array technology provide a means of sending thoughts from one person to another?'

Mike clapped his hands together. 'Instantaneous transfer of information! The ultimate communication network. Just think of it: no infrastructure! Pure head-to-head dial-up. Can we do it?'

What they were proposing was infinitely more barmy than anything Ringer had heard from Don; yet he found himself agreeing with them. 'Since consciousness is indivisible,' he said, 'no thought is truly unique to ourselves. We're all effectively hitching a ride on the quantum computation of the universal wave function. So yes, I don't see any reason, in principle, why telepathy shouldn't be possible.'

'That's great!' said Mike. 'You know, John, we could have a very attractive package lined up for you, if you'd be willing to let us develop these ideas further.'

'You do appreciate,' Dave continued, 'that the Rosier Corporation is devoted to the furthering of human knowledge by means of research conducted in the widest possible range of topics. By agreeing to become a consultant with us on the quantum telepathy project, you would naturally have to forgo any work in other areas of telepathy research which might impinge on the Corporation's interests.'

Ringer had very little idea what they were talking about. It sounded like they were hiring him, but a renewed bout of dizziness interrupted his attempt to keep up. Then he heard Mike's voice again.

'One final thing we need to know. Is there any danger in this prism effect you mention?'

Ringer had feared multiple versions of the same event, spread across time and space like spectral colours cast upon a wall. He had feared that people's lives would be reduced to accidents of frequency; that their thoughts would no longer be their own. Yet he had recalculated, and convinced himself of his own mistake. The machine was already running somewhere, and the world was safe. None of the great horrors had come to pass.

'There is no danger,' he said.

'Splendid,' said Mike. 'It's good to know I won't bump into myself on the way out of here.'

Mike and Dave laughed; Ringer laughed too. He had the vague intimation of an important matter left neglected; like the worry that haunts a person who has forgotten to bring his keys, or who left the bath running when he stepped out of the front door. There was nothing to be afraid of. Why, then, was Ringer afraid?

Mike grew serious. 'I hear you're scheduled to give a talk tonight in one of the villages near here.'

Ringer had almost forgotten about it, but Mike clearly thought it worth mentioning.

'Obviously you'll want to call that off,' he said. 'Given your state of health. And in any case, you realize negotiations here are quite delicate. We wouldn't want anybody going public before the time is right.' He and Dave stood up in unison. 'Good to speak with you,' said Mike, extending his hand. It was only when Ringer grasped it that he discovered how weak he had become.

'Goodbye,' he said falteringly.

'Until we meet again,' Dave added, patting Ringer's back as he ushered him out of the conference room. Then he closed the door, and as Ringer stood alone in the corridor, he found himself reaching out for the wall so as to steady himself. Everything was swaying, as if he were in the bowels of an ocean liner at the mercy of a rolling swell. Where was the library he had been in earlier? He should go there again, sit down, regain his strength.

No other soul was in sight, neither Don nor the receptionist, as Ringer rounded the corner and scrutinized the phalanx of indistinguishable doors, wondering which to choose and finally selecting one, neither knocking or even pausing before he grasped the handle and opened.

It was a room in a hospital. There was a steel-framed bed, a polished floor, a look of clinical detachment appropriate to a place where lives begin and end in anonymity. The hallucination did not frighten him; he was prepared to study it closely, feeling almost calm as he took in what he knew must be a view of the forbidden interior of Burgh House. It was a premonition of what lay ahead; and together with what Don and the men from the Corporation had said, and the pages he had found in the library that were still in his pocket, it told Ringer everything.

The vacuum array was already running, and there was marvellous danger in it. Spheres of fright were ready to encompass the world and show to its astonished gaze the sort of vision Ringer now beheld. He was perceiving a phenomenon denied by reason, yet as vivid to his senses as the spectrum that once told Newton he was right, and all others wrong. Logic, Ringer realized, is mere monochrome. The world of authentic existence is a piercing white noise, a blinding all-colour.

The paradox was there before him; a superposition of life and death. It was himself he saw, lying on the cold floor beside the bed, with Laura who was also lifeless. Two figures wrapped in hospital gowns, slumped in what looked almost like an embrace.

He was seeing Helen's double, and his own. His life's book had cracked ajar to reveal a looping narrative, a jumbled story. This was the only sense he could make of it: his other self was a fiction, and so, by the sublime symmetry that guides all science, he too must be a fiction.

This room was really a library, he reminded himself. Its shelves were infinite, containing every possibility, arranged in alphabetical order without regard to truth. He need only reach out, take the first volume he found, and open it at random.

FROM *PROFESSOR FAUST*
by Heinrich Behring*

Schrödinger went to the Villa Herzen's dining room, where Dr Schwarzkopf had promised to join him. The tables were laid in readiness but the place was still empty – it being a little early – save for a young woman sitting alone, with neither food nor drink to occupy her, at a small table near the window. Schrödinger made a bow towards her, but she ignored him, continuing instead to stare into space with a steadiness that soon unnerved him, so that he decided to sit well out of her line of sight. He had already selected a location from which her face was reduced to an easily inspected profile, when a waitress appeared, in a black dress and white apron, and invited him to be seated. Half glancing at his strange fellow diner, Schrödinger asked the waitress for some white wine; she began suggesting bottles, and noticed her customer's unease. Leaning towards him, the waitress – a plump, healthy-looking girl – whispered, 'Don't worry

* English translation by Celia Carter. Cromwell Press, British Democratic Republic, 1954

about her, she's always like that,' then straightened. Schrödinger thanked her, made his order, and watched the plain, cheerful waitress retreat before turning his attention once more to the stranger. Like Schrödinger, who had so foolishly left his reading matter on the train, she didn't even have a book for company, instead maintaining her vacant gaze as if in a state of catatonia. When he finally saw her blink, it almost made him start.

The waitress reappeared, but not with Schrödinger's wine. Her tray bore a glass bowl, which the waitress took to the other table, placing the bowl before the curiously lifeless guest, whose stone-like demeanour somehow added to an intriguing physical attractiveness. She made no response to the waitress, who glanced towards Schrödinger as she turned, offering him the resigned look of someone participating, through occupational necessity, in a disagreeable ritual. Once more the waitress vacated the dining room, and Schrödinger saw the stranger move at last, lifting a spoon with which to begin her meal.

At first he couldn't tell what was in the bowl; but a few spoonfuls, drawn out with mechanical precision by his fellow diner, quickly replaced his curiosity with incredulity. She was eating raw eggs. Whole yolks rose on her spoon, dripping clear trails of egg white before she pushed them into her mouth, scarcely moving her jaw as she allowed the cold slime to slip down her slender throat. Half a dozen of them perhaps, cracked straight into the bowl as if to make a cake, and served instead to the mesmerized guest who hadn't even added a dash of salt, or felt the need to stir them with a fork.

The waitress was coming back now with a trolley on which Schrödinger's bottle of white wine stood open in an ice bucket. She poured it for him, standing so as to obstruct any view of the strange feast at the other table. Whispering again, she said to him, 'Best not look.' When she moved aside, the meal of eggs was already finished; the young woman touched her mouth with a napkin, then resumed her former motionless state. The departing waitress left the empty bowl where it stood, and Schrödinger watched the diner pause a moment, then stand to leave.

Rising and turning, the young woman could now be studied in greater detail by Schrödinger, who had lost any inhibition he felt about staring at her. Fine featured and of pale complexion, her blue eyes might have been beautiful if only they were alive. Her dark hair deserved the care and attention of a skilled coiffeuse, but instead had been hacked, it appeared, with shears, since its rough style was almost peasant-like, and hardly fitted the elegance with which she walked, solemnly and purposefully, towards the door. Schrödinger watched her, admiring the curve of her figure, until she vanished from view like an evaporating cloud, leaving him with the sense of having seen something wonderful yet absurd – Maya and Brahman combined.

As soon as the waitress returned, he decided, he would ask her all about the strange young woman; however, the next person to appear, entering the room and searching it with his probing gaze before quickly finding his goal, was the Villa Herzen's new psychoanalyst, Dr Hinze.

'Ah, here you are already, professor,' said Hinze, approaching and accepting Schrödinger's invitation to sit down. 'Doctor and Frau Schwarzkopf will join us a little later. I see you are enjoying an aperitif.' He nodded towards the wine in its ice bucket; Schrödinger took the bottle and poured some of the straw-coloured liquid into the empty glass that stood at Hinze's elbow, then the doctor raised it in a toast. 'To the coming year, professor. Let us hope it holds good fortune.'

They both took a sip, then fell silent. For Schrödinger, a man on whom fame had thus far refused to fall, the future looked uncertain; and from the manner in which Hinze made his toast, it seemed he too felt much the same. Schrödinger filled the gap by asking Hinze about his time in Zürich. They spoke of favourite haunts, sought common acquaintances, and found several which nonetheless failed to animate their conversation. There were few professional or academic connections for them to identify, since Hinze had been associated with the medical school, not the physical sciences faculty.

'You must surely prefer the fresh air here to the atmosphere at the Burghölzli,' Schrödinger said to him.

'Of course,' Hinze agreed. 'The hospital was stimulating, but exhausting. It was wonderful to work under old Professor Bleuler – but when my intellectual progress reached a certain stage, I realized that in order to advance further I must take myself to the mountains. Like Nietzsche in the Engadine, no?'

Schrödinger put down his glass. 'And have you had your great insight yet?'

Hinze rubbed his hands with some embarrassment. 'Not quite. But I think I'm almost there.'

The two had more in common than Schrödinger had supposed. 'I have also come here to try and solve a problem. It concerns waves.'

Hinze's expression was one of admiring incomprehension. 'Long live physics! That's what Nietzsche proclaims in *The Gay Science*. Though perhaps with some irony.'

Schrödinger said, 'You clearly admire the great philosopher.'

They had at last found a topic that Hinze could warm to, as if Nietzsche were the only mutual acquaintance in whom the doctor had any interest. 'My affair with Nietzsche has been long and difficult,' he explained grandly. 'It began when I read *Zarathustra* at the age of fifteen, not long after Nietzsche died. What knowledge could be so deep and terrible, I wondered, that the search for it could render a man completely insane?'

'I believe it was syphilis that caused Nietzsche's madness,' Schrödinger said.

Hinze shook his head. 'That version of events, which Paul Möbius has proposed, is far too simplistic. Even before the crisis came, Nietzsche was showing symptoms quite unlike tertiary syphilis. I once met a psychiatrist who knows a great deal about the case, and he told me of an incident that occurred when Nietzsche was only twenty years old.'

Hinze sat back, as if retelling a favourite anecdote. 'It was New Year's Eve, and Nietzsche – a theology student in Bonn – was alone in his lodgings. He had dreams of becoming a novelist, or perhaps a composer. He had rented a piano, and spent so much time shut up alone playing it, that the other students thought him crazy. Well, we know that creative minds grow best in isolation; so there he was, looking through musical scores, wondering what to play for himself while the year drew to a close.'

At that very moment, Schrödinger heard the sounds of a piano. He gave a start, and Hinze laughed. 'A dramatic coincidence indeed,' the doctor said. 'Look behind you.'

Schrödinger turned and saw, through an open doorway at the far end of the dining room, a salon in which part of a grand piano was visible, black and solid as a hearse.

'Brahms, I think,' said Hinze, catching the music. 'Do you play, professor?'

Schrödinger shook his head. 'My wife does, and she once persuaded me to get one of those things in the house, but the racket made it impossible for me to concentrate. I got rid of it.'

'How curious,' Hinze observed. 'Physicists are so often musically gifted. Such as Einstein with his fiddle. Though I suppose that could be as much a Jewish trait as a scientific one.'

'Oh yes,' Schrödinger grumbled, 'it's true that the physics community is full of amateur musicians. Planck, I'm told, used to play duets with Joseph Joachim.' Schrödinger felt envy rising in his throat. Einstein had been lured from Zürich by an offer to join Planck's far more prestigious Berlin group. 'But perhaps we should return to Nietzsche.'

'Of course,' Hinze agreed. 'He looks through the scores, wondering what to play. Some Brahms perhaps? No. Or . . . let's see . . . what will we have now?' The pianist in the other room had fallen silent again; and as Hinze listened, a new piece began, slow and delicate, with trills and ornaments that enabled Schrödinger to guess its antiquity.

'A little Bach?' said Hinze. 'No, my friend, not these tones. Nietzsche mixed himself a hot punch, then decided he must play Schumann. A significant choice, don't you think?'

'I don't see why,' said Schrödinger.

Hinze now looked like a schoolteacher whose pupil has failed to fathom a multiplication table. 'Was it not Schumann, after all, who died in an asylum near that very town of Bonn, only eight years earlier? Schumann, who became detached from reason, just as Nietzsche would one day become equally detached?'

'Sounds to me like another dramatic coincidence,' Schrödinger said.

'Dramatic?' Hinze retorted. 'Or else perhaps psychic? There are many kinds of coincidence, professor. Nietzsche chose Schumann: the requiem from *Manfred*.

Think of Byron's poem, on which the opera is based. Think of its Alpine spirit, its metaphysical scale; its first moment of inspiration, when Byron heard *Faust* read at Villa Diodati, then began to write about a similarly Promethean character. For Nietzsche, Manfred was an *Übermensch*. Already it was as if the young student knew that seventeen years later, walking in the Engadine mountains, he would receive the vision of another *Übermensch*: Zarathustra. And he knew that like Schumann, he would pay for his vision. In this single incident, recorded in his diary, Nietzsche's whole future lies mapped like the notes of a score.'

Schrödinger was unconvinced; and the music next door only added to his irritation, having by now grown fast and loud, like the sound of someone being kicked down a flight of stairs.

Hinze continued. 'I discussed this episode with my colleague Dr Jung. You know of him?'

'Of course,' said Schrödinger. 'One or two of my friends have even been analysed by him.'

'He left the Burghölzli long before I arrived,' said Hinze, 'but I got to know him through the Psychological Club, where I read a paper about Nietzsche. Since Jung is himself a Nietzschean, I was fully aware that my paper would arouse controversy.'

Schrödinger had little appetite for an account of professional rivalries, about which he already knew enough from his own sphere. The waitress was returning to their table, her peasant-like features and rounded breasts a welcome sight to Schrödinger. She came and stood close to him while asking Hinze if he would like anything. Hinze appeared mildly annoyed by the interruption, but Schrödinger, to his delight, noticed that the waitress had inadvertently positioned herself in such proximity that the merest motion of his leg would bring it into contact with hers. And by placing his hand on his own thigh before moving it, he found his finger alighting upon the side of her knee, where she allowed it to stay.

'Shall we order another bottle of wine?' Schrödinger suggested, only so that the waitress would remain a little longer at the end of his finger.

'I shall have no more than another glass,' Hinze told him. 'I have work to do later on.'

'Indeed,' said Schrödinger, 'there is much for all of us to do.' And his finger slid invisibly along the back of her thigh and then into empty space, as she left them with a nod.

Hinze said to Schrödinger, 'You know about Jung's theories, then? And his battles with Freud, who initially supported him? Freud and his Jewish colleagues have made some profound discoveries; but while Freud was granted the commandments of the unconscious, he knew there still must be a Messiah. He thought he had found it in Jung.'

'And do you agree?' asked Schrödinger.

Hinze gave a mocking frown. 'I think I might call Jung our John the Baptist.' Then he said, 'What about physics? Do you not have a similar situation with Einstein? From what I hear, he has only found half the answer, perhaps leaving Aryans to make the final step. Quite a challenge for you!'

Schrödinger remained silent.

'Well,' said Hinze, 'let me tell you about the meeting of the Psychological Club where I spoke of Nietzsche, and that strange incident when he played *Manfred* at the piano. Jung sat there, looking very thoughtful as I explained how Nietzsche's choice unconsciously fore-shadowed his later vision of Zarathustra. I said to the assembled company, "Do you recall Manfred's great love, Astarte? Amidst the Alps, Manfred summons up a vision of her – she is Byron's own sister, with whom the poet had an incestuous relationship."

' "Ah yes," Jung piped up, pulling his spectacles down from his forehead onto his nose in order to look at me, now that he had something to say. "In Manfred and Astarte we have a perfect illustration of the anima principle."

' "Certainly," I replied. "Moreover, I can offer an even more perfect illustration of the principle." I had pre-pared for this moment in advance. I said to Jung, "Do you know the passage in *The Life and Opinions of Tristram Shandy*, where Sterne speaks of 'the two souls in every man – the one being called the animus, the other, the anima'?" Silence fell upon the room. I had revealed Jung to be a plagiarist, secretly passing off Sterne's insight, unacknowledged, as his own! But then, from one corner, came the cry, "Remarkable!"; and from another, "Well done!". Jung nodded to both men in approval, then said to me, "I was not aware of the passage in question, Dr Hinze, and I am so grateful to you for unearthing it. For we have here one of the clearest examples so far discovered of my theory of the collective unconscious." Murmurs of congratulation ran round the congregation before me; I was considered the bringer of good tidings.'

At that moment, the rotund Dr Schwarzkopf and his elegant wife Helga came into the room which was slowly filling with other diners. 'Ah, there you are!' Schwarzkopf declared as Hinze and Schrödinger stood to greet the couple. 'My apologies for our delay, which was entirely my own fault, and not, I can assure you, my dear Helga's.' Dear Helga bore the face of a woman who'd been kept waiting. 'I had to attend to one of our patients,' Schwarzkopf explained. The company all sat down, and pleasantries were exchanged. Frau Schwarzkopf asked after Schrödinger's wife, expressing sorrow at her absence.

'Professor Schrödinger has come here to think, my dear,' said Schwarzkopf. 'That is correct, is it not?'

Schrödinger nodded and felt renewed relief that his lover had failed to join him as planned. She would have been welcome here at the dinner table, and her relationship with Schrödinger would have elicited no comment whatsoever. But after the mistake of the forgotten book with its enclosed love letter, Schrödinger was glad to be alone.

'Just the four of us, then,' said Schwarzkopf. 'I believe, Dr Hinze, that you Jungians consider the number a good omen!'

Hinze shrugged, and Schrödinger explained they had been in the middle of a story about psychology.

'In that case,' said Frau Schwarzkopf, 'you must please carry on.' Her ample cleavage had already established itself as an item of interest for Schrödinger when Hinze began to repeat his narrative, eventually reaching the point at which it had been interrupted.

'By discovering Jung's idea in an earlier book,' he said, 'I had supposedly validated an even more important idea of his, which is that memories are unconsciously shared between people.'

'That is hardly original,' said Schwarzkopf.

'Certainly not,' Schrödinger agreed. 'In my student days I made a very detailed study of Semon's mneme theory, which says something similar.' He raised his glance from Frau Schwarzkopf's bosom to her face, and said to her, apologetically, 'Perhaps we should not allow ourselves too much philosophizing in mixed company.'

'On the contrary,' she said. 'I consider it the greatest privilege of our existence here, that we can devote ourselves – men and women alike – entirely to matters of the mind.'

'As you wish, my dear,' Schwarzkopf laughed. 'But while we cultivate our minds, let us not neglect our bodies. Or each other's bodies!'

Schwarzkopf slapped his thigh and threw Schrödinger a manly wink, which only confirmed to him that Schwarzkopf and his wife no longer shared a physical relationship. Schrödinger knew Frau Schwarzkopf to be the more cultured of the two; for despite her husband's impressive medical credentials from Berlin, he was, Schrödinger felt, at heart little more than a horse doctor or army sawbones who had risen through German ranks made thin by the battlefields of the previous decade. Frau Schwarzkopf was the one who had filled the library, provided the musical instruments, and hung the walls with paintings inherited from her grandfather. Even the villa itself, he guessed, was her family's gift to her jovial, harmless husband.

The waitress returned and once more stood close to Schrödinger, while Schwarzkopf confirmed with her the arrangements already made for their meal. Again Schrödinger's fingertips stretched out, like the horns of a snail, until they were allowed to trace a small, inquisitive circle on the waitress's leg before she departed.

'Now then, Professor Schrödinger,' said Schwarzkopf, 'let me suggest to you some walks you should try.'

'Darling, you have interrupted Dr Hinze's story,' Frau Schwarzkopf reminded him. 'I'm sure Professor Schrödinger is as eager to hear the rest of it as I am.' And with this remonstration, she invited Dr Hinze to continue.

'Well, there I was at the Psychological Club,' said Hinze, 'describing how Nietzsche played the piano one New Year's Eve.'

'Speaking of which,' said Schwarzkopf, interrupting, 'don't you think we ought to ask for something more pianissimo next door?' The whirling counterpoint in the adjoining room had dulled Schrödinger's aural sense so much that he had almost stopped hearing it, like the guns at the Italian front when he served there. But

Schwarzkopf stood up and marched next door, his movements ignored by Frau Schwarzkopf, who instead inspected the cutlery on the table while Schrödinger stared at the expensive necklace that lay across her bosom. For whose benefit, he wondered, had she put it on? Must it not be the most stifling existence, for a handsome and intelligent woman to inhabit a hotel for the condemned?

The piano playing had stopped; words were being exchanged. Schwarzkopf's voice could be heard as it rose to a growl, but the only reply was a single loud chord, hammered petulantly as the pianist stormed off. Schwarzkopf returned.

'Music is all very well in its proper place,' he said to the others as he sat down. 'But not when people are trying to have a decent conversation. And why did it have to be that infernal Bach? If it had been something nicer, I wouldn't have minded. But please, Otto, don't let me interrupt you again. Helga, I'm sure, will not permit any further intermission before you reach the final act.'

Hinze then picked up the tale. 'Nietzsche, a lonely young student, played music evoking an incestuous love affair. Manfred, having summoned up the deepest forces of nature, sought neither power nor immortality, but only the sublime gift of forgetfulness. Nietzsche rose from the piano and went to sit on the sofa. He could think only of his recent failures: the novel he was unable to finish, the musical compositions he could improvise so easily, yet not preserve. Then he looked up, towards his own bed. And there was someone lying on it!'

Schwarzkopf gave a start. 'Someone on Nietzsche's bed? Who the devil was it?'

'A man,' said Hinze, 'that's what Nietzsche wrote in his diary; a man moaning and gasping, as if close to death, a man whom Nietzsche could not recognize, but whom he nevertheless could plainly see with his own eyes.'

'The young fellow must have been too free with his brandy and cigars,' Schwarzkopf suggested.

'Shadows surrounded the ghostly invalid,' Hinze continued, 'attending the ghastly patient's final moments, murmuring to him from every direction. And then, in an instant, the entire vision evaporated. This, my friends, is the hallucination that the twenty-year-old Nietzsche recorded in his private journal. How then, I said to Jung and the others, are we to interpret it?'

Frau Schwarzkopf had followed this story with rapt attention, her hands clasped beneath her delicately pointed chin. 'And what did Jung say?' she asked.

'Nothing about cigars, I suspect,' her husband muttered.

'Jung was pensive,' Hinze explained, 'then said that in choosing to play *Manfred*, Nietzsche revealed his struggle with his own sister, who ultimately became his carer and literary executor. To reconcile himself with this anima, Nietzsche would one day discover – while walking in the Engadine mountains – his own shadow, Zarathustra.

'"Very well", I said to Jung, "but how could this destiny already have been present, when Nietzsche had his vision? And who was the dying man?"

'"It was Manfred," Jung declared. There was an audible intake of breath from one or two of his followers, who might have reached a different conclusion if left to think it through for themselves, but Jung said he was quite familiar with the sort of paranormal event that Nietzsche witnessed. Some years earlier, Jung experienced sustained spiritual visitations, of which he has written extensively. His children regularly saw ghosts in their house; and Jung acquired a spirit guide named Philemon, who had the wings of a kingfisher and a club foot.'

'The wings of a kingfisher?' Frau Schwarzkopf exclaimed, softly and with evident fascination. She was by now leaning more closely towards Hinze.

'I don't think I'd like to meet this Philemon chap!' Dr Schwarzkopf laughed.

Hinze continued, 'Jung told me he transcribed his conversations with Philemon in several notebooks; and that once, after painting a picture of the kingfisher-spirit, he went for a walk – and what do you think he found? A dead kingfisher. As you will know, Professor Schrödinger, kingfishers are seldom seen around Zürich, so it was a coincidence that is hard to explain as dramatic or even psychic. Where had the bird materialized from?

'When Jung told us this anecdote, his friends tried to fit it into Nietzsche's story. Someone pointed out that Byron had a club foot, just like Philemon, but he was quickly told by his superiors that the observation was irrelevant. Nietzsche's dying man, they concluded, arose from the guilt Nietzsche felt towards his sister, whom he both loved and hated.'

The waitress and a male colleague had brought more wine and an asparagus soup which was being discreetly served while Hinze continued his story; now told, it seemed, largely for the benefit of Frau Schwarzkopf, whose lips had fallen slightly open, as if in unnoticed anticipation of a kiss.

'Jung believes that human consciousness has a collective basis,' Hinze explained. 'This is how, for example, when he began drawing random figures as part of his own therapy, he discovered that he had produced the Eastern mandala. In Indian philosophy, the collective unconscious is Brahman.'

'We know this from Schopenhauer, of course,' said Schrödinger.

'Certainly,' Hinze agreed. 'It is a thread that runs through all the philosophy of the German *Volk* since the time of Kant. There is a world of knowable phenomena, and another that is unknowable; the transcendental, noumenal realm of the "thing in itself". This is where we find what Fichte called "self", Schelling called "nature" and Hegel called "spirit". It is what Schopenhauer called "will", and Nietzsche called "the will to power". This is what the Vedic philosophers called "Brahman", and what Jung now calls "collective unconscious". And it is what I call "universal mind".'

Dr Schwarzkopf raised his eyebrows. He had already let Hinze talk far too long; but it was a licence that offered the company some amusement, even at Hinze's expense, since the analyst was now beginning to reveal the true scope of his ambitions, none of which had initially been apparent to Dr Schwarzkopf when his young colleague had first applied for the post. It was only through Frau Schwarzkopf's recommendation, in fact, that Hinze was ever appointed. Well, listening to Hinze lecturing them while they supped their asparagus soup, thought Schwarzkopf, was no worse than being subjected to too much music from the now silenced instrument in the next room. Hinze's narrative was a music that had its own logic, its own internal significance, and above all a tenor that was soothing and undistracting, like those nice Brahms waltzes Schwarzkopf enjoyed so much after a hard day's work.

'As soon as Nietzsche experienced his vision,' Hinze was saying, 'he began to interpret it for himself. The dying man on his bed, he decided, was the expiring year. Time personified. It was a message to Nietzsche to stop wasting his energy, and get on with the creative act of living.'

Frau Schwarzkopf was nodding. 'Yes. The creative act of living. That is a beautiful message – and Nietzsche was lucky to receive it so early, and so clearly.'

'I'm sure we could all benefit from such nightmares from time to time,' Schwarzkopf observed, finishing his soup.

'According to Jung,' said Hinze, 'Nietzsche's vision exemplifies the process of individuation – a term which Jung in any case has coined from Nietzsche. For most people, the life crisis occurs in the thirties or forties; with Nietzsche it was unusually premature.'

Frau Schwarzkopf said, with a playful smile, 'Do you think, then, that we are all now in our time of crisis?'

Her husband patted her arm. 'I can assure you, my dear, that I left such nonsense behind a long time ago. Plumbing the depths of one's soul is the business of youth, when there is nothing better to worry about – no work or children or business affairs.'

The other three were silent. Then Hinze said, 'I offered Jung a different version of events. How is it, after all, that a man can paint a kingfisher, then go out and find one? How can we sit here, speaking of piano music, when suddenly the piano springs into life in the next room?'

'Is that what happened before we arrived?' Frau Schwarzkopf asked.

'Most assuredly,' said Hinze. 'Was it only a coincidence? Or is there some deeper meaning, some transcendental explanation? I believe there is, and it can be found in Nietzsche's doctrine of eternal recurrence. Nietzsche said that since we are destined to repeat our lives endlessly, we must embrace our fate and live without fear. Our species is still hardly better than the apes from which we descend; but a new species will arise, or is already arising – the *Übermensch* – for whom eternal recurrence holds no terrors. Nietzsche describes a shepherd boy, lying helplessly on the ground while a snake's black tail dangles from his mouth . . .'

'What a loathsome image!' Schwarzkopf exclaimed. Frau Schwarzkopf, Schrödinger noticed, appeared on the contrary to be fascinated.

'Zarathustra encounters the stricken boy,' Hinze elaborated, 'and tells him: bite off the snake's head! Take hold of fate, conquer fear, and you will conquer death itself. For really, there is no death; only an endlessly repeating cycle of existence.'

Frau Schwarzkopf said to him, 'Do you truly believe, Dr Hinze, that the four of us have sat round this table an infinite number of times in the past, and will do so again and again forever?'

'I do, madam.'

'So that the rest of this evening has already happened, and we cannot change how it will end?'

'That is correct. Nietzsche proved it to be the case, using – I believe I am right in saying, Professor Schrödinger – valid arguments of physics.'

Schrödinger slowly nodded. 'My colleague Professor Zermelo has, it is true, provided some support for Nietzsche's idea that the universe must repeat itself.'

Frau Schwarzkopf's face had acquired the dreamy look of someone seduced by an idea – by the thought, in fact, simply of being seduced. She had found, in Hinze's table talk, the metaphysical vindication of her own idle, frustrated existence. If a man should seize her tonight, it was only because he had seized her countless times before, and would do so again; and the thought of it made her body light, her stomach and breasts weightless, as if floating in a warm pool. Then, as though a grey cloud were suddenly piercing the sun's light, she said, 'But if the idea is true, does it not make everything we do ridiculous and pointless? If everything is doomed to repeat itself, then we're like characters in a story, hardly real at all.'

Dr Schwarzkopf interjected, 'It's certainly true from what you've told us, Otto, that the world's great philosophers have spent a lot of time repeating one another's ideas, dressing them up in new definitions. Personally, I say to hell with philosophy. Give me a loaded shotgun and a fine clear morning for the shoot!' Schwarzkopf laughed, and as the waiter and waitress cleared their table, he returned to the more interesting matter of the mountain walks that could safely be pursued in the vicinity of the Villa Herzen.

'There's too much snow for it now,' he said, after listing a few beneficial ambles which Schrödinger already knew from previous visits, 'but a summer favourite of mine is the long hike over the pass to Davos. Helga and I have done it on several occasions. Do you remember the last time, dear, when we went there and stayed with my friend Behrens? How long ago must it be?'

Frau Schwarzkopf began a calculation based on temporal markers that presumably did not exist in her husband's own mental landscape. By means of a winding footpath that took her past the children's various illnesses or changes of school, and through several phases of building work on the villa, she arrived at a figure of thirteen years.

'My word! So long already?' Dr Schwarzkopf spoke like someone surprised by his own reflection; as if the simple facts of his existence were somehow inaccessible to him except during moments of sudden and disturbing insight. 'How time flies, living up here. Well, we went and stayed with Behrens, who has a sanatorium of his own in Davos, very well equipped. You remember, dear, that Jewess you befriended? What was her name?'

Frau Schwarzkopf was still gripped by Hinze's philosophy of repetition. Perhaps she would be walking over that mountain pass again, millions of years from now, seeing the same endless peaks, the same gentians nodding in the breeze.

'And her husband,' said Schwarzkopf. 'Called himself a writer. Wonder whatever happened to him, eh?'

Now a roast had been brought and was being carved for them by the agile waiter who stood beside their table; a youth who bore, Schrödinger felt, an untrustworthy look, of the kind that certain women find irresistible. Frau Schwarzkopf, who hadn't been listening to anything her husband was saying, suddenly asked Dr Hinze, 'How does eternal recurrence explain the story of the kingfisher, or the dying man?'

Schwarzkopf was irritated but gave way, concerning himself with the waiter's performance in serving the guests, while Hinze told Frau Schwarzkopf, 'If the future, as Nietzsche asserts, has already happened in the distant past, then we might, under exceptional circumstances, be able to remember the future. Jung drew a spirit with kingfisher wings, because he remembered the dead bird he was destined to find. Neither event – the painting or the bird's discovery – precedes the other, since both occur infinitely many times. The past is just as much dependent on the future, as the future is caused by the past.'

Dr Schwarzkopf, who was gesturing to the waiter about where to place the vegetables, exclaimed, 'Otto, really, what nonsense! Where is the evidence for any of this theory of yours? Where are the data? Science must have facts, my dear fellow, not mystical speculation.'

Schrödinger – who had, during much of the preceding conversation, been absorbed by scientific thoughts of his own - said, 'Actually, there is some basis in physics for what Dr Hinze says. Quite recently I attended a lecture by Professor Sommerfeld in which he pointed out something very interesting. When an atom emits light, it does so because an orbiting electron has fallen from one energy level to a lower one. But the energy levels are quantized – that is to say, their values form a discrete series which allows for no intermediate steps. So when an electron tumbles from one level to the next, it must reach its destination instantaneously, having somehow "known in advance" where it will end up. It's not like falling out of a window; more like taking an infinitely fast lift between floors. Clearly, the radiation process involves a different kind of causality from the one we're used to – one in which the present is dictated by the future. Sommerfeld calls this "teleological causality", and your story of the kingfisher, Dr Hinze, may – for all I know – provide evidence of it on a macroscopic scale.'

Hinze appeared simultaneously delighted and pained by what was both confirmation and precedent for a theory he hoped to claim as his own. Dr Schwarzkopf, dissecting the meat on his plate and finding it to his satisfaction, was sceptical. 'Do you mean that our physicists are going to become mystics too? Is this to be the upshot of the great intellectual tradition of the German-speaking people? It sounds like madness to me.'

Hinze, having had time to decide how to respond, said, 'I find it encouraging that the behaviour of atoms might in some way mimic the evolution of universal mind; but I can tell you, Professor Schrödinger, that my theory already has far firmer evidence. For I have been able to demonstrate, quite incontrovertibly, that certain individuals perceive both the past and the future, in ways that no orthodox notion of time and space can explain.'

'Ah, we're talking about the Invisible Girl, aren't we?' Schwarzkopf interjected.

'The Invisible Girl?' said Schrödinger. 'I should very much like to hear about her.'

'Oh, it's a fine tale,' Schwarzkopf said with an ironic rolling of his eyes. 'A mystery and a headache. Some months ago, her case was brought to our notice by a schoolmaster in another village not far from here. She had shown up on his doorstep, looking as though she had walked a very considerable distance, and she had absolutely no idea where she came from, where she was going, or who she was.

'You mean she's amnesic?' Schrödinger asked.

'The case is far more subtle,' said Hinze. 'This young woman – Clara, I call her, though Dr Schwarzkopf and others in this establishment prefer the tasteless nickname you have heard – would appear to be engaged in some profound psychic flight from her own identity.'

'And in the meantime,' Schwarzkopf interrupted, for Schrödinger's benefit, 'she is being cared for here, at our own expense.'

Hinze quickly resumed, 'There is so much to learn from her! Clara's case, if we can properly fathom it, might make the Villa Herzen famous!'

Dr Schwarzkopf was shaking his head. 'Ah, yes, fame. You know, Otto, it strikes me that some men talk of fame in the way that many women speak of love. What they mean in both cases is an impossible dream. You think with your Invisible Girl that you can make a name for yourself, don't you, Otto? Good luck to you, then. But don't forget how much this experiment of yours is costing me.' Schwarzkopf stuck a piece of meat into his mouth and washed it down with wine. Frau Schwarzkopf was looking sourly at him, clearly stung by his remark about love, and eventually Dr Schwarzkopf noticed the disapproving silence that had settled over his companions.

'You surely cannot disagree with me!' he said heartily. 'Oh, I grant you, when I was much younger I had grand notions of winning renown. But look now at the happy life we enjoy here! Why should I yearn for anything else? Why should I crave the admiration of strangers? That, after all, is the dream of fame, and of love: it is the childish wish to be admired from afar, and to be "appreciated". Professor Schrödinger, I'm sure you must see this phenomenon in your own younger colleagues, new to the profession, who fancy they might be the next Einstein. And I've no doubt you tell them that a little maturity will teach them the folly of their ambitions.'

Schrödinger nodded quietly, which only made Schwarzkopf expand even further on a topic the physicist found distasteful.

'It was just the same with that writer fellow at Davos. I remember now, his wife the Jewess was called Katia: she was taking the rest cure and her husband was visiting. Whatever was his name?'

'Thomas,' Frau Schwarzkopf reminded him.

'That's right, Thomas. Well, talk about lofty ambitions! This fellow reckoned he had the makings of a bestselling author – and what were his credentials? None. No education or qualifications whatsoever. Nor had his books made any impact at all. Said he'd written some big long novel about a family in northern Germany – I think he came from Lübeck or some such provincial town. Oh, and of course this novel of his was a masterpiece. He didn't say it directly, but he obviously thought it was; but have any of us ever heard of his novel? No. I can't even remember the title he told me – it wasn't at all memorable, which I suppose was half the problem.'

None of Schwarzkopf's companions particularly wished to hear this tale of failure, so typical, so familiar, and therefore so depressing. Frau Schwarzkopf would have preferred to recall poor Katia, whom she had rather liked, sensing the wealthy, gifted woman's marriage to have been as loveless as her own. Schrödinger wanted to hear about the Invisible Girl; and the reader might likewise feel teased by the postponing of her tale, which fortunately was soon to be picked up by Dr Hinze, thanks to a natural logical progression that shall be made clear in due course. First, however, we must allow Dr Schwarzkopf to complete his anecdote; we must also let the brilliantined waiter lean across Professor Schrödinger's shoulder in order to replenish his glass; and we must permit the plump, plain-featured waitress to scrutinize Frau Schwarzkopf's pale and beautiful face in search of further instruction, finding there instead only further confirmation of the apathy that forms the hub of Schwarzkopf philosophy: an apathy that can at times overwhelm whole nations.

'He said to me, this writer fellow,' Dr Schwarzkopf continued, 'that if only the publisher had adequately advertised his first novel, then it would surely have been an enormous success.' Schwarzkopf laughed. 'You see, it had to be the publisher at fault, or the public. Never the author or the book!' He slapped the table jovially. 'How often have I heard some young guest, out on the shoot with us, who hardly knows one end of a gun from the other, loudly complaining that his line of sight has been blocked, or the weapon was inadequate, or the devil knows what else? You never hear them admit that they're simply a lousy shot! And so it was with this writer. If only the publisher had sent it to the right reviewers, and if only they'd then brought out a cheaper one-volume edition, then the book would have become a

bestseller, and the author's name would have been established. History would have been so very different –
and all because of other people's mistakes!' Again
Schwarzkopf laughed heartily, clearly amused by the
writer's failure.

'Who knows, perhaps recognition is yet to come,'
Hinze suggested. 'Some artists find their true audience
only long after their death.'

'Romantic nonsense!' Schwarzkopf retorted. 'Professor
Schrödinger, was there ever a physicist who achieved
renown posthumously?'

Schrödinger could think only of far-sighted Greeks
like Democritus or Aristarchus, who were in any case
far from obscure when they proposed their theories of
atoms and geocentrism. 'Sometimes a scientist chances
upon a correct idea of nature which is validated only
later. Regarding glory, though, I think I must side with
Dr Schwarzkopf. If a man does not win fame in his lifetime, then he must settle for oblivion.'

Frau Schwarzkopf gave a yawn, hiding it behind a
delicate hand. After meeting the writer in Davos, she'd
tried to get hold of his novel, and had searched for it in
a bookshop. It was not on any shelf, and the bookseller
had never heard of it. He said he could order it for her if
she really wanted it so much; but she declined, left the
shop, and forgot all about Thomas and Katia, until now.
Clearly, the intervening thirteen years had done nothing
to advance his literary career.

'Oh, the pompous fellow told me all about this
damned novel of his,' said Schwarzkopf. 'And I said to

him, if you want a good story, why not do one about a sanatorium? You get all sorts in places like these, I can tell you. He said he was more concerned with ideas than plots; in which case I'm not surprised nobody has heard of him. Said he was thinking of doing something based on Goethe – you see how high he set his aim! Still, for all I know he possibly took me up on my suggestion about a sanatorium, so that Helga and I are in some book of his right now, which no publisher can sell. And as far as he's concerned, it's all because of not enough advertising, not enough reviews, and no one-volume edition. Just think, my friends, supposing he was right? Suppose that his first novel had been the bestseller he reckoned it ought to be? Where would he be now? Giving lectures all over the place, I expect. Writing articles for newspapers. Being asked for his opinion about society, politics, culture. Winning prizes, handing them out, stuffing his face at banquets. Being treated as though he actually knew something, when he was nothing but a damned story-teller!' Then Schwarzkopf threw his head back and guffawed so vigorously that he almost began to choke on a fragment of meat lingering unnoticed in his wine-washed gullet.

'Which only goes to show,' Schrödinger remarked, 'that everything comes down to chance. When I think of Boltzmann or Maxwell or Newton – or indeed Einstein – I admit I find it inconceivable that contingencies such as good advertising or portable editions had anything to do with the success of their theories. Yet there were, I'm sure, other accidents that played their part. Newton's apple is doubtless as apocryphal as the stories Einstein now tells the press concerning insights I know were the fruit of many years' profound meditation. Still, the secret history of a man's thoughts – a tale of fortuitous remarks, idle speculations and countless dead-ends – would, I am sure, be a more accurate account of discovery than the neatly heroic legends we are invariably taught.'

'And that's just what I tried to explain in my talk to the Psychological Club,' Hinze said with renewed animation, while the waiter and waitress removed some empty dishes from the table. 'History itself is hinged on chance and coincidence. The question is whether such things really are as random as they seem. Or else do they reveal the necessity of eternal recurrence? This is what I'm trying to fathom, with the help of Clara.'

'Yes,' said Schwarzkopf to Schrödinger. 'And in order to achieve this philosophical insight he must make the poor girl survive on raw eggs and milk!'

Schrödinger had already guessed that the woman he saw earlier must have been Clara. Her abstract demeanour could belong only to someone who had lost contact with her own identity; a woman who had forgotten how to be herself. 'Why the raw eggs?' Schrödinger asked.

Hinze, mopping his greasy lips, said, 'For all of us, diet has both a nutritive and a symbolic dimension. We could easily feed on worms and houseflies; yet we do not. We choose a diet that affirms our position in the natural hierarchy. With Clara, as I rebuild her psyche, I must seek to recapitulate phylogeny through ontogeny. In other words, she must progress once more through the entire race memory of the species. She is currently at a pre-cooked oral-pastoral phase, requiring mainly eggs, goat's milk and a small amount of lettuce.'

'Does she speak?' Schrödinger asked.

'Oh yes,' said Hinze. 'Just like an adult. This, of course, is a complicating factor in her development; hence, as part of her therapy, she is allowed to speak only during her sessions with me. At other times she mustn't even use sign language. We have to break her in gently, you see. Soon she'll be allowed a degree of pre-linguistic humming at meal times.'

Schrödinger was appalled by what he heard. Clara was Hinze's toy, in a game that only added to the Villa Herzen's sense of unreality; a sense that in other respects was the villa's prime attraction. The thought of the disturbed woman and her raw eggs unsettled Schrödinger's stomach, making him suddenly queasy. He stood up. 'Please excuse me for a moment,' he said with a polite bow to his host, then walked towards the door leading to the kitchen, since he knew there to be a toilet beyond. In truth, he needed a break from Hinze's theories, from Schwarzkopf's coarse jollity and from Frau Schwarzkopf's dreamy indolence, all of which were more troubling to him than his digestion. He could feel the wine in his veins as he walked, and it occurred to him that he could look in at the kitchen in order to ask the waitress for directions that he did not really require. He might catch her there alone. Then, by entering into conversation with the girl whose leg he had tickled, he could decide whether it was worth chasing matters further. Her plainness only added to his sense of confidence as he exited the dining area, turned to the right and followed the bend of the corridor to a swing-door that hung ajar.

Looking through the open crack, he saw a white-tiled wall, a large stone sink and a wooden drying rack filled with plates. And from another, hidden part of the room, he heard the sound of a girl's suppressed laughter. The partly open door offered only a small angle of visibility; but at its hinge, where it met the door frame, there was a gap wide enough for Schrödinger, applying his eye to it, to survey some of the room's secret inner region. This was how he now saw waiter and waitress, standing against a far wall and surrounded by hanging copper pans and culinary utensils, locked in a passionate embrace.

The shifty, brilliantined lad was pummelling the girl's left breast like dough. With his other hand he had unbuttoned her enough to be able to pull down the upper part of her dress, helped by the girl who willingly slid her limbs through the armholes, wriggled herself free, then let him tug at her camisole until a large white breast plopped into his grasp like a landed salmon, stroked and teased by him so that its chestnut nipple stood firm before Schrödinger's fascinated gaze. Other fingers then entered her crotch, while the lovers' tongues lashed each other with the steady, single-minded hunger of grazing cattle.

This, Schrödinger reminded himself, is the world that lies beneath the illusory surface. It was those love-tainted fingers that prepared and served the food being eaten next door. The shared saliva, vaginal secretions, carelessly wiped nasal mucus and spilled semen of these two young people were what graced the plates of all Dr Schwarzkopf's slowly dying guests, who would look out across ice-covered peaks, think of the families and the hopes they had left behind, and console themselves, like Frau Schwarzkopf, with the vain belief that they were enjoying purer lives now, of lofty visions and mental abstraction.

He had the girl against the wall, her naked buttocks propped beside the dumb waiter that stood idle before its next delivery of food from the cooking area below. She was dangling ecstatically from a shelf whose purpose was the final cosmetic presentation of dishes; two gleaming fingers were sliding in and out of her, as if she were a pheasant being drawn of its wet entrails. For this little moment, Schrödinger told himself, she is alive.

Naturally he was aroused by the strange spectacle. He would enjoy it more fully afterwards, in memory. For the present moment, it was no more than a startling apparition to be glimpsed and noted, but not to be watched for too long. Schrödinger retreated from the door and went on until he reached the toilet.

Standing inside, idly passing water that echoed in the enclosed space, he imagined – it was mere fantasy – that he could hear the waitress's climactic moans. He thought of the two of them hurriedly wiping and restoring themselves while the dumb waiter brought up a variety of cheeses. The sight of Clara eating raw eggs had been revolting; but now, as he imagined putting into his mouth the residues of lovemaking, Schrödinger felt strangely elated, as if the meal were blessed and sanctified by divine power, transubstantiated by sex into the food of gods. He finished urinating and was about to wash his hands, then decided not to. The dinner table, he suddenly realized, was a place where an altogether different drama was being played out, wholly unnoticed by the diners themselves; more vital than anything they could ever envisage.

He went back to the dining room, where Dr Hinze and Frau Schwarzkopf were in conversation.

'I met him recently in Munich,' Hinze was saying to her. 'He edits the party newspaper, and I said to myself at once: this man will go far! Then he came over to me, and do you know what I saw? He walks with a limp! Like Mephistopheles, or Byron, or indeed Philemon. He has a doctorate in Romantic literature, so he understands the significance of such details. But the limp is no affectation; it is perfectly genuine. Mark my words, Frau Schwarzkopf, that fellow will one day lead his party – just as soon as they can get rid of Hitler. And then, who knows, maybe the nation itself!'

Schrödinger took his seat, and Hinze said to him, 'Let me tell you now about Clara. We have been unable to discover anything about her origins. There is possibly a foreign influence in her way of speaking; but this might only be another manifestation of her psychic struggles, mimicking a general process of unconscious evolution. I would not be surprised if suddenly she were to begin speaking French or Italian; for really, her vocalizations betray – I'm sure of it – an inherited memory of some lost Indo-European source. Now, professor, you might be sceptical of all this . . . '

'On the contrary,' Schrödinger told him. 'I have long been sympathetic to the sort of ideas you are presenting.'

'Well then,' Hinze resumed, a little gruffly, once more irritated by Schrödinger's failure to acknowledge his originality. 'Let us consider what Clara has said to me under hypnosis. She has described her walk through the mountains, on her way to a place of refuge. In other words, a sanatorium.'

'You mean she was seeking help even before the schoolmaster discovered her?' Schrödinger asked.

'What she was seeking,' Hinze declared proudly, 'was this very place where she now resides. She does not know why she had to come here; yet like a moth impelled by some nocturnal fragrance, she came. It is indeed,' he announced, 'as if my meeting here with her was decreed by fate itself. In other words, by the divine inevitability of eternal recurrence. She came because she has been here infinitely many times before.

'And there is far more to report,' Hinze continued. 'More than once, Clara has spoken of a brilliant flash of light, tearing through the mountain valley where she walked, almost blinding her. A radiant, blue-white wave of energy, enfolding and transforming her. What might this mean? I can assure you, Professor Schrödinger, that

I gave many long hours of study to this enigma, for I knew it must be some collective memory – a fragment of universal mind – that would help me unlock Clara's secret. During one hypnosis session, I asked Clara to be more specific about the mountains. Where exactly were they? She said, "In the land of Ossian." Well, was this not a startling example of the Nordic-Aryan race memory? Here was a direct link to Thule itself!'

Frau Schwarzkopf, who was familiar with this part of the story, then said to Schrödinger, 'Dr Hinze might still be groping in darkness, were it not for the assistance I have been able to offer him.'

The waiter and waitress were returning. They looked exactly as before, Schrödinger noticed, as if nothing had happened. Around the waitress's cheeks there was perhaps a flush of quiet fulfilment, evident only to the informed eye; but the couple went about clearing the table without arousing any interest from Schrödinger's fellow diners. When the waitress reached her closest point to him, Schrödinger found her leg to be beyond his touch. Instead he inhaled, imagining odours of which she could have had no time or opportunity to divest herself. He watched her rump as she retreated, picturing all the white flesh he had briefly been allowed to witness.

'Dr Hinze told us about Clara's hypnotic memories,' Frau Schwarzkopf explained, 'and not long afterwards, I came across exactly the sort of thing she was talking about!'

'Jung would call it a clear example of collective unconscious,' Hinze interjected, and Schrödinger began to listen to them once more, now that the waiter and waitress were out of sight.

'We had an English woman staying here – a very dear lady, whom we were sorry to lose,' Frau Schwarzkopf continued. 'She spent the last eighteen months of her life at Villa Herzen – in fact, Professor Schrödinger, you might have seen her during one of your previous visits, if she was not already too ill. Her name was Dorothy; she had never married, and had no close relatives left in the world, nor any friends beyond the ones she found here. When she died, she bequeathed all the possessions she had brought with her to my husband and me. This necklace was hers.'

Schrödinger had gazed at it many times during the course of the meal, and at the bosom beneath it. Now, when he looked again, he saw the breasts of an old, forgotten woman, soon to be laid to rest in an Alpine cemetery by people who never knew her.

'Pretty, don't you think?' Frau Schwarzkopf was tugging at the necklace, displaying both the jewels and her own breasts for Schrödinger's benefit. 'Well, there were lots of other things besides, including a great many old letters she had held on to over the years. They were mostly in English – which I read well but slowly – and I had no time to study them properly. I did notice, however, that some bore dates as far back as the middle of the last century; and since Dorothy's father had apparently numbered many distinguished people among his friends, I thought they might be worth saving. Then we happened to acquire another English patient, and I suggested he might like to have a look through these old letters.'

Schrödinger freed his eyes from the dead woman's necklace, and saw the young lovers returning with fresh wine, fruit and cheeses. He observed their nonchalance as they filled the table, and wondered if some further residue had been applied to the food during their last brief absence.

'This was around the time that Dr Hinze told me about Clara,' Frau Schwarzkopf explained. 'And only a few days later, the English patient – Mr Porter, also now sadly no longer with us – told me with excitement that among the letters were some addressed to a prominent American writer who lived in England for a few years, which I suppose is how Dorothy must have acquired them.'

'The writer's name is Nathaniel Hawthorne,' Hinze interjected. 'Perhaps you've heard of him, Professor Schrödinger. He was American consul in Liverpool for four years. And one of the letters – which is of most interest to me – was written to him by another author called Herman Melville, who published adventure novels and was quite popular in his day. Though in fact,' he said, turning to Dr Schwarzkopf, 'I've recently discovered there are now one or two American critics who reckon this Melville was a neglected genius. Which is why I believe you were a little too rash earlier on, sir, when you dismissed the idea that a writer – or indeed a scientist or a philosopher – might achieve due recognition only long after his death.'

Schwarzkopf offered a grunt in reply, and began slicing a piece of cheese that his guests apparently found less interesting than a story of old letters.

Hinze told Schrödinger, 'Frau Schwarzkopf pointed out to me that Melville, in his letter, describes a mountain walk, using language that is strikingly similar to Clara's. There is a blue-white flash, for instance.'

'Thunder is not uncommon in mountains,' Schrödinger suggested.

'Ah, but there's more,' said Hinze. 'Melville even speaks of Ossian! It is as if Clara had somehow read the letter beforehand. But she could not have. She arrived here after Dorothy, its owner, had died; and the letter had then remained locked in a secret compartment of Frau Schwarzkopf's desk until she gave it to Mr Porter.'

'I didn't know that your desk has secret compartments, my dear,' Dr Schwarzkopf interjected. 'Though it seems you know all about them, Otto.'

Hinze, somewhat ruffled, chose to ignore this comment. 'Melville's letter, I believe, may be the best evidence I have yet found for the existence of universal mind. He describes a vision of a woman – a hallucination as vivid as Nietzsche's. The woman he saw, I maintain, was Clara.'

Schrödinger laughed. 'How on earth can that be possible? Are you telling us this man Melville saw a ghost?'

'What he saw,' said Hinze, 'was the future. Just as I believe Nietzsche may have done, without knowing it. The experience is not unique to writers or artists; it can happen to anyone. But writers record the evidence, and we can now look through history in search of it. I am discovering many examples, and they explain so much. Was it purely a coincidence, for example, that Dorothy should have brought Melville's letter with her here to Villa Herzen? Was it a coincidence that Clara – so curiously linked to the letter, as if by an electromagnetic field – should likewise have found herself here? I have conveyed my thoughts on all of this to Dr Jung, who rejects my notion of universal mind, and also my theory of coincidence, which I call "synchronicism". I've no doubt he'll rediscover them for himself, under different names.'

Schrödinger was sceptical. 'It's easy to establish links between things. The hard part is deciding what's genuinely connected. That's the basis of the entire scientific method: discovering, for instance, that the swing of a pendulum is not affected by the time of day, or the weather, or the mood you're in, but only by the length of the pendulum itself. You say Clara's hypnotic ramblings resemble a letter between two writers; but surely the resemblance is one you've identified for yourself, while no doubt ignoring many conflicting elements.' Schrödinger could see that he was in danger of rousing Hinze's anger, and since his purpose was only to pass the time, he decided instead to offer Hinze's views further support. 'As a matter of fact,' he said, 'I've thought a good deal about the issues you raise, which really concern causality. Einstein worried about this too, but the best that relativity can offer is to say that some things must always happen prior to some other things, and this is the extent of the causal link between them. There is no frame of reference, for instance, in which an observer would witness the cheese reaching our table before the asparagus soup. But ever since I first began to study general relativity, I confess I've been dogged by the idea that under certain circumstances, gravitational fields might cause a disruption of normal causality. You see, Einstein has provided certain equations that allegedly describe the universe as a whole, and he has derived from them a model in which the universe is static, as we currently believe it to be. But what if this belief is wrong? What if the universe is growing or shrinking at some presently unmeasurable scale; or else rotating, or distorting itself? What if it is not uniform and homogeneous, but is instead a patchwork of different conditions? All sorts of strange solutions might then arise, which I have pondered, though I have not been able to reach definite conclusions. Einstein supposes that a traveller, if he were to venture far enough through space, would eventually return to his point of origin. What, though, if the traveller were to return not only to the same place, but also to the same time? Or what if he were to return and find the universe altered somehow? I have, for example, privately considered what one might call a Möbius universe, whose circumnavigation would bring about a reversal of parity. A left-handed glove, tossed at great speed from the earth, would return millions of years later – or else at the very same moment – as a right-handed one.'

If this was meant to offer encouragement to Dr Hinze, the effort was a failure, since it provided only bewilderment. Schrödinger therefore added, 'Ever since the work of Boltzmann, whom all of us physicists revere as the true founder of our modern subject, there has been a realization that much of the world is statistical in nature. Perhaps time and causality are phenomena of this type. My major criticism of your version of eternal recurrence, Dr Hinze, is that it fails to allow for this statistical element. We may indeed find ourselves one day sitting at this table again, having exactly the same conversation. Equally, we may be destined to participate in every possible conversation, with every possible permutation of fellow diners, in an ensemble of possible universes that is without end. Leibniz, as I'm sure you're aware, Dr Hinze, thought about such things a very long time ago, and proposed a criterion for selecting just one possible world from the many available ones. Perhaps, though, there is no selection: everything happens eventually. In which case your visions of past and future may really be strange, transcendental flashes of pasts that never happened, or of futures we can avoid. But I wouldn't know, Dr Hinze. I'm only a humble physicist who has done some respectable work on the theory of colour and the behaviour of gases.'

Frau Schwarzkopf gave a polite laugh. 'You are too modest, professor. I'm sure your scientific theories will one day have much to offer cultural life in general, if only we can all learn to understand them. But really, you ought to read the letter we've been speaking about – I take it you know English?' Schrödinger nodded. 'Well then, I must let you see it. Who knows, it might even give you some ideas for your next theory.'

There was a curious rasping noise, like a saw becoming snagged in a log. Dr Schwarzkopf had allowed himself to nod off. He spluttered back into wakefulness, examined his companions with the small moist eyes of a startled hedgehog, and said, 'Bet you thought I was asleep, eh? Well, I may not be too hot on philosophy these days, but there's one thing I do know, which is that coincidences aren't worth a damn unless you seize and make use of them. And I'll say this for you, young Otto,' he leaned towards Hinze, more evidently inebriated now that the wine had run through sleeping veins. 'You know an opportunity when you see one. Coming here, for instance. Good for your career, in the long run. And Jung? No hope: you've ditched him. I like that. A man's got to know who's on the up, and who's going down. Your new friend the newspaper editor, for example; I like the sound of him.'

'Indeed,' said Hinze, 'Dr Goebbels has asked to see the evidence of universal mind that I've gathered so far. He, at least, appreciates the significance of it.' This last barb was meant for Schrödinger, but by now they'd all had enough. Schwarzkopf rose, unsteadily at first, to his feet, and the rest followed his example. In the salon, the piano was coming to life once more, joined now by the pleasant strains of a violin. Schwarzkopf invited the men to smoke with him there, but Hinze said he had work to do, and Schrödinger decided to retire to his room.

'As you wish, gentlemen,' said Schwarzkopf. 'Helga, I bid you goodnight.' He kissed his wife's hand, then went through to the salon, leaving his three guests to supply their own formalities before bringing the evening to a close. Schrödinger quickly excused himself and went out to the staircase, ascending as swiftly as the wine and food in his body allowed, running his hand along the thick, polished banister as he made his way up to the floor above. It was a relief to find himself back in his room, alone, and able to think once more about the scientific problem that brought him here.

But there was also the lost book, of course, with its incriminating love letter. It had fallen from his mind during dinner; now it returned, showing up in the railway compartment where he left it, thumbed by a passenger who just happened to be a journalist on the hunt for a story, any story, with which to fill a space. Yes, everything comes down to chance, and chance could make or break him. His colleague Debye had suggested he seek an equation for matter waves; perhaps Debye would find it first. The answer might be worth a research paper or two, or might prove the summit of a man's career. It was all hardly more than the toss of a coin.

He had devoted himself to seeking new laws of nature; yet Schrödinger had to concede that perhaps those laws are themselves statistical. The force of gravity or speed of light might be mere local customs, collectively observed yet of no more profound or durable significance than the current levels of taxation, or the rate of inflation, whose astronomical levels had so recently made the world itself seem insane. For his inaugural lecture in Zürich four years previously, Schrödinger had taken as his theme the notion that perhaps everything in nature, without exception, happens by accident. Where Hinze saw relentless necessity, Schrödinger saw contingency, and a multitude of possible worlds.

He loosened his tie and sat down at the desk where already, before going down to dinner, he had laid his notebook in anticipation of a night's labours. In front of him, where he sat, hung the heavy red curtain he had looked behind earlier, whose only purpose was to hide a door that could never be opened. It was almost like some insipid metaphor; the kind that might appeal to Hinze and his psychologist friends.

When he first stayed at the Villa Herzen, stricken with tuberculosis, Schrödinger had completed only two short papers in a period of seven months. One of them was about electrons orbiting atoms, and their quantized energy levels which he had mentioned to Hinze during dinner. Schrödinger had applied a discovery made by his colleague Weyl – his wife Anny's lover – concerning an ambiguity of nature called gauge invariance, and Schrödinger found that for electrons, this led to the introduction of terms involving the so-called imaginary numbers, such as the square root of minus one. What did it mean, for these unreal objects to enter into physical descriptions?

Then Schrödinger heard a noise. It came to him through the sealed door behind the curtain, and it was unmistakably the kind of sound that earlier in the evening he had summoned only in fantasy, while relieving himself in the small toilet beyond the kitchen. It was a woman, moaning in sexual ecstasy. Schrödinger, frozen at his desk, listened to the silence that followed, until it came again, rising like a wave that swells and discharges itself against the shore in a burst of rolling foam.

'Ooooo-AHH!'

Schrödinger softly drew back the red curtain. The door, he realized, led to an adjoining room. If he were to pull the desk clear in order to investigate more closely, he risked disturbing the woman, whom he took to be the waitress, finally enjoying the completion of an act that had been teased out over a span of hours. The neighbouring guestroom, he supposed, lay empty and hence available to the more adventurous members of staff. Or else it was indeed a cupboard in which the waiter and waitress had managed to install themselves, there to howl like cats on heat throughout the whole long night!

Schrödinger gently pulled his chair aside, careful not to scrape it on the floor, and switched off the light. He now could see that another light still glowed beyond the door, its luminescence seeping round the thickly painted edges. This time, however, there was no space through which Schrödinger could study the waitress's copulation; instead he was left to imagine it, seeing in his mind her large, soft breast, kneaded in her lover's hand.

'Ooooo-AHH!'

There was something almost forced about it; like an exercise meant to improve the capacity of the lungs. Perhaps this was Schwarzkopf's latest gimmick. And then Schrödinger heard a knock so loud he thought the door being struck was his own. It came from the next room, however; an abrupt rap, followed without pause by the rattling of a key, the door's opening, and then a voice that Schrödinger recognized at once.

'Very good, my dear.' It was Hinze, closing the door behind him and advancing, Schrödinger surmised, towards the room's solitary female occupant.

'Ooooo-AHH!' she repeated, as if for his benefit.

'Now then, Clara,' he heard Hinze say. 'That is enough for the time being. You can practise again later. Meanwhile, let us go back into the mountains. Let us ascend the stony path together . . . That's right, watch it sway to and fro . . . let your limbs relax. One . . . two . . . three . . . There, it's done. Where are you?'

'Walking.' Schrödinger heard her voice for the first time, and it was like the heavy murmur of one who has been drugged. Hinze had hypnotized her.

'Where are you walking?' Hinze asked her.

'In the mountains.'

'That's right. And it's a beautiful sunny day, isn't it? You're very warm, Clara. Let me help you cool down a little. There . . . it's easier to move now, isn't it?'

'Yes.'

'You're walking along the path. Can you see the bare, grey rocks?'

'Yes.'

'And can you see the withered tree?'

'Yes.'

'And are the clouds like white fingers against the sky?'

'Yes. Like fingers.'

'Very good, Clara. But now what's this in front of you? Go on, look at it. Can you see what it is?'

'A snake.'

'That's right, Clara. Are you afraid of it?'

'No.'

'And do you know what you must do with it?'

'Yes.'

'Go on, then. That's right . . . yes . . . oh, yes. Thus says Zarathustra.'

Schrödinger listened with horror as the sounds of sexual gratification from the next room became unambiguously Hinze's own.

'Taste your fate, Clara. Is it not sweet? All of human history is in your mouth, my child. Mind your teeth, though. Don't want to be too much like that shepherd boy, do we? Yes, my love . . . that's right . . . Ahh!'

After a moment's silence, Hinze spoke with complete nonchalance. 'Well, where have you been today? Was it the sick man again?'

'Yes.' Her voice was still as flat and lifeless as before.

'And was there a piano nearby?'

'Yes.'

'Good. Your hallucination makes a great deal of sense. Now, were you able this time to see the features of any person present? Was there a man with a big moustache?'

'No.'

'Hmm.' Hinze sounded dissatisfied. 'We really must try a little harder, Clara. Next time this particular vision of yours occurs, I want you to try and take in as many details as possible. I'm quite sure you ought at least to notice the music that's open on the piano – I'm certain you'll find it says *Manfred* somewhere.'

'No music,' said Clara. 'Only pages near bed.'

'Oh, not all that again,' Hinze said with growing impatience. 'Clara, you really must understand that the only way to resolve your problem is to trust my judgement, not your own. I suppose you saw the old lady again?'

'Leaning over sick man in bed.'

Hinze was exasperated. 'It makes no sense at all, Clara. There was no old lady when Nietzsche saw it, so I'm damned if I'm going to let you get away with making one up.'

'Old lady,' Clara repeated. 'Two men. And the third one, sick in bed. Schumann.'

'Are you talking about the music on the piano, Clara? Well, at least we've got the right composer at last!'

There was another knock, only this time it was on Schrödinger's door. Hinze must have heard it too, since he fell silent. Schrödinger quickly pulled the curtain back in place, moved away from the desk and switched on the light. 'Come in,' he said, speaking softly so as not to alert Hinze to the ease with which sounds were shared between the adjoining rooms.

Schrödinger's door opened and he saw Frau Schwarzkopf, holding a sheet of paper in her hand and bearing in her features the expression of one who had not long ago been crying. Her eyes were rimmed with sadness, her make-up blurred; the lines of her handsome face were etched deeper than before.

'I hope I am not disturbing you, Herr Professor,' she said meekly.

'Not at all,' he told her, straightening his necktie as she walked into the middle of the room, there to inspect it briefly with a few quick glances from her sorrowful eyes.

'I brought you the letter,' she said.

'Letter?' Schrödinger thought for a moment she meant the one he had left on the train.

'I told you about it earlier,' she said. 'From the American writer.'

'Of course,' said Schrödinger. 'How kind of you to bring it so promptly. It could have waited until tomorrow.' He had no interest in seeing it, and would have preferred to listen for further activity in the next room.

'Well,' Frau Schwarzkopf said with a note of disappointment, 'perhaps I should put it here on your desk for you to look at another time. I'm sorry to have bothered you.' She laid the letter beside Schrödinger's notebook, then withdrew towards the open door, pausing there.

'No, please,' said Schrödinger, 'I'd be very interested to read the letter now.'

Frau Schwarzkopf closed the door behind her. 'As you wish,' she said, leaning back into the door so as to seal it. As she did so, her bosom swelled beneath her silk gown in a signal Schrödinger thought unambiguous. And at almost the same moment, he heard the opening and closing of the neighbouring door, as Hinze slipped away from Clara's room.

Frau Schwarzkopf came towards the desk where Schrödinger stood. 'Please, sit down,' he told her. There were three chairs in the room, but she chose the edge of the spare bed, crossing her legs when she placed herself upon it. There was no need for subtlety, Schrödinger reflected. They were both old enough to know that once the sexual contract has been agreed, even by the merest glance, completion should not be delayed. He lifted the page on his desk, noticing it to be typewritten.

'It's a transcript of the original,' Frau Schwarzkopf explained. 'The handwriting was very hard to decipher. For all I know, it's full of mistakes. But then, life is full of mistakes.' Schrödinger looked round at her and saw how carefully she had positioned herself, the better to display her cleavage. He came and sat down next to her, and a moment later they were kissing.

Her lips tasted of alcohol and cigarettes; her breasts, when Schrödinger reached for them, were as full and heavy as the waitress's, only drier, he fancied, reminding him of fine leather. The necklace was still there, that had once hung round an old woman's gizzard; but Schrödinger, like Frau Schwarzkopf, was too preoccupied to worry about removing it. The two of them were soon stretched fully on the bed, pulling at whichever items of clothing formed a hindrance to the sex act. He had never expected anything like this to happen; he had never in the past found Frau Schwarzkopf particularly attractive, nor had he received any previous suggestion of interest from her. But everything in this world is an accident; and through sex, we can momentarily break free of Maya, allowing us a glimpse of Brahman. In sex, Schrödinger had always firmly believed, all men become one man; all women become one woman. Thus it was the young waitress beneath him; it was Clara he was penetrating, and also the distant beloved who should have been here with him now, and who was instead being serviced by her own husband, freshly harassed from a parliamentary debate and thinking about his mistress. In such moments of transitory delight, visions flit between lovers everywhere, joining them in a secret union. This, for Schrödinger, was life and death in purest form, a brief taste of the infinite.

Too often, though, the act falls short of its mystical potential. As Frau Schwarzkopf clutched him with her thighs, his mind chose to portray for him the complex phase factor of the electromagnetic gauge transformation. And then he was finished.

They both got up, neither looking at the other as they each restored their dignity. Frau Schwarzkopf made use of the washstand while Schrödinger contented himself with his handkerchief. Then from the next room came a sound he'd heard before.

'Ooo-AH! Ooooo-AHH!'

He looked round towards Frau Schwarzkopf, who was now more naked than when they were making love together, and the two of them broke into a laugh.

'Do you know what that noise is?' Frau Schwarzkopf questioned him.

'I think I can guess.'

'Oh no you can't,' she said. 'It's not what you think. According to Otto, it's the sound of a whale. He makes Clara pretend to be one.'

'A whale? What on earth for?' Schrödinger asked.

'So that she can rediscover the species memory, or something like that. Apparently we all evolved from sea creatures.' Frau Schwarzkopf clothed herself once more, and as she checked herself in the mirror to the floating accompaniment of Clara's marine vocalizations, said casually, 'Have you read *Tomcat Murr*?'

Schrödinger froze. It was the novel he had left on the train. 'Why do you ask?' he said, wondering if he was about to be blackmailed.

Frau Schwarzkopf, still looking at the mirror, directed her gaze towards his reflection. 'It's why we call her the Invisible Girl,' she said, then turned. 'It comes from the book.'

Schrödinger could not recall having reached that part; he remembered only the philosophical musings of a cat, which had sent his mind along paths of its own during the slow, meandering train journey to Arosa. The coincidence, far from being dramatic, was merely laughable.

'We all know what Hinze does with her,' Frau Schwarzkopf added.

'You don't mind?'

'Why should I?' On Frau Schwarzkopf's tired face there was a look of indifference bordering on callousness. 'It's his business.' She made a final adjustment to her gown, then pointed to the letter on the desk. 'Shall I take it now?' she asked.

'No,' said Schrödinger. 'I really would like to read it.'

'As you wish.' She walked to the door. 'Goodnight, Herr Professor.' Then she went out, and from the next room, the whale-moan rose as if in farewell.

Schrödinger sat down at his desk, and began to read the letter.

Herman Melville to Nathaniel Hawthorne
November [? illegible] 1856

Our meeting, friend, was not as I had wished it. Liverpool, your home, was as welcome to me, as colourful and as strange, as an Arab bazaar, but there are regions of this island stranger still. I told you of my intention to find out, for the benefit of the little book that is my harmless diversion, the ancestry of the Melville line, which task has taken me to the mountains and rivers whose praises Scott has sung so finely. I mean Scotland, where my forebears were born, and from where I write.

Let us feud no more, Nathaniel – or are we to become like the heathen clans who spilled their brothers' blood in this wild place? You were unsuccessful in your efforts to win me a consular appointment like your own. What of it? Believe me, friend, I feel no resentment. Such honours are like robes, and whose shoulders they fall upon is the domain of fortune, and of fate. Yes, your star remains in the ascendant: I see everywhere the works of the good Mr NH, and am glad of it, for your renown is well deserved. I see my Typee disappear from every shelf, and with it the last of the fame I knew ten years ago. That saddens me – but do I blame you for my misfortune? No more than sinking Sirius loathes the ruby light of Antares! When we spoke together in Liverpool about Moby-Dick, now five years closer to being completely forgotten than when first the public were granted liberty to spurn it, I was not so dismayed as you would have it. The tale was botched, as all mine are, but better books will come. Nor was its dedication to you, as you hinted, made in any hope of advancing its cause. No, a book must fight its own campaign, and if my Whale be bloodied, I wager it will sink and rise again, for ne'er was monster so incapable of being killed by critic's feeble barb!

I envy you, friend, yet still love you. Is it not the highest praise, to be envied? Were a thousandth of your gift within my grasp, would I not be blessed?

Such dark thoughts need not cloud friendship's skies. I recall the happy gathering at Stockbridge where we first met five years ago – we were already acquainted through reading one another's books, long before the shower of rain that brought us sheltering together: two souls separated in Platonic chaos, now rediscovering each other at last! Must we return to the darkness of estrangement? Alas, in Liverpool of late, I offended you, and your family. Sir, if a million apologies would make good the rift that one, it seems, can not, then you would be shipping apologies by the bushel.

I speak too much of myself and my misfortunes. Forgive me, friend, you know my foul habit of introspection well enough already. In truth, my journey from Liverpool to Scotland was made not only for purposes of historical inquiry. I desired moreover the solitude and tranquillity in which a man may weigh himself as on a scale – may judge his worth before the court of Nature, with the swoop of eagles as his counsel, and annihilation his threatened sentence.

It matters little, then, that my search for Melvilles past has turned to such a merry chase. Many there are, in every town, but what have any of them to do with me? Does the fiery blood of Andrew Melville course my veins, who sent heretics to their flaming end? How many books would I likewise put happily on the pyre! Or Jessie Melville, seamstress? Her grave is but a bookmark in the dictionary of the forgotten. And there too go I! Typee will outlast me, and perhaps my new Confidence-Man, but what else? Moby-Dick, as gravestones go, is light and easy to misplace.

The family threads, I've found, are roots innumerable and too fine to trace. Why seek them, if the plant be barren of fruit? Yet I have toiled, in the few short days since I saw you, on the book that will be my best. I do not mean the family history, that is but a trifle, nor The Confidence-Man, which is done and no longer my concern. It must blast its cannons beneath its own ensign. No, a finer book has unfurled its sails – and it is called Agatha.

Yea, this will be the work that saves me – I am filled with its promise. And do you not recall that I offered you the tale four years ago? I gave you the plot and told you to write it out, since I feared myself inadequate to the task. And you refused! Yet I bore no ill feeling on account of the matter. Instead the heroine Agatha has slept patiently and now is ready to come into the world – not on your arm, though, but on my own, and decked in all the finery I can give her. I shall write this tale; and if you would but clasp the hand of friendship one last time, my new book will be dedicated to you.

I have found myself in a hamlet called Ardnahanish. There once were Melvilles here, they've fled like rats, and not a tombstone marks their passing. The churchyard is romantic and overgrown, though the church is of but recent make, subscribing to a local Presbyterian sect more unfathomable than the Messina straits. The minister, seeing my dark and thoughtful countenance, sought to know my business in the town, and when he heard my accent, found it something comical. Even village children flock to hear the American tongue, as though I were a travelling circus inside my own coat. As for their speech, it has the thundercrack of Ossian about it – the ring of myth and legend, the hardness of winter rain. Thus speaks Carlyle, in London parlours, hammering his words as though they were rocks to be broken. Here they call a lake a 'loch', saying it like the Germans – and when the minister first spoke to me, I thought he was using Erse, which is the normal language of these parts.

He asked me, 'What is your profession, sir?' And I told him, not untruthfully: a writer. 'A writer?' says he. 'That's very fine. And what manner of books do you write?' It was, to cut it short, the conversation you and I and every other writer knows well, including a request from him that I scribble my name so that he could memorize it, for he said he had never heard of me. I then offered him the added name of Mr Nathaniel Hawthorne, author of <u>The Scarlet Letter</u> and other equally fine works, which he said sounded familiar.

He wanted to know about American religion. I said I had recently published a fat book about belief, available in his country ere my own, though when I described it to him he said, 'You mean it's really about whaling?' As much as is the Book of Jonah, I said to him. Then he told me about Ardnahanish and its simple life. I asked him about the Protestant faction he adheres to like a sour black limpet: it was born of some ecclesiastical rift here thirteen years ago, and the look of bitterness this Disruption brought to his face was of the kind that's seen in any literary circle when the talk is of other people's successes. His cause, I guessed, had taken few followers, and so he must console himself with the comical self-belief of one who jousts oblivion and calls it heroic.

He said to me, proudly, 'We have a magnificent new fountain,' and led me along the village's main street. I found a solid and attractive structure, babbling prettily as it shot a thin jet of water that splashed upon a polished bowl. How like the spouting of a whale, I thought, and soon grew sorrowful again, so that the minister said he had other matters to attend. He left me watching the waters of the fountain, thinking of my failures, and then of my Agatha. What a noble book it will be!

Tell me, Nathaniel, do you believe in predestination? I do. It was fated that I should stand there beside the fountain, fated too, that I should draw from my pocket two English coins, intending to place upon each of them a wish. I tossed them into the fountain's bowl, one landed near the rim, the other further down. And then I wondrously beheld that both slid to the bottom in equal time! I saw that the shape of the fountain was precisely one described by me before, in Moby-Dick. 'Twas the famous cycloid – the poetically named Helen of Geometry. In Moby-Dick, you might recall, the magical shape was to be found in the try-pots, where my hero is visited by thoughts of madness and despair after seeing himself transformed in the curved bowl's reflection. Now here I was, in this Scotch village, finding those same thoughts answered by that same sublime, mysterious shape! Was it not the figure of the universe itself I saw encompassed there? What heavenly hand belayed the pen, when drowsy draughtsman plotted the fountain's construction, and its fate? Did the same hand steer my own pen when I wrote my Whale, fashioning a tale whose lesson was to be not fame, but failure? There is a divinity that shapes the contours of our lives, then tosses coins upon them, of fortune or of ignominy.

It made me dizzy to contemplate. How had I been guided here, to discover a message I alone might comprehend? My ancestors brought me: but did they know? Did a thousand generations of Melville shepherds and trawler-men work for this? Looking into the fountain's gleaming polished bowl, I saw their command to me. 'Write your Agatha,' the waters said. 'And like this fountain, your book will find its way to one who understands it.'

This was the message of the fountain; yet about me I saw grey clouds – a wind rose up and parried with me as I wrapped my coat about my shivering frame. I felt transformed, as if by sacred or infernal opiate. 'I must walk into the mountains,' I heard myself decide. 'There are other answers there.'

And so I walked. The village quickly lay behind me, below me, as I trod a narrow path the hooves of mountain sheep had carved. Rough grass and heather gave way to black rock – the clouds still gathered and assembled as I reached a barren peak, unable now to see anything beyond another summit, as dismal and as blasted as my own. There was snow at my feet: it was madness to be here, in a place where better men might perish. But like the coins in the fountain, I was instructed by a gravity beyond reason.

The clouds shrouded me – the wind grew as if to topple and destroy me. And as I felt the chill embrace of destruction I called out: 'I will not be annihilated!' There on the peak, I said Yes to life – to endless, unbounded life!

And as rain began to rattle around me, all at once the scenery was transformed. From beyond the mists and clouds, a flash arose. It was not lightning, but a rosy globe that swiftly grew and sped, like a fireball, illuminating the mountain side, rending the clouds asunder. A brilliant, blue-white sheet of light, hurling itself past me like a locomotive and speeding on across the valley.

So bright was the vision, that for a moment I was blinded. Then, as my stunned eyes regained their strength, I saw the mountain anew. Far off, a fine castle stood, surrounded by other buildings and girt by a great road on which a carriage moved without horse to pull it. In an instant the mirage was gone; but now, closer to hand, a more wondrous sight arose. Rubbing my scorched eyes, I beheld beside me – a woman! I knew at once who she was. It was Agatha, the heroine of the novel I am to write, which will be my salvation. She hovered like the spirit she was, reaching towards me an inviting hand. Was I to go with her already? Or was I to climb down from the mountain, spend days and years among the living, before meeting her again?

I hesitated, and I lost my chance. She was gone, the vapours of madness were clearing. The storm had passed, and though I was drenched with rain I knew the meaning of all that I had witnessed. You refused to write the story I offered you, and your refusal was just. Yet I allowed it to sour our friendship, and the rancour I harboured made me give offence to you and your family.

My vision on the mountain told me that I must complete the story of Agatha. It will be a better tale than I could ever have made it, had I not seen before me my own doubt and jealousy personified, my fear and anger made flesh, my love and hope made female and forgiving. I shall finish my book, Nathaniel, and we shall be friends again – I feel sure of it.

Will I even send this letter? It would further arm those who say philosophy has robbed me of my senses. Damn them, then! What worth is a book, if it be not aflame with madness? Are the scriptures not filled with divine folly? And if my words offend you, then you have not understood them. There is a wisdom that is madness: I have seen it here in Ardnahanish, in this ancestral land of ghosts and spirits. Hail, friend!

H. Melville

When Schrödinger finished the letter, he noticed that the moaning next door had ceased. That poor woman, Clara, was being incorporated by Hinze into the neurotic visions and fantasies of a few writers and artists. This was 'universal mind'! A chain of chance associations. To Schrödinger, it showed only how easy it is for imagination to invent connections where none exists.

He laid the letter on the desk, then reached for the red curtain and drew it aside again to reveal the painted door. Hearing no further sound from the next room, he suddenly decided to give the door a mild rap, three times, loudly enough that Clara would hear. There was no response; so a moment later he tried again, gently, as if requesting admission. And this time, after he finished knocking, he saw the doorknob turn in reply. Clara was trying to open the door.

'Hello,' he said softly. The doorknob stopped moving. Schrödinger reached for it, then as he began turning it, he felt the resistance of her grasp on the other side. 'How strange,' he said for her benefit, providing some refuge for himself in assumed casualness. 'At first I thought this was only a cupboard, but the door appears to connect our rooms. Is there a key on your side?'

Still she gave no answer.

He said, 'Perhaps I might come and have a look. Would that be too bold a suggestion? It would be best after all, would it not, if I were to verify that the door cannot be opened. Then we both could sleep soundly, without fearing that a visitor in the neighbouring room might inadvertently—'

'Ooooo-AHH!' Suddenly she'd decided to be a whale again. Schrödinger was dismayed.

'Do you have to keep doing that?' he asked. 'As you realize, the door is not a good barrier to sound. Why don't we both agree to place a wardrobe, let's say, on each side of the door? I could come now and help you shift it.'

'Ooooo-AHH!'

He'd had enough of this weird performance. Schrödinger got up and went out of his room, stood before Clara's door and knocked hard on it. 'Hello? Might I come in?'

'Ooooo-AHH!'

'If we're to have any rest tonight, we really ought to talk.' He tried the door, and it opened, Hinze having left in too much hurry to lock it.

She was sitting on the floor, wearing a faded dressing gown, cross-legged like a Hindu sage. Her back was to him, but a mirror on the dressing table she faced allowed Schrödinger a full view of her. Her arms were held angled and aloft so that her hands met horizontally before her breast. Her eyes were closed in transcendental contemplation.

'Ooooo—!'

She stopped, opened her eyes and stared, by way of the mirror, at Schrödinger, looking as though she had suddenly been woken from a dream.

'Do you mind if I come in?' he said, closing the door behind him. He quickly scanned the room, which was an exact though transposed replica of his own. She too had a red curtain, drawn back, behind her desk. He went to the sealed door and tried its handle. The lock, as on his side, was covered with a wooden flap that had been painted solid.

'Would you like me to move the wardrobe?' Schrödinger asked calmly. She gave no reply, and he sat down at her desk, which was just like his. In fact it was as though, in reaching her room, he had himself passed through a mirror, arriving in a world whose rules of conduct, as well as its geometry, were reversed. There were some papers on the desk, which he examined one by one.

'Your drawings?' he asked. The first sheet was covered with circles of varying sizes, some having crosses or stars inscribed within them. Schrödinger guessed they were part of Hinze's therapy. The second sheet was a portrait of a man, done with evident care but so lacking in skill that it could have been a picture of anybody. Then he looked at the third sheet, which bore lines and curves, like crude symbols. One was a semi-circular arc pierced by a straight line, resembling a devil's pitchfork. Rotating the page, Schrödinger saw it as a letter of the Greek alphabet.

'Ooooo-AHH!' She was off again, moving not a muscle save those of her face as she moaned and gasped.

'Where are you?' Schrödinger asked, deciding to try Hinze's method.

'Waves,' she said immediately. He was startled and intrigued.

'Where are the waves?' Schrödinger asked.

'Everywhere.' Her eyes were closed again now, her body still immobile.

'Are you swimming?' he asked her.

'Yes.'

Then he said to her, 'Are you naked?'

'Yes.'

He had a sensation of terrible power. He could will her to submit her body to him, as she did to Hinze. Yet his own body was already sated by the abrupt copulation with Frau Schwarzkopf, which Clara must have heard. Schrödinger's desire now was purely abstract.

'You're beautiful,' he said to her. He reached out and stroked her hair. She appeared not to notice. 'What's your name?'

'Agatha,' she said.

'Not Clara?'

She paused. 'Helen,' she told him.

'Well, you're a lovely woman, Helen,' Schrödinger said. 'I'm sure you could launch a thousand ships.' He looked again at the portrait she must have drawn. 'Who is he?' Schrödinger asked. 'The man in the picture?' There was no answer. 'And what about this?' He was contemplating the other sheet, with its Greek letter like a pitchfork.

'Waves,' she said. 'Stories.'

Schrödinger asked, 'Are there stories in the waves?'

'Yes.'

'What sort of stories?'

'Everything at once. Real, imaginary.'

'And you're swimming in them?'

Slowly, she swung her head, opened her eyes, and looked at him. 'You too,' she said. The words chilled him; it was the first time she had addressed him directly. She used the familiar *du*, but Schrödinger could not tell if it was truly meant for him. She had the same vacant expression he'd seen in the dining room, like that of a somnambulist, unaware of her surroundings and instead inhabiting a landscape of dreams while fixing her blue eyes, almost accidentally, in his direction.

'Are we both swimming in the waves?' he asked.

'Why should we be doing that?'

'Because the waves are everywhere.'

It was what he had come here to Arosa to ponder. Waves. And now this strange, disturbed woman was talking about them. Suddenly it was as if he were in mystical consultation with a fortune-teller in a fairground tent.

He said to her, 'Will I find the equation I'm looking for?'

'You already have.'

'Then where is it?'

She turned her head back to its former position, closed her eyes, and at that moment, Schrödinger realized he did indeed have it. Looking at the sheet of paper on the desk, he saw that there was not one pitchfork, but two, and that the symbols could be read, with only a little effort, as a crudely scribbled formula, like one copied by an uncomprehending child. $H\psi=E\psi$.

'It's an eigenvalue problem!' he murmured. 'The answer is no more complicated than that!' At once he understood the ultimate form that the equation for De Broglie's matter waves must take. All that was left was for him to find a way of deriving the correct answer he knew he must reach. He was like a crafty pupil, peeking at the back of nature's book where every problem is solved.

Had Clara already seen the last pages of that great book? Was she the oracle of universal mind after all? Schrödinger, examining her wondrous scrawls, convinced himself they could be interpreted in countless other ways. What he had seen in them, he would later decide, was an equation already written in his own imagination that had been waiting for the right moment to emerge from its secret cocoon into rational thought. In Clara's random scribbles, a poet might find an elusive rhyme; a lover might see his beloved.

'Ooooo-AHH!'

She was still swimming in her endless Platonic ocean. Might De Broglie's matter waves likewise exist everywhere? What would it mean, to say that an electron is borne on waves extending across galaxies? The flotsam of this cosmic sea is the Maya we call reality. Schrödinger realized that the falling of a single quantum of light, in the room where he sat, might be instantaneously linked to some hidden event among the stars. Then there could be no meaningless coincidence in the world; everything would be correlated, everything would have significance. This, perhaps, was the real basis of Hinze's universal mind.

Schrödinger rose. He would leave Clara to her mental roaming, across distances he could not contemplate. At this moment, she might be visiting the sick man she had told Hinze about; giving him a message from the unwritten book of the future, like the one she had offered Schrödinger. And in this same moment, the young Friedrich Nietzsche was seeing the same sick man, finding in the vision his own message. And through some strange juxtaposition of time and possibility, Clara was simultaneously materializing on a Scottish mountain, where an American writer was consoling himself over his failure.

'OOOOO-AAAHHH!'

Schrödinger left her, closing her door as he emerged into the empty corridor, then turning to his own adjacent door, likewise closed. From the salon below, he could hear voices, and music. A violin and piano, linked in a lyrical duet that seemed to be moving towards a final cadence, driven by the tonal logic that makes every bar somehow dependent on the one that is to be the last. Schrödinger swung open the door to his room. And what he saw was not his room. The floor was smoothly tiled, the bed steel-framed, the furnishings brutish in their functional simplicity. On the floor, their faces hidden from his view, a man and woman lay slumped and entangled as if in the aftermath of sexual congress.

Schrödinger blinked, and in an instant it was gone. He was tired, that was all. Now he would spend the night deriving the equation he felt sure would make his name. And down below, the music faded to its conclusion.

ARRIVAL

He woke to see a white-uniformed nurse – stocky, over-weight and perspiring – standing beside his bed.

'Where am I?' he said to her.

'You're in Burgh House Hospital,' she replied. The name meant nothing to him. He had surfaced from a dream that still clung to his senses, deadening them. All he could remember from it was some music playing in another room. And the nurse. Had he seen her in his dream, making love in a kitchen? How could he possibly have been aroused by such a loathsome sight?

'It's Wednesday,' she said. 'You took a bad turn and they brought you here from Craigcarron.' She could see puzzlement and incomprehension on his face. 'Craigcarron. Village up by the coast. Can ye no remember any of it?'

'I was at the villa,' he told her. 'My name is . . .' He fell silent.

'You're called John Ringer,' she told him, exuding a locker-room odour as she reached above his bed to attend to a part of the world beyond his gaze. 'You were lucky you fell ill so near here. Anybody loses their

memory, this is where they come. Fly them in by heli-
copter frae as far away as Edinburgh, so they do.'

It was hardly worth trying to make sense of it. He had
passed from one dream into another, and his progress
through this latest illusion could be equally unhindered
by curiosity. Lying on his back, staring at the nurse's
grotesquely enormous bosom as she fiddled with whatever it was that occupied her, it was as if he were floating on a raft of indifference.

What concerned him more was the nurse's unpleas-
antly sweaty smell, which was beginning to make him
feel nauseous. He was glad when she finished what she
was doing and stood clear of the bed.

She said, 'I sometimes wonder why they didna put the
hospital in Edinburgh instead. It would save a' they heli-
copter trips. I reckon it's likely something to do wi' Red
Zone, though I'm not supposed to talk about that. It's
below the basement, mind.' She was tucking in his bed
sheets while beads of perspiration began to glisten on her
fleshy forehead. 'We're never allowed there, but you
know what I've heard?' She leaned towards him, wafting
her farmyard scent over his nostrils again. 'They've got
some kinky social club doon there. There's men come up
the hill frae time to time – in big fancy cars!' She leaned
back, stood straight behind her proudly jutting bosom,
and was evidently pleased to have dispensed the information.

Ringer's complete lack of interest was no deterrent to
her, now she had begun to air her views on a subject she
had said she was supposed not to discuss. 'These men

that come,' she continued, leaning towards him again, 'they're no the type frae roond these pairts, I can tell you. Nice suits, some o' them. We see them frae the canteen windae, comin' alang the road in broad daylight, if you please. And there's us slaving all day long, and all we get is a wee KitKat and a cup o' tea while they're doon in Red Zone watching a' their naked table dancers in that strip club they've got. Well, that's what we reckon. Wee Elsie – one o' the cleaners – she swears blind they've got great big mirrors in there, so that when the lassies dance in front of them – stark naked, mind – the men in suits can get a good view. That's what Elsie says. Though she did tell us once that her pet dog just had kittens, and that turned out to be no quite right.'

For a brief moment, Ringer's attention was snagged like a drifting net by the thought of those naked breasts and buttocks, ballooned and multiplied in a hall of mirrors. Perhaps there was only a single woman down in Red Zone whose many reflections populated the illusion of a cavorting crowd.

'Hospital's damn near empty, mind,' said the fat nurse, continuing her monologue. 'I tell you, it's no way to run a business . . .' She suddenly stopped herself as another person entered the room and came to Ringer's bedside. 'Eh, he's woken up, Dr Blake.'

'I can see that, Maggie.' This second visitor was tall and slim, wore metal-framed spectacles and had flaxen-blonde hair that gave her a Nordic appearance. For an instant she looked familiar; Ringer had the same sensation he initially felt with the nurse, of having seen her already in a dream. But there was something different about this blonde woman that Ringer could not identify.

'Hello, John,' Dr Blake said to him. 'Do you know what day it is?'

'Monday.'

'And can you remember what happened?'

'There was snow.'

Dr Blake was carrying a clipboard. She wrote something, then peered at him again through her spectacles. 'Can you tell me the name of the First Minister?'

Ringer attempted to push his lethargic mind into activity. 'Goebbels?'

Dr Blake turned to Maggie. 'You can leave us now,' she said curtly, and the nurse disappeared from Ringer's field of view, taking her perspiration with her. Dr Blake lifted the uppermost page on her clipboard so as to inspect the next. She said to him, 'I'd like to ask you a few questions. How many minutes are there in an hour?'

'Which hour?' he said.

'Any. The one that's just passed.'

His mental inertia was unconquerable. 'None,' he said.

'Which day comes after Friday?'

'All of them.'

'What colour is Wednesday?'

'Red.'

'Are you sure? Think carefully.'

He tried again. 'Green? White?'

Dr Blake jotted a few notes. 'What's one and one?'

'One.'

'There are four socks in a drawer. How many pairs is that?'

'Six,' he said. Then, 'Where's Clara?'

Dr Blake looked up from her clipboard. 'Do you know her?'

'Who?'

'Clara. You asked where she is.'

'Did I?'

Dr Blake stared at him as if he were an unexpectedly subtle calculation. 'We have another amnesic patient who was brought here yesterday,' she explained. 'We call her Clara. Did Maggie mention anything about her?'

'I think she's my wife.'

Dr Blake's smooth brow became creased with doubt. 'Your wife's coming up from England to be with you as soon as she can make child-care arrangements.' She continued to watch his face, intrigued by the apathy she saw on it. 'Would you like me to tell you anything else about your family?'

He felt no urge to reply; instead, dimly recapturing part of his dream, he said, 'She got lost on the mountain.'

Dr Blake tapped her pen thoughtfully against her lip.

'What's in Red Zone?' Ringer asked.

Dr Blake was still more intrigued. 'We're getting some new brain-scanning equipment installed down there,' she said cautiously. 'Physicists from the Craigcarron plant are setting it up for us. Who did you speak to when you were there yesterday?'

'The Invisible Girl,' Ringer murmured.

'What?' Dr Blake was trying to unscramble a problem her scientific training had left her unequipped to deal with. 'Is this some kind of code?'

Ringer gazed blankly at her.

'There's something I want to show you,' she said. 'I'll be back in a moment.'

She went out, leaving Ringer to stare at the ceiling, whose emptiness was more reassuring than anything else he had seen since waking. What was he doing here? The question hovered briefly in his mind but was soon submerged by renewed waves of listless torpor.

His mind was swirling. Dr Blake's absence may have lasted a considerable time; but there was no question of boredom, since Ringer had no interest in what would happen when she returned. Instead, for what may have been seconds or hours, he watched the flat expanse above his head; the ceiling that after a while began breaking and crumbling into tiny fragments unable to remain aloft. They were dropping down on him: countless flakes of snow. His bed, he noticed, was gone. Instead he was lying on solid, frozen earth, beneath an infinite sky. A man was looking down at him, shaven-headed and malnourished, bearing a shovel in his dirty hands. Ringer was about to speak to him; but the man, seeing the movement of Ringer's lips, appeared shocked. *He's still alive*, he called. Some way off, a uniformed guard stood with a rifle slung casually over his shoulder and an expiring cigarette dangling from his lip. *Dig!* the guard barked. *But I tell you, he's alive, it's the truth.*

Then it was over. Dr Blake was with him again, holding what Ringer saw to be a book. She opened it at a place marked with a slip of paper, then presented the page to him. The words were mostly too blurred for him to read, but he saw a phrase that had been underlined. *The Invisible Girl.*

Why was she showing him this? All he could recall was the snow, which perhaps had come from some other story he once read. The book was in his hand as he prepared to cross a road. In his other hand, a phone. He had to call someone.

Dr Blake pointed to a footnote at the bottom of the page, circled in pencil. Ringer was unable to focus on the small print at the end of Dr Blake's polished fingernail, so she read for him.

'*The Invisible Girl is possibly based on a real-life woman exhibited as a fortune-teller in fairgrounds throughout Germany, who would fall into a trance in front of a mirror and speak in many languages. Schumann's piano piece "Chiarina" may be a portrait of this enigmatic figure, rather than of Clara Wieck as is commonly supposed.*'

Dr Blake closed the book. 'Does that mean anything to you?'

The ceiling above him was solid now. What had felt like hours must have been no more than a minute or two.

She said, 'This book – *The Life and Opinions of Tomcat Murr* – was in the bag of the woman found wandering near here yesterday. We call her Clara because of the name in the footnote. She'd marked the page, as if it were important. I think you know who she really is, and what she was doing.'

Dr Blake then moved closer and lowered her voice. 'I hear the rumours, like everyone else. Perhaps Craigcarron is the cause of all the health problems round here, which is why they're so keen to help treat them. Maybe it's really a new reactor they're putting in Red Zone, and this entire hospital is simply a way of keeping it hidden from nosey journalists or terrorists. Oh yes, I hear the gossip, and then I wonder if all the private research funding I've been getting is no more than a way of making me play along with the facade. So I need to know: what was Clara doing? What happened at Craigcarron? You can trust me.'

He made no reply, and she stood back, convinced of the genuineness of his ignorance. She said, 'I once read somewhere that ninety-nine per cent of the people involved in the Manhattan Project had no idea what they were really doing. Who knows, perhaps Red Zone is the same. For me it's a brain scanner, for the Craigcarron people it's something else. You might be the only person who knows the truth. Yet you've forgotten.'

Her words were as insubstantial as the snow that had fallen on him from nowhere and had just as quickly evaporated. Time itself was equally volatile, so that after she left him, the succeeding minutes or days passed quickly. The colour of a wall, the texture of a bed sheet, were of far greater concern to him than the faces he sometimes saw, or the question of who he was, or why he should be here.

At one point he noticed a woman beside his bed on whom his eyes were able to focus with unexpected clarity.

'Hello there!' she said brightly. She had closely cropped hair and a ring protruding from her nostril. 'Priss Morgan. Writing therapist.'

His senses were sharper now; it was as though he had woken from a drugged sleep. He could concentrate well enough to wonder what was happening. 'How long was I unconscious?' he asked.

She looked puzzled. 'I don't know. You must have been awake to talk to the visitor I saw coming out of your room when I arrived here a moment ago.'

'You mean Dr Blake?'

'No. Might have been your wife.'

'What day is it? How long have I been here?'

'It's Wednesday. I think you've been in since last week. Now, Dr Blake reckons it'd be a good idea for you to put your thoughts on paper. Maybe you could keep a diary. Or we might try poetry.' She took some blank writing paper from her leather briefcase, then laid the pages on a table that she wheeled over Ringer's bed, placing a pen there too. 'Jot down anything that comes to you,' she suggested.

He didn't want to write; he wanted to get out of bed and discover what was going on. He was like a drunkard suddenly grown sober. Yet as soon as he tried to raise himself, his head began to pound with a force greater than any hangover. He fell back, stunned, and was once more in the windswept landscape, where the shaven-headed prisoner was wielding his shovel with a look of terror while the guard called to him, *Dig!*

What restored him to consciousness was a noise out-side his room; a banging and rattling as the door was pushed open and a trolley entered, pushed by a fat nurse who seemed familiar. It was Maggie. Ringer's mind was clear again, his head free of pain. Priss Morgan was gone, and the blank paper she left him had moved. The pages were on top of his bedside locker, all filled.

'Feeding time,' said Maggie, taking from the trolley a brown plastic tray bearing an unappetizing meal that she deposited, along with a side-helping of bodily odour, on Ringer's table. He stared at the food-shaped mess on his plate. 'Have I been eating this every day?' he asked incredulously.

Maggie looked surprised. 'Feeling like a chat, are we? That makes a change. Usually all I get frae you is a lot of mumbling while you scribble your story.' She nodded towards the pages Ringer didn't recall writing.

Still contemplating the meal he had been offered, he said, 'Is there anywhere I could buy a sandwich?'

There was the hospital shop; but Ringer couldn't go there, she said, because whenever he tried to get out of bed he swiftly fainted.

'I'm sure I can manage.'

'On you go, then, if you're so smart. Let's see ye get-tin' oot o' that bed.'

Ringer promptly swung his legs to the floor and stood up in his pyjamas.

'Wonders will never cease,' Maggie said sarcastically. 'And I suppose you want me to take you to the shop now. Just as well for you I'm goin' past there on my way tae Clara's.'

She produced a robe and slippers that were apparently his own, then presented him with his wallet which she retrieved from the bedside locker. He was perfectly steady on his feet, and keen to find out what sort of place he was being kept in.

'Off we go,' she instructed, leading the way as she pushed the rattling trolley through the open door.

The corridor outside was empty and spotlessly clean. Everything Ringer saw looked new and hardly used. Walking slowly and to one side of Maggie's unpleasant slipstream as she marched in front, Ringer saw open doors leading onto single-bedded rooms, none of which had any occupant. There was a complete absence of the constant hum and chatter, the endless sound of wheels and footsteps, the blur of passing faces, that would characterize any genuine hospital. This one was a clever fake, though not so clever that its creators had thought to include the most vital and convincing ingredient of all – the human souls, wrapped in private concerns over their own infirmity, whose presence would have been enough to make Ringer doubt what Dr Blake already suspected.

They came to a small shop. It had bunches of flowers at its entrance, racks of newspapers, a counter covered in untouched confectionery, behind which stood a woman who must come up here every day, Ringer reckoned, to earn her living selling sweets and magazines to the few nurses and cleaners who might make her task worthwhile. They too – those idle staff members – would make the journey here, from all the villages round about, finding artificial employment in a place whose purpose they need never question; a job-creation scheme inhabited by sleepwalkers, happy to share the make-believe.

'Enjoy your lunch,' Maggie said to him, nodding towards the chilled shelf where a row of pre-made sandwiches stood neatly to attention in triangular packages. 'I'll take the rest of this food where it's wanted.' Then she went puffing on her way, pushing the heavy trolley that served to transport a single meal.

Ringer watched her go towards what, according to a cheerfully cluttered direction board, was called F Wing. But as she disappeared round a bend, he decided that food was not uppermost among his present concerns. His body and mind were returning to strength; so too were his curiosity and scepticism. He wanted to meet Clara. And so he followed the nurse, seeing her some distance ahead as he turned the corner, and keeping well clear of her as she proceeded to Clara's room.

It was through a series of heavy double doors that Ringer was led. None was locked; each swung as freely for him as for Maggie, who simply rammed her trolley against them in order to gain access, as if she were barging through a gate in a field. But Ringer, wishing to remain unnoticed, had to move more slowly and carefully, sometimes waiting behind a set of doors until the nurse was well beyond him before continuing his pursuit. During all this journey, he encountered no one.

Eventually Maggie arrived at her destination. She rapped the door, swivelled the trolley and pushed it into Clara's room. Ringer, hiding at the end of the corridor, waited until he heard Maggie emerge and move on. He saw her proceed until she reached a bend far ahead where she turned and went out of sight. Now Ringer could pay a visit to the only other patient he knew of in the entire hospital. Once he was sure the nurse would not return, he walked gently to Clara's door and knocked.

There was no reply. He waited, and was about to knock again when he heard a noise inside.

'Ooooo . . .'

It was a woman's low moaning; and as he stood there, the sound was repeated, growing in intensity each time, becoming more and more regular in its inscrutable rhythm; more and more urgent, determined and single-minded in its unfathomable purpose.

'Ooooo-AHH!'

Standing outside the door, Ringer heard a sound of ecstatic mystery; a deep, reverberating music, limitless in possible meaning.

'Ooooo-AHH!'

Recklessly, he opened the door and saw a white-walled room quite at odds with the rest of the hospital. There was a handsome wooden desk, a wardrobe. A woman sat facing him, cross-legged on the floor, and beside her, with his back to Ringer, a strangely clothed gentleman was adjusting his trousers, saying something in German.

Ringer immediately closed the door. What had he just witnessed? How could Maggie have walked in so calmly, only moments before? His recovery, he realized, was still incomplete.

Ringer knocked again. And again he opened the door, impelled by an urge he was powerless to resist. Now everything was changed; it was a room much like his own. The man was gone; the same woman still sat on the floor, though now he saw her to be wrapped in an unflattering hospital robe. Her meal had been left for her, and she was ignoring it. His previous hallucination hardly mattered to him, however, for all that concerned him was the startling familiarity of the woman, who with her eyes closed and her arms held bent across her chest repeated her rhythmic chanting.

'Ooooo-AHH!'

Ringer entered and closed the door behind him. He watched her sitting there, wholly oblivious to his presence, and he waited while her performance continued.

'Ooooo-AHH!'

At last he said to her, 'Hello.'

Her exhalations ceased, though her eyes remained closed when she spoke. '*Guten Tag, Herr Schumann.*'

'I know you, don't I?'

Still her eyelids were lowered, her head was motionless. '*Toujours.*'

With a clarity that felt startlingly new, he had the blissful experience of remembering, of truly recollecting, of being suddenly confronted with a beautiful past that was his own. It was in her face, her shape, her breath and in her very presence. He knew who she was, and had some dim sense of the way her life had intersected his. Seeing her there, cross-legged on the floor, a small but crucial part of his own true self was resurrected. He came and stood beside her.

'Helen!'

She opened her eyes, swung her head only as far as was necessary, and gazed listlessly at him.

'It's me,' he said. 'John. I knew you once, I'm sure it wasn't only a dream.'

She stared at him with eyes that looked drugged and uncomprehending. Her dilated pupils, Ringer noticed, were of unequal size, making one eye look darker than the other, so that her face was like an unsettling composite of two separate halves. She closed them and re-adopted her placid, yogic pose.

'Ooooo-AHH!'

Ringer watched in fascination; but then she suddenly ceased her meditation, opened her eyes and looked at him.

'Who are you?' she said. 'What do you want?' Her pupils were normal now; it was as if she had instantly woken from a bizarre alteration of mind.

'Can you remember anything?' Ringer asked her.

'What are you talking about?'

He wondered if his own lapses of consciousness were as drastic as Clara's. 'My name's John Ringer,' he said, kneeling beside her. 'I'm a patient like you. As far as I can tell, we're the only two in the entire hospital.'

'What about Harry?' she said.

'Who?' The name was somehow familiar.

'He's here too – I've been to see him.'

'Where's his room? How can I find it?'

Clara's face bore a dreamlike calmness, as if she had been stirred from visions far more pleasant than anything the rational world could offer. 'Close your eyes and let your mind slip,' she said. 'Then you can go anywhere you like.'

'Are you telling me you've seen Harry in a dream? Or have you met him in reality?'

Clara shrugged. 'What's the difference?' Her inability to separate fact from fiction, Ringer realized, was a sure symptom of the condition that was also his own. 'We've got to fight the hallucinations,' he said.

She beamed at him with the vacuous joy of a cult member. 'Why fight?' she said. 'Don't you like being everywhere at once?' Her pupils were dilating again, spreading their uneven pools as she started lapsing into another trance. He was losing her, and Ringer could feel the return of his own dizziness. Unable to remain upright, he leaned against the woman beside him until they both fell over in a clumsy, intoxicated embrace.

'Ooooo-AHH!'

They rolled onto a floor that was beginning to undulate beneath them like an ocean swell. Furniture was floating free of its moorings, bobbing and drifting, transforming itself while Ringer, drowning, watched helplessly.

The bed was making and unmaking itself like rapidly melting and recongealing wax; a picture on the wall had transformed itself into a window, then started migrating in search of a more favourable location before declaring itself a picture again. Everything was in flux; and when the process subsided and the metamorphosis was at last complete, Ringer had no way of knowing if he had been returned to his original starting point. A second or a century might have passed; he might have slid a hair's breadth or a light year across the smooth floor. His companion, bearing an expression of serene contentment, lay asleep beside him. Ringer, though, was filled with unease. His eyes told him that the room was unchanged; the upheaval it had undergone existed only in his mind. Yet his mind itself had suffered a distortion that was far greater. He had the inescapable sensation of being somehow elsewhere; he was not really here. The planks of time and space had come apart, dividing him between its separating pieces.

All was quiet, and Clara, slumped beside him, dreamily raised an arm across her sleeping face, resting the back of her hand on her forehead. It was a gesture he thought he recognized. 'Helen,' he murmured.

Suddenly the door opened. Ringer swung his head to see who was there. It was himself.

That other Ringer, the intruder, stood aghast as he beheld the two figures on the floor. Wearing jacket and tie, he looked pale and unwell; his collar was unbuttoned and his tie askew. Without a word, this other Ringer stood watching, paralysed with shock, until eventually he entered the room, closed the door behind him and approached. Standing over them, as if about to faint, the Other finally reached down and touched the top of Ringer's head.

'You're real!' he gasped.

The Other knelt down on the floor and extended a trembling arm towards the sleeping woman, but drew it back, as if terrified.

'Laura!' he whispered to himself. 'Now I understand everything!' He looked again at Ringer. 'This isn't a hallucination – you really are me.'

Ringer was doing all he could to resist the vision, but finally surrendered. 'How can I be in two places at once?'

The Other smiled. 'Have you forgotten everything you ever learned? Photons manage; it seems physicists can too.' He coughed, gagged, looked as if he might throw up, but then recovered his composure and brought his sweat-smeared face close to Ringer's, looking at him with bloodshot eyes. 'You really have forgotten, haven't you?'

'Yes, everything,' said Ringer, looking at his hideous reflection. 'Tell me whatever I need to know.'

The Other, swallowing hard, said, 'You and I belong to different worlds. You're one of my potential futures; I'm one of your possible pasts. We aren't meant to overlap, because wave functions are supposed to . . . collapse.' He looked as though he himself might collapse, but then he reached into his jacket pocket and brought out some printed documents. 'I found these in the library here not long ago. They fell out from between the pages of a journal. The Rosier Corporation know all about the dangers of driving the vacuum array at full energy. Non-collapsible wave functions are exactly what they're hoping to create.'

The Other's words, though spoken with such urgency, meant nothing to Ringer.

'The hospital is only camouflage,' the Other told him. 'So's the Q-phone network. At least that's my guess, though I don't think they've told Don Chambers.'

With a trembling hand, he gave the pages to Ringer, who looked at the printed words and was surprised by what he saw. 'I can't read this,' said Ringer. 'Everything's back to front.'

The Other, puzzled and sweating, stared at Ringer with an expression bordering on outrage. Then a look of understanding swept across his face. He smiled with private delight, nodded, and by way of silent explanation, took hold of Ringer's left hand, where a wedding ring shone. The Other, Ringer saw, wore his identical ring on the right. Almost laughing, the Other made Ringer feel his own scalp. Ringer found that the two of them parted their hair on opposite sides. They were mirror images.

The Other was murmuring excitedly to himself. 'How extraordinary. I never anticipated parity reversal.' His discovery appeared to satisfy him so much that he could briefly forget his sickness. He nodded towards the unconscious woman. 'Now I understand why Laura is right handed, when Helen wrote with her left.'

Ringer, too, gazed at the woman beside him. 'Are you saying she's Helen's reflection?'

The Other suddenly retched, catching hold of his mouth and swallowing. New droplets of perspiration had begun to glisten and trickle at his temples. Again he recovered. 'Reflection?' he said, then shook his head. His brief joy was restoring itself to sorrow. 'No, Laura's a human being, as alive and real as you. It's Helen who was her image. I understand it now. Helen never truly existed. Nor, in a sense, do I.' He trembled, shivered, grew still once more and said, 'We're one of your pasts. We live only in memories you've lost.'

Bewildered by what he was being told, Ringer began leafing through the pages he held. Among the documents was a map.

The Other, still trying to frame events within a logic Ringer by now felt inclined to abandon, said, 'It's like being in a cinema, coming in halfway through the movie.'

'Yes,' said Ringer, still gazing at the map. 'That's how it feels.'

'There's a woman on the screen: she's sitting down at a table in the university canteen.'

'Is this woman Helen?' Ringer asked, looking up.

'Give her any name you like,' said the Other, speaking more calmly now. 'She's placing a novel on the table, beside her plate. While she talks to the man sitting opposite, she taps this novel with the fork in her hand.'

Ringer began to see it in his mind, as if he had been the man at the table. Was it only a movie he'd once watched?

'Tell me,' said the Other. 'Which side of her plate is the book on?'

Ringer wondered what was the purpose of the Other's strange conundrum. Some days or weeks previously, Ringer realized, it must have been he himself who asked the question.

'It's on her left,' said Ringer. 'The fork is in her left hand.'

'Very well,' said the Other. 'The film goes on. We see the same woman, lying unconscious on the floor of a hospital. We keep watching, and eventually there she is again, sitting down at the canteen table, placing the book beside her.'

'Is life an endless loop?' said Ringer. A fragment of his dream was resurfacing: he was in a dining room, gazing at a woman's necklace where it lay across her ample bosom.

'Watch more closely,' said the Other, wiping the perspiration from his face now that his nausea had abated. 'Helen is sitting at the table with the book beside her; but this time you see it to the right of her plate. Her fork is in her right hand, her knife in her left. The lettering on the book's cover is reversed, so is a sign above the serving hatch in the distance. Everything – the entire film – is running back-to-front, though none of the actors can possibly notice, because from their point of view nothing has changed. Only we in the audience know what has happened. When the ends of the film were fastened together to form a continuous loop, they were given a twist. The film is a Möbius strip.'

'But we aren't characters in a film,' said Ringer. 'I'm alive: I have thoughts and feelings.'

'Perhaps,' said the Other. 'I have no way of knowing. You could say that we've been granted a moment together in the darkness where the audience of the universe is allowed to sit. From that perspective, our thoughts matter little.' He pointed at the documents in Ringer's hand. 'This map shows the layout of Burgh House Hospital. Right now, you're on it somewhere. And down here, at the lowest level, is the vacuum array you must destroy.'

Ringer was shocked. 'Destroy? Why?'

'The array enables multiple realities to exist simultaneously: letting a person be in two places at once, or projecting a living image backwards in time. I don't know why we – you and Laura – appear to be the only people to have experienced the effect, but if the machine runs at full power it could happen to every atom in the planet: the whole world could be duplicated and multiplied; even annihilated.'

Ringer still doubted a message coming to him by means, he reminded himself, of a particularly convincing dream. 'Why should Laura and I have been chosen?'

'The explanation must lie in your future,' said the Other, 'which is to be our beginning.' Then he retched again, swaying as dizziness gripped him. Ringer, too, felt a return of his own giddiness. 'You have to destroy the machine. Trust me, and for God's sake do what you must.'

Then the floor began to rise and fall, slowly at first, with long, rolling waves. Gradually they swelled until Ringer toppled again and found himself prostrate, watching the Other disappear intermittently behind the smooth crests of a floor turned molten.

'Remember what I've said!' the Other called to him, trying to reach out for his double but finding himself already drifting too far. The room was melting; a picture was dripping from the wall and weaving itself into a rug. At the far end, the Other stood at the door of the office in Craigcarron where all of this happened, and before he could float beyond sight, Ringer saw two men take hold of him, subduing him as he struggled. They're going to kill him, Ringer thought, as he watched the Other's flailing limbs and his assailants' violent response. And yet, Ringer reminded himself, they can't have killed him; for this was how Ringer got here. They had knocked him unconscious, and he had woken up in hospital.

All was still. The visions had fled, and beside him, quietly, lay Laura. He could call her that now; it was her true name. In other places her image might be Clara or Helen, but Laura was who she really was; the rest belonged to the world of vapours and dreams that it was his duty to extinguish.

'Ooooo-AHH!' As if rising from a great depth, she gasped herself into wakefulness.

'Why do you keep doing that?' Ringer asked her.

'Doing what?'

'Never mind,' he said. 'Right now, we need to visit Red Zone.' He got to his feet and found himself free of dizziness. Laura too was steady as he helped her stand.

'Why do we have to go?' she asked, with something of the dreamlike calm that was the mark of her illness.

Ringer held her by the shoulders and spoke sternly, as if trying to rouse her from slumber. 'Your name is Laura. If we go to Red Zone then perhaps you can be cured.'

Her expression changed. 'Laura,' she said softly to herself, mouthing it two or three times with such touching sweetness that Ringer felt his grip on her softening into what was almost an embrace.

He let go of her, then reached down for one of the pages he had dropped on the floor. 'This is how we'll get to Red Zone,' he said, lifting the map and showing it to her. He took her hand and led her to the door. The corridor outside was deserted; Ringer looked one way and then the other, expecting Maggie or Dr Blake to come into view at any moment, but he soon decided it was safe for the two of them to set off. 'If anybody challenges us,' he said, 'we're taking a walk together, that's all.' After a while he saw a stairwell, closed off behind double doors marked *Authorized Personnel Only*. 'Come on,' he said to her, and they both went through.

It was dark and cool here. The stairs were dusty; the walls were bare concrete, uninterrupted by windows or any other feature. In passing from the brightly lit corridor, Ringer and Laura had forsaken an environment of clinical cleanliness for one of utilitarian sparseness. There was no lighting on the stairs; the only illumination came from the swing doors' small reinforced panes, which projected some light from the corridor the couple had left. Ringer held the map up and examined it, tracing with his finger the route he thought they'd followed. 'These must be the stairs marked A,' he said.

'Hold on,' said Laura, tugging the map into her field of view as she stood beside Ringer in the feeble light. 'No, I think you've got everything back to front.'

It was true; the writing on the map was reversed, as Ringer already knew, but so too was the map itself, showing a hospital transformed in space. They tried to match the lines they saw with the real corridors and rooms they had passed.

'We're at R,' Laura finally decided, pointing on the map to a reversed letter that looked as though it belonged in the blueprint of a Russian cargo ship.

'No,' said Ringer, 'I'm sure this must be J. We only have to swap left and right, not up and down.'

'What about front and back?' she suggested, adding another level of complexity that had not occurred to Ringer. The map he held had passed between universes; it bridged not only different points of time and space, but also different realities.

'Perhaps we should just go downstairs,' Ringer suggested at last.

And so they descended. With no windows to the outside world, and no lighting on the stairwell, what lay beneath them was almost total darkness, pierced feebly at intervals by whatever light escaped from the hospital's illuminated levels. The next floor down offered them locked doors, through whose glass panes they saw an empty laboratory, unmanned workbenches and idle equipment glimmering palely, as if in expectation of the thousands who would one day pray that a cure might be found here for the madness that had engulfed them.

'Keep going,' Laura told him. 'This isn't Red Zone.'

Ringer was startled. 'You mean you've already been there?'

'I don't know,' she said. 'But I think I'm starting to remember it.' Somehow she knew what she must find, though on the floor below, she still did not see it. This time it was the entrance to an underground car park where three vehicles stood among room for as many hundred. 'Further,' she told Ringer, though beneath them now the darkness was absolute. It was a lightless shaft they ventured down; and when they had passed what felt like another two or three floors without any door to punctuate their journey, Ringer wondered if there was anything he could drop into the blackness in order to assess its extent. Having nothing to hand, he paused, leaned over the stair-rail into the void, and let a drop of spittle fall from his lips. He didn't hear it land, but felt a slight breeze, a barely perceptible air current rising upwards from the unseen depths.

'Are you getting cold?' he asked Laura, whom he could no longer see, but whose arm he held. The two of them were wearing only their robes and slippers; and by now, he thought, they must be a hundred feet or more beneath the ground, still spiralling down the endless stairwell that reminded Ringer of a castle tower, taking them far into the mountain. Beyond the cool dark air they breathed, and the concrete walls, lay miles of solid rock, encasing them like a tomb.

'Don't stop,' she said. 'I'm sure we're nearly there.'

And then they were at the bottom. They could see nothing; they knew only that the stairs had terminated on a smooth floor. 'Keep hold of me,' Laura whispered, as the two of them began to grope their way around the invisible walls in search of an exit. At last they found one.

'A door!' Ringer hissed. He could feel no handle; nor was there any window on the door, or even a gap around its edge that might offer them some light. What lay beyond, Ringer knew, was Red Zone. 'We've got to get inside somehow,' Ringer whispered, but then felt Laura's grip on him grow weak. She was sliding to the floor. 'Laura!'

She slumped at his feet, and as Ringer stooped to help her, unable to see a thing, he heard her moaning softly. 'Ooooo . . .'

'Please don't start all that again, Laura; somebody will hear us.'

'-AAAHHH!'

He put his palm over her mouth, but wondered if he risked suffocating her. He let go.

'OOOOO . . .'

What if anyone in Red Zone heard? There was only one possible reason why two patients might be making strange noises in the dark. Perhaps, in the interests of not arousing suspicion, Ringer ought to undress both of them.

'-AAAHHH!'

Suddenly there was light. A painful whiteness filled his eyes, flooding from the slowly opening door as Laura regained her senses and Ringer tried to prepare a plausible excuse for them both. A figure stood in silhouette, motionless, saying nothing, partially eclipsing the vast and sterile chamber of Red Zone that now was revealed. The figure – a man – appeared unperturbed by their presence. In fact he was welcoming them, waving slowly as if in greeting. It was Ringer.

This second Other could not be from the past, Ringer realized, resolving in the space of a second or two the man's face and his apparel, identical to Ringer's own. Without a word, the Other was beginning to walk slowly backwards, like a film in reverse, retreating among the control panels and towering equipment until he vanished from view. Ringer and Laura stood up and looked into the great gleaming room.

'Is this the place?' he said to her. She nodded, and the two of them walked inside.

There was no one about; the Other was gone, and Ringer began to inspect the rows of computer screens, the metal stairs and walkways, the notice boards and signs warning of high voltage, or the need for hard hats and protective goggles. At the centre of the chamber, a tangle of wires and pipes converged on what, to Ringer, might just as well have been the workings of an enormous refrigerator or air-conditioning unit. Its appearance was industrial yet immaculately clean; and at its heart,

Ringer observed, was a huge, tapering white cylinder, like a great whale caught in a tangle of rigging.

'Is this where you've been?' he asked Laura.

'I can't say for certain,' she told him. 'But somehow it's as if part of me has always been here. Look, there's the door.'

It was marked *Maintenance*, and lay open at the side of the cylinder like the entrance to a spacecraft. A stepladder took them up to it; Ringer first, then Laura. The two of them climbed inside, and saw at last the vacuum array.

'Yes!' Laura whispered with pleasure and satisfaction. 'This is the place!'

There were hundreds of her, perhaps thousands. Ringer too was reflected in the circular mirrors, each a couple of metres in diameter, at either end of the small chamber they had entered. These were just two mirrors among countless others beyond view, all of a smoothness and rarity that would have delighted an emperor, fashioned from rare metals, polished to perfection, aligned with astronomical accuracy. Not a speck or mote was on them, not a stain or scratch. Gently curved, the mirrors magnified what they reproduced, like the star-catching surface of a great telescope. Yet their curve was no common parabola; Ringer understood this at once with an insight he could not explain, a memory he could not account for, seeing his distorted face first in one mirror, then in the other, and noting how the world itself, by means of these bright sheets, was in some enchanted way inverted. Their figure was a cycloid; beautiful yet monstrous. Time and madness lay within their caustic grasp.

Laura reached out to touch a mirrored surface. 'No!' Ringer gasped, and she drew back. The thought returned to him, like a puzzling echo, that the destruction of this perfect machine was the sole reason they were here. 'It might be dangerous,' he explained to her. 'We don't know if the mirrors are charged.' The mere breath of his words, floating invisibly close to the mirror beside him, turned the caution he had voiced into a patch of condensation, grey and transiently flickering over a small part of the mirror's face, clouding for a short moment his own perplexed reflection and all its multiplications. Perhaps it would be safe after all, to place a hand on the polished metal; to leave a fingerprint that would betray them, when the crime became known.

Yet it was surely important that no one discover they had been here. 'Wait a moment,' Ringer told Laura, climbing out of the service hatch and back down the ladder.

'Where are you going?'

'Stay here. I want to find the best way of putting this thing out of action.'

First he decided he should close the stairwell door which presented such an obvious indication of their intrusion. He walked tentatively towards it, treading as softly as he could on the polished floor, but as he drew near he had to stifle his own startled exclamation. In the shadows beyond the open door, at the bottom of the stairs, something moved. Ringer froze for an instant, then understood. Arriving at the door, he saw the two figures lying at his feet: himself and Laura, only a few minutes earlier. Now Ringer was the Other. Here in Red Zone, time's loops and contortions were shrunk to mere moments.

Ringer saw himself look up, dazzled by the light. Standing there, confronted by a past that was his own yet now belonged to someone else, Ringer waved to the confused strangers on the floor; a gesture of final farewell before closing the door on them, and on his life. Ringer knew what they were doing now, in the dark stairwell. Soon those two hidden figures would rise and begin to walk backwards up the stairs, growing a little younger with each difficult step. Eventually they would reach a level with light enough to read by; and as their words congealed out of the vibrating air into their mouths and lungs, they would puzzle over whether the map they held was back to front. Thinking in reverse, oblivious to the strangeness of their orientation, they then would go to Laura's room, and Ringer would walk backwards to his, returning at last to sleep, and to dreams that perhaps, just occasionally, might betray to him the paradox of his existence. And this other Ringer would be released from his clinical prison, to pursue shrinking years that would culminate in the oblivion of his mother's womb.

This was the life to which Ringer bade farewell; the entertainment of a cosmic projectionist, played in a darkened, empty theatre. Now he had to deal with the vacuum array – but how? He heard a sound: it came from high up, at the far end of a walkway. Someone was entering Red Zone, and this time Ringer felt sure it could not be himself.

He hurried back round to the stepladder that took him into the service hatch. He found Laura sitting inside the vacuum array, cross-legged, her arms bent across her chest.

'For God's sake, Laura,' he whispered, 'whatever you do, don't start that "oo-ah" business now!'

The sounds were growing louder; Ringer could hear the metallic clang of footsteps on the overhead walkway, and he could hear a voice, a man speaking confidently, though as yet unintelligibly, to some companion.

The footsteps ceased; Ringer now could make out the man's words.

'You'll be left in no doubt of the medical significance, Dr Blake, believe me.'

'All I know,' said Dr Blake – Ringer recognized her voice – 'is that this machine of yours is possibly what's been causing the mental disorders in the first place.'

'That's wholly unfounded, doctor.' The footsteps resumed; Ringer heard the two people coming down a flight of steps less resonant than the walkway. 'You have to appreciate,' the man continued, 'that work of this kind will have applications in every area of science. I'm a particle physicist: I don't care very much about mobile phone networks! But the energies resulting from the vacuum array will produce physics of a kind we've never witnessed before, and that's why I'm all in favour of what the Rosier Corporation is trying to do.'

'New physics, Dr Chambers?' said Blake. 'Like non-collapsible wave functions?'

Chambers laughed. 'You've obviously been doing your homework, but I think you need to be more discriminating in separating fact from speculation. Don't believe anything you might have heard from John Ringer or read in his papers – there's absolutely no risk, as he himself conceded before he fell ill. Just get him back to health, Dr Blake, so that he can carry on his work with us. Rosier are very keen to have him as a consultant.'

Ringer then heard Dr Blake say, 'I'd find it a lot easier to treat my patients, Dr Chambers, if I could find out exactly what medication was given to them before they came into my care.'

'What are you talking about? Do you think we drugged them?'

Dr Blake spoke firmly. 'Both Ringer and Clara have suffered a mental impairment far more devastating than anything I can explain medically. And both of them happened to be involved with your work in one way or another: Ringer was with you at Craigcarron, and Clara was found unconscious here in Red Zone.'

'She was outside on the mountain!' Chambers snapped.

'That's what you and the Rosier people tell me. I've heard otherwise. Which makes me wonder if my patients' memory loss, so convenient for your need for corporate secrecy, might have had a little pharmacological help.'

Then Ringer heard a change in Chambers' voice. He spoke politely but with unmistakable menace. 'Dr

Blake,' he said, 'if there were any truth in what you were saying, and if you chose to say it to anyone else, then you might expect to be next in line for some "pharmacological help".'

She laughed in nervous disbelief. 'Are you threatening me?'

'On the contrary,' Chambers reassured her. 'Surely only a mentally disturbed person would make the sort of ludicrous accusations you've just aired – hypothetically of course – against the Rosier Corporation.'

Both fell silent. Ringer waited inside the vacuum array, surrounded by the endless reflections of himself and Laura.

'Now,' said Chambers briskly to his companion. 'Let me show you what all the fuss is about. This is the main control panel – look, it's all in test mode. Then we click on "standby".'

Suddenly Ringer heard a new sound; a deep humming that sent its vibrations through the entire machine, and through himself. It was the sound of a great animal slowly coming to life.

'The safety procedures are absolutely foolproof,' Chambers said, continuing his presentation for Dr Blake. 'This check here, for instance, screens for any maintenance personnel who might happen to be doing work inside the array. We wouldn't want to go shutting someone up in there, would we!'

Now Ringer was sure he was about to be discovered. Should he simply lunge at the mirror and shatter both it and himself? But before he could even decide what to do, he heard another sound, close at hand and whining disconsolately, as if aware that no protest could possibly overwhelm the great rumbling of the dormant array itself. Beside him, Ringer saw the origin of the noise. The service hatch was sliding shut. The safety procedures were far from foolproof.

Taking the last of the outside light with it, the hatch closed with a judder and bump. Ringer and Laura were sealed in total darkness within the array. He could no longer hear the voices outside; instead there was only the constant hum of the machine. Then it too ceased.

All was silent. Perhaps the control panel had, after all, detected the human contaminants trapped between the mirrors. Ringer waited, hearing his own rapid breath and Laura's beside him, which was slow and calm. He was terrified, and he envied her. He reached out and put his arms around her.

'It's all right,' she said softly. 'Don't worry.'

Then there was light. It came from all around them: a dull, red, uniform glow, as in a photographer's developing room. It was suddenly warmer, too, and the thought occurred to Ringer that their tomb might be no more than a grandiose microwave oven.

'We're going to die,' Ringer whispered.

'No,' said Laura. 'We're about to be born.'

She was free of fear; as if she had seized her fate in all its multiplicity, and had conquered it. What he had previously considered apathy was to be her soul's final mercy. In the blood-red light, Ringer saw the endless reflections on either side; and among the numerous figures, now that dizziness and faintness were beginning to rescue him from terror, he began to discern curious differences. The reflections, he noticed, were not all synchronized. There was a gap of time between them, which was growing larger.

'Something strange is happening,' he said. 'Can you see it?'

'It's always like this,' said Laura.

There he was, a few minutes ago. He saw it – one of the closest reflections – himself, walking across the smooth floor. Beyond lay earlier times; he was in the hospital corridor, or back in his room. And as his eyes grew more accustomed to the dull glow, he saw the reflections move closer to one another, like the folding of a deck of cards. He supposed the mirrors must be sliding together; the space between them was shrinking. Perhaps Ringer and Laura would be crushed before being boiled alive. Whatever the outcome, Ringer realized that, in the accepted manner of the doomed, he was seeing his life before him, in infinite, time-lapsed layers. At the furthest distance, almost invisible, he was a child.

'We've always been here,' Laura told him. 'This is why we've existed.'

Their lives had been sucked from empty space, and to the same void they would be returned. A sudden loud hiss engulfed them; the chamber was whipped by wind.

'We're decompressing!' Ringer saw it as another kindness; to be unconscious before the end. The reflections by now had detached themselves altogether from the unflinching geometry of the mirrors. He could see Laura with her husband and children; he with people who must once have been his own family. At exactly the same time, elsewhere, she was Helen, and he was someone who thought he loved her. Beyond, in the same limitless moment of non-being, she was being hypnotized by the swinging pocket watch of a man in a waistcoat; and as the reflections increased in number and variety, there were other men, other women. All of them, perhaps, throughout human history, were the spectral images of this captured couple at the end of time.

'I am Life – creator of worlds.'

It was the last thing he heard before the attenuating air of the hull they lay trapped in attained the emptiness of outer space, and they passed beyond the bounds of mortality. The mirrors were quickly spattered and ruined, the machine was whirring itself to destruction; but the reflections would live on, their ebb and flow traversing the cosmos. The array was erupting in a brilliant whiteness; a vast ball of radiation that might one day faintly illuminate a distant sky, a twinkling amendment to a constellation. The infant fireball was still only taking its first steps during the split-second that saw Red Zone evaporated, Blake and Chambers dissolved, Burgh House Hospital turned to atoms, and with it the story John Ringer had written and left beside his incinerating bed. It was called *Harry's Tale*; and on the small planet that now melted as swiftly as a snowflake, none survived who might have read it.

HARRY'S TALE

'I ordered a book,' he was saying to the T-shirted youth behind the till.

'Uh?'

'I'm here to collect it. My name is Harry Dick.'

There were few other customers in Rosier Books; though enough, apparently, to make the lanky teenage assistant too busy to be of immediate help. 'Hang on,' he said, consulting the computer screen on his desk while Harry idly gazed at his surroundings. Founded in the nineteenth century, the grand old shop had retained its original name even throughout the Time of Restructuring. Then came the Change, and six years later the place had been saved from bankruptcy by Rosier Media, who had refitted it as a branch of their retail chain.

'Yeah, here we are,' said the assistant. '*Professor Faust.* I'll go and get it for you.' He came out from behind the counter and loped off in the direction of a door marked *Staff only.* Probably paying his way through a university degree in television studies, Harry supposed. Better than tossing burgers.

'No service?' a voice said behind him. Harry turned to see an elderly gentleman.

'He'll be back in a moment,' Harry explained. His companion looked nearly old enough to remember the Patriotic War, but still had a youthful twinkle in his eye.

'It's just not the same, is it?' he said to Harry. 'This place, I mean. Look at that big pile of cookery books they've got beside the door. That's where the history section once was.'

'I remember,' said Harry. 'Though you surely aren't nostalgic for the Cromwell Edition we used to queue for.'

The old man shrugged. 'No worse than cookery or gardening, if you ask me.'

There was still no sign of the assistant. 'I seem to have caused him a problem,' Harry remarked. 'I ordered a copy of *Professor Faust*.'

'Oh yes,' said the old man. 'Heinrich Behring: a fine writer. I remember reading him at school. Totally out of fashion now, of course.' He waved his arm, indicating the surrounding shelves with their countless books. 'One minute you're in; the next, you're out. Like you never existed. Stalinism didn't die, it only got a new name. "Dictatorship of the free market".'

Harry was beginning to feel uneasy. His elderly companion was evidently some old Party man; a former union official or civil servant perhaps, or a retired secret policeman who'd once made a good living spying on his neighbours. He hoped the absent shop assistant would hurry back.

'I'm meant to be meeting my wife soon,' Harry said, glancing at his watch. He took out his mobile phone. 'I'd better call her.'

The old man watched as Harry pressed the phone to his ear. 'Don't go frying your brain with that thing,' he said, his eyes still gleaming with mischief. 'Haven't you heard of AMD?'

Harry was getting no reply. 'AMD?' he said, deciding to text her instead. 'What's that?'

'I read about it in the paper,' his companion told him. 'People lose their memories, make things up. They've got a hospital somewhere studying it. There's a theory it might be caused by these new phones.'

'You mean Q-phones?' said Harry, looking at the one in his hand.

'That's right. Signal's too powerful, or something like that. Holding it next to your head mixes up the electrons in your brain.'

Harry was beginning to wish he'd never entered this conversation. He started keying a message for his wife; but before he could even reach the end and select a recipient, his phone informed him it had been sent already.

'I wish it would stop doing that,' Harry muttered to himself, then explained to the old man, 'It keeps sending texts before I'm ready. I've no idea where they go.'

The old man shrugged. 'Technology, eh? Never trust it. No, you won't catch me putting one of those brain-eaters to my head. That article I read about AMD, it said that when people lose their real memories, they replace them with things they've seen on television or read in books. One patient reckoned he was a character in *Anna Karenina*. Can you believe it? Not only that, but he got the story all wrong, it was so long since he'd read it. You mark my words, these Q-phones are trouble. And it's all American military know-how they've put inside the damn things.'

Then he described for Harry's benefit how the entire phone system was really a capitalist method of mind control; as if capitalism needed any further power over people's minds than it already held. The old man spoke with the depressing conviction of a crank, and Harry was relieved to see the assistant returning.

'Here we are,' the lanky youth announced, placing a copy of *Professor Faust* on the counter, having presumably used his absence as an excuse for a coffee and a fag. He took the credit card Harry offered him.

'What age are you, young man?' Harry's elderly companion asked the assistant, who looked slightly startled at being invited into an interaction his sales induction programme had clearly never prepared him for.

'Er, nineteen,' he said, swiping the card. 'Why?'

'Well, nineteen years ago, anyone walking into this shop would have seen a whole shelf full of books by Heinrich Behring. He was on the school curriculum. Some towns even had a street or library named after him. He was a Hero of Socialist Labour. And now he's gone. Makes you think, doesn't it?'

'Er, yeah,' said the assistant, pushing a receipt in Harry Dick's direction for him to sign.

'Isn't it wonderful to be able to forget so easily?' the old man said, then began walking towards the shop's exit, limping slightly as if from an old wound.

'Aren't you waiting to buy something?' Harry called after him.

'Hardly worth it,' the old man replied, and walked out into the street.

Harry felt unnerved by the enigmatic exchange. Was it a warning? He'd been wondering if his Q-phone might be bad for him; he'd noticed a recent tendency to forget the simplest things. The other day his wife had been reminiscing to him about when they all had to recite the Seven Articles at school. And for a moment Harry was unable to remember the Seven Articles, or even his school. Was it only a case of growing older, or was it something more sinister?

The assistant handed him his book and was about to resume staring at the computer screen he appeared to find more fascinating than any human who might ever enter the shop, when Harry, prompted by the old man's earlier boldness, decided to make his own remark to the young lad.

'Have you heard of AMD?' he asked him.

A smile briefly disrupted the assistant's narrow lips. 'Moby fever? Don't believe the scare stories, mate. I'm on my moby every hour of the day and it hasn't done me any harm.'

Harry was hardly reassured by this advice, coming from a teenager who looked as if his brain had been replaced by a silicon chip. 'I read *Professor Faust* when I was at school,' Harry said, continuing his experiment in conversation. 'It was a set text in our philosophy class, for the paper on historical dialectics.'

The assistant wasn't even listening now; his glazed eyes were still directed at Harry, but his mind, if he had one, was more probably focussed on the pub he'd be sitting in as soon as his shift ended.

'Then last week,' Harry added, 'I realized I could hardly remember anything about the book. A few names, one or two incidents, nothing more. One thing I did recall, though, that had struck me so much when I first read it, was that Behring began his story in an alternative past and extended it into an imaginary future. Now I've lived through those years Behring depicted. He got it all wrong, of course: that was his point. But I wanted to remind myself how he pictured the Sixties, the Eighties, the new century.'

'Enjoy your book,' the assistant said with the voice of a robot for whom any life form over the age of twenty-five might as well be in a geriatric home.

'Yes. Goodbye.' Harry turned and began heading for the door. His own history was crumbling away to dust. Human souls were being quietly revamped and redecorated, just as this shop had been. One day he'd be redesigned out of existence.

He was at the entrance, looking at the road he'd known for years as Karl Marx Avenue until it had suddenly become Princes Street again, as if none of the intervening period ever happened. There was the busking bagpiper; and in the distance, on the rock, was the castle whose highest point once held a red star no one thought could ever be extinguished. Already there was a whole generation for whom such things were meaningless.

He brought out his phone again. He needed to talk to his wife; but still there was no reply. And so he began his text message again: *Call me: Harry.* And again it disappeared before he could even complete it, into the void where all our lives, all our memories and experiences, are ultimately sucked, like water spinning down a plughole.

So he tried once more, wholly absorbed in the task as he stepped into the road. A witness later said he looked neither right nor left before launching himself from the kerb, as if he didn't care, or had simply forgotten that Edinburgh in the middle of the day is a busy place, and its drivers don't take kindly to any obstacle. The witness saw him bounce; another denied it, saying the car gave Harry no more than a glancing blow that sent him back onto the pavement, where he landed on his side and then lay perfectly still. Whatever the truth of the matter, it looked to all concerned as if a man had died: there were screams, heads turning, faces becoming ashen, and a clutching of young children to adult breasts.

A bystander picked up the stricken pedestrian's shattered phone. Another crouched beside Harry, taking his pulse and insisting to the gathered crowd that everything would be all right. He was the one who saw Harry's face now, the injured man's open eyes directing themselves towards the book that had escaped his grasp and was flapping and fluttering in the breeze on the pavement beside him. It had fallen open at its final pages; and as Harry gazed at it, oblivious to the approaching whirr of an ambulance siren, he looked like a man at peace.

AUTHOR'S POSTSCRIPT
by Heinrich Behring

Four decades ago, in the 1920s, I lived in Switzerland and took a number of low-paid jobs while seeking my artistic vocation. For a time I worked at an Alpine sanatorium, where I saw at first hand the opulent, sterile lifestyle of the bourgeois consumptive, which I took to be indicative of a more general malaise, invisible even to an X-ray machine, that was slowly spreading itself throughout the entire social organism of the German-speaking people. The place where I worked – near Arosa – was completely unexceptional, and I would not have troubled the reading public with its existence, but for one curious fact; which is that, in my capacity as chauffeur, I had the opportunity to meet and converse with most of the patients and staff; and among them there was one figure who was to cast a significant shadow over history. This was Otto Hinze.

I need not tell his dreadful story here: it is well known. Let me simply point out that if, while driving Dr Hinze to the sanatorium to take up his new position there, I had inadvertently rounded a familiar mountain bend too sharply, then Hinze and myself might both have perished. The loss of an as yet unpublished novelist would be a cause of sorrow only to his own family; however, the death of Hinze, tumbling down a hillside as the gleaming black car in which he was travelling rolled and shattered itself, would mean the sudden salvation, the retrospective resurrection, of all those innocent souls who were to die at his behest.

Our paths crossed again nine years later, when he was the Reich's Minister For Education, and his book *Evolution Towards Perfection* became compulsory classroom reading. I was by this time a science instructor in a Hamburg school, where I refused to teach my students that Darwin's natural selection and Hinze's 'progress theory' were equally valid, with neither being definitively proved. I was consequently suspended from my post, and wrote directly to Hinze to appeal. The reply came from a lowly official in his department, informing me that I was henceforth dismissed from my position, and banned from teaching for five years.

These details are personal and contingent; I would not even speak of them, were it not for the kind invitation of my esteemed comrades on the British Board of Literature, who have requested some explanatory remarks regarding *Professor Faust* – the novel in which Hinze appears in fictionalized form – intending them as a postscript to the fifth and all future editions of a book which the people of my adopted country have, to my surprise and embarrassment, chosen to embrace as a work of merit and significance.

Barred from teaching, I next found employment with a publishing house that had first hired me many years previously as reader of unsolicited manuscripts; and this gave me access to a few brave journalists willing to help publicize Hinze's abuses of the education system. The theory of cosmological expansion, for instance, was to be taught equally alongside the Aryan doctrine of primordial ice. Even astrology was to be considered a suitable university degree subject.

My protests led first to fines, then to periods of imprisonment. When Germany began its war on European civilization, I was declared politically subversive and sent to a series of concentration camps throughout the burgeoning Reich.

The last of these was a mine in the Highlands of occupied Scotland, where rare minerals were extracted – though we did not know it – for Heisenberg's atom bomb project. The mining process yielded radioactive substances which ultimately contaminated the area around the camp's location at Ardnahanish to such an extent that long after our liberation by the People's Army, the whole vicinity had to be cordoned off. Indeed, to this day, I believe the local inhabitants still see strange glowing lights during the gloomy evenings, believed to be luminescent exhalations from the boggy soil that holds so many irradiated corpses – the remains of people I knew and worked with, brought there from as far as Bulgaria or Palestine, to the harsh and desolate wilderness of Ultima Thule.

It was while in the camp that I began to compose, in my head, some of the books that I would write after my release, and that would bring me fame. Thus I conceived *The Angel Returns*, my novel about Goethe's lover Bettina von Arnim, in which I included a somewhat fanciful episode about her friend Robert Schumann, based in fact on Hinze's analysis of the composer's madness in his book, *The Teleology of Mental Degeneration*. My aim, naturally, was to expose the folly of Hinze's theory that certain states of mind might be caused by events in the future. In my novel, Schumann receives a composition in the twentieth-century atonal style; a comic effect not lost on the Union of British Writers, when they awarded my debut novel the Lenin Prize at a gala dinner in London's Guildhall in 1949.

Following that success, I was encouraged to begin work on *Professor Faust*. My novel is based on history, yet distorts it. We all know that in reality, Hinze left Arosa for Berlin, where he became the right-hand man without whom Goebbels could never have taken control of the National Socialists. In my novel, however, he dies at Arosa; though even here I lack the courage to kill him with a twist of the steering wheel. Instead the task is given to Hinze's mentally disturbed patient Clara, who stabs him to death after enduring the most loathsome extremes of sexual degradation. Historically, we know that Clara (whose psychiatric affliction inspired Hinze's theory of universal mind described in *Synchronicism and Coincidence*) killed only herself, using a shard from a broken mirror.

The physicist Erwin Schrödinger is likewise grounded in fact. In December 1925, I drove him to the sanatorium from the railway station where he arrived. A few days later, taking him back down the mountain after he had enjoyed a pleasant Christmas holiday, Schrödinger told me he had come in order to work out a new theory of quantum mechanics. He had failed. But I knew, looking at the beautiful companion who sat beside him and was clearly not his wife, that he'd probably had other things on his mind. In my novel, this forgotten physicist – who never did any work of lasting significance, and apparently died soon afterwards from a recurrence of his tuberculosis – is resurrected, and allowed to make his discovery.

Rewriting history is an easy matter; rewriting science is not. Seeking expert advice, I contacted Academician Paul Dirac, professor of theoretical physics at Cromwell University in Cambridge, who kindly explained to me, in a number of letters, the elements of dialectical matrix mechanics. I asked Professor Dirac if some other, equivalent theory of quantum mechanics could be constructed, which my Schrödinger (whose historical counterpart Professor Dirac had never heard of) might have unearthed. It is to the ingenious Professor Dirac that we owe the absurd 'wave mechanics' outlined in *Professor Faust*. According to Dirac, this version gives precisely the same answers as Heisenberg's original matrix theory in all calculations, yet is based on a wholly different physical interpretation, involving 'quantum waves' that are actually quite meaningless. As an illustration of the esoteric and physically impossible nature of these waves, Professor Dirac pointed out to me that the wave function of a single hydrogen atom would be six-dimensional, involving the square roots of negative quantities.

Professor Dirac considers his theory a mere curiosity of no more than pedagogical value; nevertheless it proved crucial to my novel, and I am thus deeply indebted to the fertile virtuosity of his scientific imagination. Sadly, my relations with the distinguished physicist – recently named Hero of Socialist Labour for his work on Britain's nuclear deterrent – became strained as soon as *Professor Faust* was first published twelve years ago in 1954. Among the characters featured in the book is one whom Dirac took to be an unflattering portrait of himself; an accusation (first aired by him in an essay on matrix mechanics in the *Radio Times*) as unfortunate and untrue as the allegations of plagiarism raised against me elsewhere, with which I shall deal in due course.

It will be recalled that my novel alters history to the extent that it is Hitler, not Goebbels, who leads Germany in a war of conquest equally doomed to failure, though differing in detail. Britain is thus imagined to repel German invasion, thereby enabling its monarchic and undemocratic institutions to retain power in a post-war Europe still dominated by capitalist hegemonies. Thus there is no Time of Restructuring; even the Father Of The Nation, Esteemed Comrade Vernon Shaw, is written out of history.

Some outraged critics have wondered if my purpose here was to deny the truth of the Marxist-Leninist theory of historical determinism. Surely, they argue, though the specific facts of the past might be altered (the life or death of a man, for instance), the broad sweep of history – in particular the triumph of world socialism – must remain unchanged.

I do not dissent from this orthodox view. The purpose of *Professor Faust* is a strictly dialectical one, concerned with the historic opposition between left and right, materialism and idealism, and the necessary triumph of the former in both cases. The world I describe in *Professor Faust* – with its altered past and imaginary future – is quite deliberately one that could not possibly exist. Who could believe such a thing as a female Prime Minister of Britain, or a movie actor elected President of the United States? It would be difficult to be more evidently ironic without lapsing into farce.

My narrative, it will be recalled, also describes Schrödinger's supposed rise to fame, his confrontation with Heisenberg, and the crisis of physics this provokes. In the fanciful post-war world I describe, this scientific debate is resolved in the most ridiculous and decadent manner imaginable: by inferring the physical existence of a multitude of universes. Every observation of nature, it is argued, creates a branching of realities. The simple tossing of a coin is then enough to sunder the cosmos, bringing two worlds of equal possibility into being.

Critics intent on exposing my so-called plagiarism have naturally sought historical antecedents for this 'many-worlds' theory, whose discovery my novel places in 1957. Academician Cyril Connolly, for instance, has unearthed a vanishingly obscure story penned in Argentina in 1944 that discusses 'an infinite series of parallel times'. An even earlier ancestor could be found in Leibniz: the idea's antiquity is its sole virtue.

Equally, it has been pointed out that the arguments debated by my hero Schrödinger and his antagonists, about a cat that is simultaneously alive and dead as long as it remains unobserved, are merely a reworking of Berkeley, Fichte and others. I do not deny this. It will further be recalled that I make my hero read (and mislay) *Tomcat Murr*, precisely so that the fanciful feline paradox might be planted in his head.

More serious are allegations made against me concerning the brief mention in *Professor Faust* of a fictitious writer named Thomas. Assiduous scholars, more intent perhaps on making a name for themselves than on furthering the cause of socialist literature, have discovered that a real writer existed, by the name of Thomas Mann, whose biographical details fortuitously resemble my character's. Mann's first novel *Buddenbrooks* was a commercial failure; he published nothing more, though his brother acquired a modest literary reputation, and I may indeed have heard his name in Germany before the war – I cannot now recall. Apparently Thomas Mann submitted for publication several other novels, all rejected, which nevertheless foreshadow in some uncanny way various features of my own output. It is alleged, in short, that I must have seen these manuscripts, and that they – not the labour camp at Ardnahanish – were the source of my ideas.

When these outrageous claims were first made (in the *Daily Worker Literary Supplement*), I confess they caused me considerable unease. For I suddenly wondered if this strange, unconscious replication – albeit so feeble and imperfect as to be discernible only to experts – might somehow be a manifestation of the very plurality of worlds my novel jokingly posited.

Could there be a universe in which Thomas Mann genuinely found fame? Might there even be some telepathic means of communicating ideas between his world and ours?

It is the kind of hypothesis that would have appealed to Otto Hinze: the kind we must reject at once. My critics attack me with a coincidence I cannot deny. I vigorously refute the significance they attach to it. Do these critics prefer many-worlds theory to Marxist-Leninist historiography? No: let them fall silent.

With all its patent impossibilities, my novel can only be a work of fiction, and to think otherwise is folly. History, like gravity, has laws that cannot be resisted. In his *Dialectics of Nature*, Engels wrote: 'For one who denies causality, every natural law is a hypothesis.' In a world where everything is considered a mere state of mind, we would be reduced to relativism and chaos.

And if that sounds too abstract, let me be more specific. I have already mentioned the labour camp, but have said little about it, since the most fitting memorial for those who perished there is reverent silence. Nevertheless, I shall mention a single incident among countless horrors that occurred there. It was during the particularly severe winter of 1943, when many prisoners who had hitherto proved so stubborn in their struggle for survival finally surrendered to the temptation of death, expiring in unusually large numbers from typhus, malnourishment or pure despair. My work party was ordered to bury a day's worth of victims, and after turning the rock-hard earth we prepared to dump the laid-out row – their emaciated faces bearing a look of enviable calm – into their communal grave. But as snow began to fall gently all around us, I saw that one of the dead men appeared strangely discontented with the peace he had been granted. His lips were moving. He was a corpse filled with the horror of continued existence.

I called out to the guard: 'This man is alive!' The guard, irritated by my interruption of the cigarette that so pleasantly occupied his attention, commanded me to shut up and dig, calling me a lazy swine. 'But he's alive,' I repeated, 'it's the truth!'

The guard came and looked at the figure on the ground. Like me, he saw the twitching lips, the pleading eyes, the desperate attempt to summon forth pity in a place where such weakness was ruthlessly banned. Too obscenely indifferent even to be prepared to put a bullet through the sick man's head, the guard instead jabbed me harshly with his rifle butt. 'Here there is no truth. Dig!'

I had learned a simple and terrible formula from that uniformed youth with his smouldering cigarette. Truth is hope. Hell is the place where all truth is abandoned.

I grant that there are many truths: those of lovers or of poets, of physicists or of ship builders. To say that there are many is not to say there is none. The camp existed: I am its witness. I never knew the name of the man I saw buried alive, his lips still trying to frame a cry for help as the earth was piled upon him. But I know he was a creature with thoughts, feelings, dreams; not some philosophical enigma, some fiction easily erased. The only person who could have believed otherwise was the guard, and only because at that moment, halfway through his cigarette, it suited him.

Imagine a world where the guard's indifference to fact became the norm. Would it not be the subtlest and most terrible hell of all? Are you not glad the revolution succeeded, and that we do not live in the sort of world the Nazis wanted; one where people quietly accept that since every newspaper lies, it is best to read none? Are you not glad that evolution is after all still taught, and that people cannot do a university degree in astrology? Are you not relieved that scientists do not advocate a multiverse of realities; that university professors do not claim a pop song is worth as much as the symphonies of Beethoven; and that political leaders – holding offices bought for them by big business, and considering themselves personally guided by divine right – do not wage war against helpless nations whose dictators are fictions, possessing weapons of mass destruction that are fictions? Is it not a blessing that the world I have described, and its characters, are but a fable?

Forget them now. Unless all that was ever thought or written has life in some Platonic heaven, they are no more than pictures on a screen, shadows soon to fade. See: already the film is winding itself to an end, we count the final moments of the reel. Three, two, one . . . then nothing.

How vivid it all was. How soon the dream is finished.